Praise for Claire Knows Best

"Through Claire, Tracey Bateman leads us in and out of the corners of *real* life where children misbehave (and triumph), trees fall in unfortunate places, and a romantic kiss can still be a doozy of a good one. What I love about the Claire Everett series is that through it all, Claire knows best, even when she doesn't—which is so relatable."

—Charlene Ann Baumbich, author of
the Dearest Dorothy series
www.welcometopartonville.com

"I love Claire Everett! With poignancy and humor, Claire confronts life, romance, and mothering with an authenticity and nerve that grabs my heart. I just wanted to climb inside the book and hang out with her. A delightful read that charmed me and made me believe that, indeed, Claire Knows Best!"

—Susan May Warren, award-winning author of
Everything's Coming Up Josey

"Whether you're eighteen or eighty, you will find something to love about Claire! She is everygirl, and I loved sharing in her life and can't wait to see her again. Tracey Bateman is a wonderful, snappy voice in women's fiction."

—Kristin Billerbeck, author of
What a Girl Wants and *She's All That*

Claire
Knows Best

Tracey Bateman

WARNER
Faith®

New York Boston Nashville

Warner Faith

Hachette Book Group, USA
1271 Avenue of the Americas, New York, NY 10020
Visit our Web site at www.warnerfaith.com.

Warner Faith® and the Warner Faith logo are trademarks of Time Inc. Used under license.

Printed in the United States of America

First Edition: June 2006
10 9 8 7 6 5 4 3 2 1

Library of Congress Cataloging-in-Publication Data
Bateman, Tracey Victoria.
    Claire knows best / Tracey Bateman.— 1st ed.
        p. cm.
    Summary: "Claire Everett, an overwhelmed single mother, enlists the help of a life coach to get a grip on the chaos in her life"—Provided by the publisher.
    ISBN-13: 978-0-446-69606-7
    ISBN-10: 0-446-69606-4
    1. Women novelists—Fiction. 2. Single mothers—Fiction. I. Title.
    PS3602.A854C57 2006
    813'.6—dc22   2005035341

To Susie Warren.
Sometimes a girl needs a best friend to laugh with.
Thank you for loving life with me.
Sometimes I think we were twins
separated at birth.

Acknowledgments

First of all to Troy King, owner and operator of America Tree in Grand Lake, Colorado: Thank you Troy for your expert information on how to remove a tree from a house. On a day when I was frantic for something fresh, God spoke through you and gave me exactly what I needed to get over my block. From the bottom of my heart, thank you.

Debra Ulrick: Thanks for being a voice of praise when I need to hear nice things. And thanks to your husband, Rick, for putting up with contracting questions.

Leslie Peterson for great editing.

Cara Highsmith: I would have been lost without you during the edits of this book. Thanks for being an ear and a voice of encouragement as well as offering good insights that made the book much better than I could have done alone.

My great agent, Steve Laube: Thanks for believing in me.

My mother-in-law, Vivian: You're always there for your grandkids and for me. You raise the bar for mothers-in-law everywhere.

My mom, Frances: As always, you read for me, you watch kids, you provide much needed prayer and pep talks.

Angie and Eldon Shivers: Thank you for feeding my kids, driving them places, and convincing me that I'm doing you the favor by letting you do it. God breathes His goodness through you two. I've never known anyone with such a spirit of generosity. I'm blessed to call you friends.

Rachel, Chris, Susie, Susan, and Anne: For helping in so many different ways. Just for being my friends.

Kris B: Thanks for long, honest e-mail conversations. You're a treasure.

Jesus, You make this all possible. I live for You.

Claire
Knows Best

I have a bad habit of laughing at the wrong times. Like last Tuesday during prayer meeting. Eddie Cain, a sweet, elderly man who has attended my church for twenty years, stood up and asked for prayer. Nothing humorous about that. But for ten whole minutes—and for the record, ten minutes can be agonizingly long—he shared every detail of his medical malady and then excused himself and headed for the men's room.

Let me just say that incontinence is a serious issue facing many seniors, and I know it's not funny. Only, the way Eddie said, "Preacher, I need y'all to pray for me. I'm having trouble holding m'water these days," just sort of gouged my funny bone. I pressed my lips together and bowed my head like I was getting ready to pray. But the truth was that laughter bubbled just below the surface. I knew if I looked anyone in the eye, I'd lose it.

The heavy silence that followed this man's request and subsequent exit didn't help matters. I kept waiting for *someone* to say something to ease the tension. Pastor, maybe? Our leader, the shepherd of the flock. But the pin-dropping silence lingered . . . lingered . . . Then, as I sat there replaying poor Eddie's words in my mind, the inevitable happened: I felt a dreaded giggle coming on. I pushed it down not once, but twice. Oh, all right, at least ten times. Fervently, I prayed that

Pastor would just end the service already before I made a complete fool of myself. But alas, that was not to be.

Still, to my credit, I was totally winning the battle for control. I really was. That is, until my fourteen-year-old son snickered next to me. Oh, my goodness! Spit-flying guffaws burst forth from my innermost being. First I tried to cover them with a cough. That never works. Next I pretended I'd been moved by the Spirit. You know what I mean. Just above a whisper I resorted to the word that remains the same in every language: "Hallelujah." Hey, I'm not proud of it. But in the heat of the moment, I caved in to Christianese.

I don't think anyone was fooled by either diversionary tactic, anyway. Imagine a high-pitched, way-too-forced "Hallelujah" and you can guess why no one bought it. Oh well.

I didn't wait around after the final "Amen." Instead, I bee-lined for the door and got the heck out of Dodge before anyone could give me that way-to-blow-the-whole-service glare.

And then, of course, I was too embarrassed to come back. I begged off Wednesday-night Bible study, then faked the flu on Sunday. To make matters worse, my best friend, Linda, phoned Sunday afternoon to tell me they'd cancelled Tuesday-night prayer meetings for an indefinite period of time. Pastor Devine claimed it was because of low attendance, and I can't help but feel responsible.

Believe me, I know poor Eddie Cain's plight was so not funny in the first place. But like I said, the stupidest, unfunniest things make me laugh.

Moral of the story? It is quite possible that laughter is *not* necessarily the best medicine. Because I just feel sick about the whole thing. Although, in my defense, let me just say that with four pregnancies under my belt, it's not like I haven't experienced the same problem. I mean, you try sneezing with nine pounds sitting on top of your bladder. And heaven forbid anyone should make me laugh at the wrong moment during the last trimester.

Not to make this all about me or anything, but I *do* empathize on some level with the poor man.

Fresh from the memory of such a mortifying experience, you'd think I'd be on my guard for a while. Instead, I made another huge mistake merely a week later when my editor, Tanya, called me from home to break some potentially life-altering news.

I'm thinking, really, after five years of working with Tanya, who edits my books with the touch of Midas, why I was the last to know about her obsession with *Star Wars*? She had to have a baby (of which I had no clue until a week before her maternity leave) in order for me to know this.

If she'd have mentioned it in the first place or even hinted that she enjoys the Lucas-film mega-movie empire, I'd have been prepared for her boldly going where no parent has gone before. Oh, wait. That's *Star Trek*, not *Star Wars*. Well, either way, if I had known she had a penchant for sci-fi, I would have been prepared for her announcing the child's name.

Anakin Skywalker Gordon.

So, there I was, laughing like a lunatic at her little *joke*. Only to find out, um . . . she wasn't joking. To make matters worse, Anakin is a girl. Although from the photo Tanya proudly e-mailed to me, Anakin Skywalker Gordan looks more like, well . . . Yoda. But I suppose it's not fair to judge. No one else in the world can have babies as beautiful as mine. Besides it could have been worse as far as names go. Flash, for instance, would have been worse, considering her last name. So, that little "Anakin" fiasco happened yesterday when Tanya called to tell me she had decided not to return to work.

Apparently, she doesn't have the heart to leave little Ani (on second thought, I guess Ani works for a little girl). She wants to be a full-time mommy. Admirable, but leaves me in a bit of a lurch.

And after I mocked her choice of a name, even though she knows I thought she was kidding, she's in no mood to go to bat for me with her replacement. Who is a man. Who hates romance novels. Which I write.

This guy will not be swayed by my ever-growing fan base. Because from what I've heard, his vision for the publishing company is about as far away from romance as a person can get. Literary something or other, I imagine. The stuff college seniors deconstruct in English 401, taught by frustrated English instructors who wanted to be authors but who didn't have the guts to live on Ramen noodles and reuse paper towels so they could afford to write the great American novel. Hmm. Maybe they *are* the smart ones.

Even my agent, who used to think I was the cat's meow, isn't optimistic about my future with this publisher. Methinks my publisher is about to cut me loose. So much for all the hype about loyalty. Guess that's a one-way street and I'm heading the wrong way.

Did I forget to mention I'm a writer? Claire Everett, writer and single mother juggling four kids ranging in age from eight to sixteen, three of whom are boys. My ex-husband and his new younger (and I promise I'm not bitter about it anymore) wife, Darcy, are expecting their first baby this summer (she may have morning sickness, but *I'm* the one who's truly nauseated by the whole thing).

My kids are excited about the pregnancy and have already started talking about spending more time at their dad's. I'm a little jealous. I admit it. I just have to get a grip and realize that they will naturally want to be around their new baby brother or sister.

Anyway, back to the situation at hand. My agent's hesitation is making me nervous.

"So, where does this leave me?" I ask, hating the tremor in my voice. I mean, honestly, I know God has my life in His hands. I know my writing career was totally His idea and that He's surrounded me with His favor every step of the way. There's no need for me to worry. But why'd I have to go and laugh at Anakin's name? Why? Why? Why?

I finished my last contracted manuscript a month and a half ago. I've been expecting a new series contract soon. Waiting, as a matter of fact, for my editor to get back from maternity leave so she can approve the new manuscript and turn her attention to pushing the review committee to approve a new contract for me. But no, Miss I-want-to-be-a-mommy turned over *her* job to a woman-hater. And suddenly *my* job security is gone.

"Look, Claire," my agent, Stu Lindale, says in a smooth voice that, to be honest, I could listen to all day. He'd make a killing reading audio books if he ever wanted to give up agenting. "You still have a name in the industry. I'm sure the other publishing houses would love to get their hands on you now that your contract has expired."

I know he's trying to mollify me, but quite frankly that bites. "What if I don't want to go looking somewhere else?"

"You've been wanting a change," Stu reminds me. "Now's your chance."

Hope, like the phoenix, rises from the ashes. "Does this mean we're going to start shopping the new series proposal?" I started it during my recovery from surgery. Carpal tunnel. Had it last year and was forced into a sabbatical. Best thing that ever happened to my family relationships. Maybe not so good for my career, though.

Stu is hemming and hawing about now, and I feel the phoenix crumbling once more into the thick dust that is my life. Stu never hems and haws. He's precise, concise, and, by the way, never charges me for mailing supplies. I like his no-nonsense approach to my career. So why, all of a sudden, is he hedging?

I just come right out and ask. "So, what's the problem, Stu? You don't like the plot idea?"

"Oh, it's a good idea. The series could easily go on for eight or nine books."

Now *that* would be job security. I'm not picking up on his reasoning here. Guess I'm going to have to push a little.

"Improbable, unsympathetic characters?"

"No. The characters are likeable." He pauses. "Well, the agent comes across a little Magoo, but . . . ."

Smirk. Let him wonder if I patterned my heroine's agent after him. I didn't, but let him wonder. Life imitating art imitating life. That's the beauty of writing. Everyone thinks you're writing about them. Very empowering.

Anyway. "So the plot's good, the characters are good. Then what's the problem, Stu? My writing?"

"No, I'd say it's some of your strongest writing so far."

You got that right, buddy.

"Good grief, then. What?"

One of those well-all-right-if-you're-going-to-pin-me-down huffs that Stu's famous for blows through the receiver, and I swear I can almost feel the breeze. "Your readers don't want this Everywoman stuff from you, Claire. They want romance. It's what you're known for, like Nora Roberts and Danielle Steel."

Yeah, minus the furs, cars, and diamonds.

Besides, what does he mean "Everywoman stuff"? Okay, my heroine is sort of real. Okay, so maybe she's a lot real—as in a lot of me went into that character. But that should be a good thing. I'm an interesting person, especially since I started getting out of the house more. And no one can argue with the fact that I have quite the quippy sense of humor. But most of all, I am so ready to move on and write another type of book. And I thought my agent was on *my* side. Creep.

"You just said, not two minutes ago, that maybe I could make a change."

"We were talking about changing publishers. Not genres."

"Well, what if this new guy who hates romance is a blessing in disguise? Maybe this is my chance to really give something else a shot."

His silence is excruciatingly loud. My heart starts beating inside my ears.

"Stu? Come on. What do we have to lose at this point? If it doesn't work out, we'll just fall back on romance."

"That's a little risky. Can you afford to go without a new contract for much longer?"

Stu knows me well enough by now to know that I am not one of those idealistic authors who write for the euphoria of creating. I have mouths to feed and that takes the green stuff, baby. I huff and stomp the ground like a bratty kid. "Not really."

"Well, then." His tone is sort of high falutin' and smug and ticks me off just a little, but I've learned to schmooze in this business, so I refrain from calling him a big jerk.

Apparently oblivious to my restraint, he says what I figured he was going to say. "How about getting a romance proposal out there? And when you get picked up by another publisher, we can mention the other series."

He poses the words in question form, but we both know he's not asking. I give one last-ditch effort to salvage my pride. "You work for me, you know. Not the other way around."

"I know, Boss," he patronizes. "So, how about that new romance proposal?"

"I'm going to have to think about it," I say, aware that I'm pouting and that he's acting like the boss (which, in all honesty, he is). "I hate this business."

"No, you don't," Stu chuckles. "You're addicted."

"Well, I hate writing romance."

"Romance readers got you where you are today."

Now Stu's scolding me? What am I, ten?

"I really hate when you're right." Really, really.

"You mean all the time?"

"Funny." Not! He may be right but he's not *right*. Know what I mean?

"Get that proposal to me soon," he says, and we hang up.

Instead of obeying his directive, I stubbornly grab my running shoes and head for the door. Irritation rumbles through me. How come he just assumes my decision will be to go ahead and write the romance? I mean, true, the heart-pounding and heavy-breathing stuff *was* my first attempt at writing and got me published. Why? Because I was in desperate need of income after Rick walked out on our eleven-year marriage. I figured if I was ever going to do anything but work three waitress jobs, I might as well give it a shot. I chose romance because that's what I read to escape my crappy, lonely life. (That was back before I realized a woman doesn't need romance to be happy.) And guess what? Turns out a lot of people think I write it well. And my wonderful, faithful readers have continued to buy my books, thereby keeping me two steps ahead of the unemployment line and government cheese.

But after providing entertainment for one and a half million romance readers, I feel like I've earned the right to do what I want. I mean, why can't I just be true to my convictions for once and write the story on my heart?

Sigh. The almighty dollar. That's why. And a mortgage, and electricity, and, oh yeah, food.

Especially pizza.

Just before I reach the door, my sixteen-year-old daughter pops down the stairs holding her cell phone to her ear. "Hang on, Paddy," she says into the receiver to her on-again-off-again heartthrob. "Where you going, Mom?"

"For a run. Do you mind starting supper? I bought a frozen Stouffer's lasagna. Follow the directions on the box."

"Yuck." She wrinkles her perky little cheerleader nose. "Why can't you ever cook a real meal?"

I guess she's forgetting about the canned chicken casserole I made night before last (and that we had again last night so as not to be wasteful). She could give me a little bit of A for effort.

Still, I hide my hurt and answer her question with my trademark rapier wit. "Because I don't want to spoil you, honey." Oh yeah. Good one. Snap, snap, and snap.

Rolling one's eyes should not be an art form, but my daughter has it perfected. "All those preservatives are killing us from the inside out, Mother. We shouldn't be eating this garbage. Especially the little boys. You'll stunt their growth."

Her concern for her brothers is truly touching. "Duly noted." I reach for the door and give her a little wave as she resumes her phone conversation. "I'll be back."

"Wait a sec, Ma. Paddy says you better stay in. He's IMing

with one of his friends in Springfield. They're getting hammered with a storm. And it's headed our way."

Yeah, like I'm really going to listen to an adolescent boy. Besides, I'm sick of people telling me what to do. I'm taking a stand. "Thank Paddy for looking out for me," I call, as I step onto the porch and shut the door behind me.

Patrick Devine is the pastor's son and the boy who has captured my daughter's heart every other month during the past six. Intermittently, she's dated Craig Miller, Nate Cooper, and Tyler Lincoln. But she always comes back around to Paddy. I think he may be the one. If not, he'll at least be the one she remembers in years to come as the first boy she ever loved.

Sitting on the step, I pull on my Nikes. The spring wind is blowing like crazy, warm and comforting, breezing up the scents of fresh grass and daffodils, honeysuckle and roses. A sudden gust whips through the gutters with a high-pitched whistle.

I like the idea of running against a strong wind. With Paddy's warning in my mind, I give momentary attention to a distant rumble of thunder. Typical for a Missouri spring. Something about it always makes me feel powerful. Woman against the elements.

Still, I glance at the sky just to be sure there are no threatening clouds. The sun is making a brave showing, trying to peek through. If the storm is moving seventy miles an hour straight down the interstate, it's still going to take almost an hour to get here. Plenty of time to pound my frustrations into the pavement before I'm forced to unplug the electrical appliances. Well, okay, there's no way I'm going to run for a whole hour, anyway. The point is I'm not likely to get soaked before I get back home.

I slide on my headphones, clip my nifty little iPod to my

shorts, and off I go. (Yeah, I should probably stretch, but I never do. Too impatient to hit the open road.) Blasting to Hillsongs Youth band, I feel my spirits lifting at the mere mention of Jesus being the center of my life.

I smile and wave at my boyfriend, Greg, as I jog by his house—formerly my mother's house before she hightailed it to Texas last fall to live with my brother, Charley. Funny, I grew up in that house, but my best memories I have from there happened this past Christmas Eve, when I received my first Greg kiss under a construction-paper mistletoe hanging over the doorway to the kitchen. (My second Greg kiss happened less than a minute after the first. My third and fourth happened on my front porch before I watched him walk back to his house.)

Things are going well, I suppose. Except Greg's been trying to pin me down for a serious conversation over the past week. Knowing the possibility is high that he will want to talk about joining our lives, I'm excited and scared all at the same time. So I keep avoiding the issue. And in order to avoid the issue, I've been forced to avoid him, as well.

Only now he's standing on his front porch with a humongous frown on his face. His mouth moves and he jogs down his steps toward me. My chest tightens. Can't a girl go for a run? Spend a few minutes alone and try to figure a way to heat up a cooling career? Bury her head in the proverbial sand so she doesn't have to discuss a future where she might have to give up a little independence?

What is wrong with me? One minute I pray for someone with whom to share my life. The next I worry about whether or not I'll be able to watch what I want on TV or be forced to watch the military channel—ugh—or football.

I need therapy. I know I do. Or at the very least I need

someone to help me point my life in the right direction. I've been thinking of looking into hiring a life coach since they're all the rage. Only all the life coaches I've found are full of New Age mumbo jumbo. I want someone whose head is, at the very least, screwed on tighter than mine—and, really, that shouldn't be a tough find.

But there's no time to think about that right now. Greg's striding my way. The closer he gets, the more my heart starts to pick up, and I forgive him for invading my personal space. Greg is gorgeous. Dark hair, Andy Garcia eyes. I think I'm in love. I really do.

He's talking, but I'm not hearing. He points to my ears. Headphones. I slip them off. "Sorry. Want to go for a jog with me?"

Jogging is something we've enjoyed doing together during the past few months. And given my desire to do some thinking, I consider it a generous invitation. I flash him my winningest smile.

Only Greg isn't liking the idea. His brows are furrowed, and his eyes look more like mean, controlling Andy Garcia in *Ocean's Eleven* and *Twelve*. Not the sweet, ever patient one in *When a Man Loves a Woman*. He gives a frustrated grunt and waves his arms like a crazy person. "Are you out of your mind?" he questions in a voice slightly above his normal tone. I get the feeling he's sort of yelling at me. "There are tornados all over the place."

Another fairly common threat during a Missouri spring.

I glance at the sky. Darkening, but still pretty bright. No telltale green clouds to indicate a tornado. "Looks okay to me," I say, with flippant disregard for his concern.

His darkening gaze is all I need to tell me what he thinks

of my answer. "The squall line is just to our west. And storms travel west to east."

I swear, if he says, "Young lady . . ."

I squeeze my brow into a frown to match his, because quite frankly, he's beginning to tick me off a little. "I know that."

"I've been trying to call you for thirty minutes." His high-and-mighty attitude isn't helping to soothe my irritation. Not one bit. "I assumed you weren't home."

"I had an important business call," I say, taking a page out of Stu's book and trying to sound superior. "I figured you could wait. That's why I didn't take your call. You do remember that I *work* from my home phone, cell phone, and e-mail?"

He gathers what I've come to recognize as a steadying breath. "Yes, I remember." His thoughtful gaze peruses my face, and he hesitates like he's going to say something, then thinks better of it—which is probably just as well. "Why don't you come inside? I have the radio tuned into the weather report. We can run down to the basement if a tornado gets close."

"I can't. The kids are home."

"Okay. How about I come over to your house, then? Sadie's at Mom's."

I hesitate. I'm not really ready to let go of my grudge, but the image of cuddling with Greg while the storm rages outside sort of melts away any memory of exactly why his bossiness bugged me in the first place.

He gives me a fake pout. "I'm scared of storms."

Grinning like a lovesick fool, I nod. "All right, come over. I'll protect you."

"Hang on while I make sure I unplugged everything." Greg's a double-checker. I'm usually running so late I barely check anything the first time.

I stay on the porch, watching the gathering storm in the west as the sky grows darker by the second. I shudder just as Greg reappears.

I take his outstretched hand and my knees nearly buckle when he laces warm fingers through mine.

"You know there's not going to be a tornado, right?" I say. "We never actually get one."

A crash of thunder hammers through the air like a sonic boom and I jump, glad that I'm not out running in it. As Greg's arms encircle me, I gather in the scent of his understated aftershave. Mmm. My stomach hip-hops and I smile into his shining face.

"I could get used to this," he murmurs, just before lowering his head. His mouth covers mine. I don't know if he's trying to make a point or not, but he's never kissed me like this before. My ears roar. I'm not sure if it's thunder or my heart pounding in my ears.

Oh yeah, I could definitely get used to this.

Let the storm beat against my house. Let the winds blow. I'm in the arms of the man I love.

Being in the arms of the man you love is little consolation when a tornado is bearing down on your house with the speed of an airplane and the roar of a train. Huddled in the basement of my home, my four children, Greg, and I are definitely in touch with our mortality.

I can't speak for anyone else, but never again will I take life for granted. No more artery-clogging food, no more skipping exercise in favor of a mocha latte down at Churchill's (the cute little coffee shop I love so much). No more driving even a block without my seat belt, or punching it at a yellow light, or going eighty in a sixty-mile-per-hour stretch of highway. From now on, it's the straight and narrow for this chick.

And these are the promises I'm making God as the basement windows rattle so loudly I'm sure they're about to blow. I lunge for the two blankets folded on the end of the couch and fling them over my children to protect them from shards of glass should that happen.

I'm glad I'm not alone, and Greg's great comfort, but sometimes a person just wants her mommy. I can attest to that, not only because I'm thinking of mine right now, but because all four of my children are clamoring about like pups around a mother dog. Snuggling and romance are the farthest things from either my mind or Greg's. I know he's frantic to call and check on his daughter and mother, who are just across town in Greg's childhood home. But for now, he's hanging on like the rest of us amid the shaking, roaring, and clattering.

Ari gives off an ear-splitting scream as an enormous boom shakes the house. For the kids' sakes, I try not to show fear, but I dread what we might find once we are able to leave the basement. Will there be anything left of my house?

Suddenly everything goes silent. "What's happening, Mom?" Tommy, my brave fourteen-year-old boy lifts his head from where it's been gouging my spine. "Are we in the eye of the tornado?"

"What are you talking about?" He always comes up with the weirdest stuff. Like the time he thought agoraphobia was the fear of gore. And hydrophobia, the fear of hydrants. The boy has his days.

"I saw it in a movie once. Everything got quiet and they thought the tornado was over so they went outside and got sucked into the vortex."

Ari lifts her head from under my left arm. "That's *The Wizard of Oz*, idiot." Nice to see that fear hasn't dampened her spirit.

"No it wasn't, *idiot*," he returns.

Oh, brother. Nipping this thing in the bud is the only thing that will keep me from screaming. I open my mouth, but Greg beats me to it.

"Hey, you two," he says, and I can hear the tension in his voice. "Knock it off. This isn't exactly the time to be fighting over movie titles."

"Whatever." Tommy knows he's not supposed to say that word in that context—mainly because it drives me nuts. But I know everyone is tense, so I'm going to let it slide. This time.

Ari jerks her chin and looks back at me like I should step in and fuss at Greg for getting on them. I roll my eyes. I mean, am I the only one who just heard a sound that, for all we know, could have been my house imploding?

It's been quiet outside for a few minutes now, so I figure it's time to check out the damage overhead. I disengage Jakey, my eight-year-old boy from my lap and pat Shawny's back. He's at my feet with his arms still clutching my legs. "Shawn, honey. Get up." He grabs on tighter. "It's okay, babe. It's all over."

Slowly he raises his chin and I capture his gaze. Love-mingled compassion squeezes my heart with one look at my eleven-year-old's tear-stained face and fear-filled eyes. I gather him up in my arms. "Come on, now. Everything is going to be fine. You're safe now."

"What a big baby," Tommy says, disdain thick in his tone.

I shoot him a shut-up-or-you'll-have-me-to-deal-with glare. "Don't be mean."

Tommy's chest swells with macho-man bravado now that the noise has subsided. "I'm going to check out the house."

"No. Greg and I will go up in a few minutes."

"Whatever," he mutters, and stares daggers at Greg.

Unaffected by the boy's hostility, Greg takes the remote and by some miracle, the cable is on. The weather guys are talking about the storm that, apparently, only hit this side of town and totally skirted off to the east without so much as a raindrop on the swanky part of town, where my ex-husband lives. (And if anyone deserves to be the victim of a freak tornado . . . ah well, best not to go there.) Besides, the weather guys aren't even confirming a tornado. Geniuses.

Shawn's body shudders and I tighten my grip on him. Settling back, I hold him for a while until he stops trembling and before long I realize he's fallen asleep. I press a kiss to his head and set him gently on the couch, carefully standing as I do so.

Greg and I exchange a glance. His brow lifts in question. I nod. "Kids, we're going up to check on things. Stay down here until we give the all clear. Understand?"

"Why can't we go up and see, too?" Jakey asks. The kid's played too many video games and seen too many disaster flicks. He has no sense of reality.

"Because it might be dangerous, bud," Greg says. "Your mom and I need to check it out first."

I stand at the bottom of the basement steps and brace myself. Who knows what we'll find beyond that door?

Greg goes on ahead and turns to look at me. "Are you coming, Claire?" I nod, taking the stairs one agonizing step at a time.

I stop short after we walk through the basement door and into the living room. Other than a few pictures hanging askew, I see no house-shaking damage. We wander into the kitchen and suddenly the noise makes sense. Okay, I'm not sure how, but the dishwasher has loosened from its cubbyhole and has rolled all the way across the floor and crashed into the fridge.

Relief swarms through me. "I guess that's the boom we heard."

But Greg's frowning and I don't think he's buying it. Which is what I was afraid of.

"Why don't you get the kids and take them outside? I'd like to check out the upstairs."

"Take them outside? Why?"

"I have a hunch." He bends and brushes my lips with a kiss. "Trust me?"

Well, what's a girl to do? I nod and head for the basement. "Kids! Come on up here. Greg wants us to go outside. And bring the blankets. It's cooled off quite a bit."

I hear Ari. "Shawn, wake up! Wake up. We're going outside before the house falls in."

Falls in? Is that what Greg's worried about?

The kids and I are ready to go out about the same time Greg is coming back downstairs. His face is a little white.

"What?" I ask. My stomach is twisted in knots because Greg doesn't rattle very easily.

"The tree fell on your roof."

"Th-the big one?"

He gives me a nod.

"Cool!" Tommy yells like only a clueless fourteen-year-old boy can in a situation such as this. He heads for the stairs. Greg snatches him by the arm just in time.

"You can't go up there. It's dangerous."

Tommy's gaze is as dark and stormy as the sky was an hour ago. He jerks his arm out of Greg's grip. "You can't tell me what to do. You're not my dad."

Now that's an original line. I've been wondering when it might crop up and which of my kids would be the first to blurt it out. If I'd have placed bets, though, I'd have put my money on Ari. Guess it's a good thing I'm not a gambler.

I look my son square in the eye, in no mood to bargain, cajole, or, for that matter, be even the least bit nice. "Greg may not be your dad, but he's right. You're not going upstairs. Get your behind outside. Right now."

He's muttering under his breath as he clods to the door and yanks it open.

I snatch my cell from the coffee table where it's been charging since I got home earlier. I'm dialing Rick and Darcy as I step out.

"Hi, Rick, it's me."

I'm a little surprised at the relief in his tone. So maybe he's not envisioning me with my feet sticking out from under the house like the Wicked Witch of the East. Ding dong, the ex is dead . . . okay, maybe he wouldn't go that far. "Thank God. I saw on the news that the storm did damage in your part of town. We barely had any wind over here. I've been trying to call, but they kept telling me circuits were busy. And there was no answer on your cell."

"Holy moly!" Tommy hollers. "Look at the roof!"

I walk down the steps, dreading what I'm going to see. In this computer-generated world we live in, it's not easy to excite a kid. And my kids are all starting to get nerved up. "It's all right, Rick. Stop freaking out. We were in the basement. The kids are fine."

"Is everything okay though?"

"Not exactly. We have some tree damage, and I need the kids to stay over there with you."

"How are they?" he asks.

"Upset, but fine otherwise. But we can't stay in the house right now until we get some repairs done."

"How bad is it?"

I turn and follow my children's gazes.

Holy moly. That is some tree.

Can I just admit something once and for all? I didn't cry when Old Yeller died. I wanted to. I knew my mom was watching Charley and me like a hungry hawk, ready to scoop us into her waiting arms for a cuddle at the first sign of distress. But no matter how hard I tried to drum up a few tears, they just weren't happening. I guess I'm too much of a survivor to have even considered any other alternative as acceptable. The dog had rabies, therefore the dog had to go. I mean, yeah, he was a good yeller dog for a while, but in the end he was foaming at the mouth and growling. Not exactly Mr. Cuddles.

I remember the entire scene like it happened yesterday . . . Mom and Dad are in their respective recliners. I'm sixteen years old, loving it that Mom roped Dad into watching a movie with us on the new VCR, even though it was the second day of trout season and I knew darn well he really wanted to go fishing. My thirteen-year-old brother, Charley, is sobbing like he just got a line drive to his shin, and I'm thinking, "Might want to plug the dog one more time to make sure he's dead. Never can be too careful."

I'm not heartless. Honest. I still cry every time Rhett leaves Scarlett (so sue me). The sweet presence of the Lord brings tears to my eyes when I worship. My children hurting or happy can make me cry for hours. But staring at the tree crushing the top of my house, all I can do is look on, dry-eyed, and try to wrap my mind around the fact that my office is gone. And following that thought is, "Thank God for the jump drive on my keychain." That little thumb-sized instrument, 256 MB of golden memory, contains all my recent work. And in this moment, that's what's important—that and the fact that my children are all safe, of course.

I tend to disconnect from emotion during times of extreme crisis. That is, while I'm *in* the actual moment. Later, reality usually sends me rushing to Pizza Hut for a deep-dish super-supreme (hold the onions and green peppers now that I'm dating and very likely to get kissed at least once a day).

Just for the record, I have a message for the weather guys who say they're not able to confirm a tornado: Come down and look at my new tree house, or house tree, as the case may be. That'll convince them. The tree was literally uprooted and dropped on my house. Only a tornado could have done that! That's my uneducated opinion, and I'm sticking with it.

"My room!" Ari whines. "My computer."

I know how she feels.

"That's what insurance is for," Tommy informs her, with a superior attitude he had to have picked up from his dad.

"Like you know anything about insurance," she zips back. "You can barely spell your own name."

He clutches his chest in mock pain. "Oh, gee, that hurt so much coming from a dumb blonde cheerleader."

"Both of you shut up," I say, in a tone just above normal but not quite a shout.

They hush, and I think I've shocked them into obedience; "Shut up" is a banned phrase in our house, and I haven't allowed it in years. But when I'm looking at a halfway demolished roof and they're bickering back and forth, it's just too much, you know?

I'm vaguely aware of Greg's hands cupping my shoulders as he stands behind me. "I'm sure it's not as bad as it looks."

Greg's sweet. He's the every-cloud-has-a-silver-lining kind of guy. And usually this attribute has a steadying effect on me. But not now. I mean, really, if the split tree on my house doesn't look that bad, how *does* it look to him? Because, not to be a drama queen, but from where I'm standing, it *looks* like my roof is caved in over my office, Ari's room, and most likely Tommy's as well. It *looks* like if my children had been in their rooms, they would probably be squashed beneath the granddaddy of all oak trees. So I'm not sure how bad he thinks it looks, but reality is starting to seep through my practical side and emotional what-ifs are about to make me barf.

Plus, I'm trying to remember whether or not I ever got around to sending payment for my homeowner's insurance. And for that matter, will the policy even cover holes in my roof due to storm-ravaged trees? Greg's hands drop, leaving two cold patches on my shoulders as I walk out from under them. I head for the house.

"Where do you think you're going?" Greg's firm tone and even firmer grip on my upper arm surprise me. He's usually such a beta male.

Okay, sidebar. Romance writers categorize guys in two ways: alpha and beta. Alpha males are the brawny kinds of guys who can fix a car, watch football, and generally take command of every situation. All the things we independent women say we don't want (but really do) in a man. On the other hand, beta guys are sensitive, sweet, content to let their women take the lead (to an extent). They're mama's boys in general, but the ones who've evolved past the wimpy stage usually make the best husbands. Unfortunately, they're not all that exciting at first glance. It takes a woman of maturity to recognize and appreciate the qualities of a beta man.

Romance writers typically combine the best of both types, alpha and beta males—brawn, sex appeal, and sensitivity— and that's the stuff romantic heroes are made of. Totally bogus, of course, but the fact that half of all book sales are from the romance category attests to the assumption that our female buyers will pay anything to escape into a world whereby men don't burp or scratch, where they live to please her and don't care if she's fat.

But back to *my* beta hero, Greg. This alpha-male-like man-handling is out of the box for him and to be honest, kind of turns me on. I whip around to face him, and he cuts me off before I have a chance to tell him off or kiss him (not sure which I was planning). "Claire, you're not going back into that house."

"I have to get the number for my insurance company."

"You should always keep your insurance agent's number with you, Claire."

Where? In my wallet with all my money? Sheesh, Mr. "Always be prepared" has fallen back into beta.

"Well, I probably should, but for some stupid reason it never occurred to me that a tree would fall on my house, and I didn't think to punch in those numbers. I'll have to work on forethought. Definitely a character flaw."

"All right. Point taken. No need to be sarcastic."

I actually do think I have a reason to be sarcastic, but now is not the time to get into an argument.

Taking the high road, I rise up on my tiptoes and kiss him. Full on the lips in front of God and everybody. I had intended to make it brief, but Greg (being a man) has other ideas.

"Stop kissing!" Jakey says, yanking on my sleeve.

Ari tosses me a scowling gaze. "Really, Mom. It's not even dark out here. The whole neighborhood is watching."

By "the whole neighborhood," she means the elderly couple three doors down and across the street, along with their two cats. No one else has ventured out yet.

"Kids, go get in the van. I'm taking you over to your dad's."

"What about my stuff?" Ari demands.

"Sorry. Whatever you don't have at Dad's, he'll get for you."

Rick's a doctor—a very successful one. He can afford it.

"Come on, boys," Ari says in a sulky tone that always gets under my skin. "They want to be alone."

I look up at Greg. "Sorry about the way they're acting. You

know they like you a lot. This is just a pretty big deal. And they've never seen us act this much like a couple."

"Claire," he says, in that husky I-want-you tone that always makes me shiver. "I don't mean to act like a husband. I just . . ." He grips my upper arms. "Do you know that you could have been in that office? You didn't even know a storm was brewing. I could have lost you."

Well, when he puts it that way.

"I just want to take care of you." He presses a kiss to my forehead.

I wrap my arms around his neck and his hands slide back to my waist. I give him a coquettish smile and run my fingers through the curls at the base of his neck. "News flash. I don't need someone to take care of me. I like taking care of myself."

He doesn't smile back. A bubble of nerves floats around my stomach. He stares down at me with smoldering eyes that leave no doubt in my mind that he's smitten. "Maybe I need to take care of you, baby. Forever." Something about the way he says "forever" makes me picture him getting down on one knee while branches poke him in the shins.

Okay, this so isn't the way I wanted to have this conversation. Not standing in front of my branch-cluttered yard. I take my only line of defense. I kiss him again. Long and slow, a kiss that leaves us both breathless. He pushes me gently from his arms and touches my nose with his index finger. Giving a short laugh, he eyes me warily. "You win this round. But as soon as you get all this house repair stuff settled, we are going to have a serious talk about our future. Okay?"

My heart flutters at this new forcefulness coming from Greg. "It's a deal."

"Good. Now wait here while I check things out again to make sure the house is reasonably safe."

He doesn't give me a chance to argue, this man of mine. Just strides with determination up the steps and into my house.

Minutes later, I've retrieved my policy from a kitchen drawer and have made a call to my insurance agent, Pat, who assures me the cost of repair is indeed part of my policy. And yes, I'm paid up.

I'm just about to head over to the van to drive the kids to their dad's when Darcy's SUV squeals into my drive. She jumps out, leaving the door flung open like a TV cop, and waddles as fast as possible to my door. Her eyes are wide with horror and as soon as she sees the house, she bursts into tears. In half a second flat, I find myself wrapped up in her pregnancy-plumped arms and fighting her little one for space. The baby's winning and I'm about to lose my balance when Darcy finally loosens her death grip. "Oh, Claire. I'm so glad you're all right. I was worried sick."

She cranes her neck. "Where are the kids? Are they all okay?"

"They're fine, Darcy." I motion toward the van where the kids are waving at her.

Relief washes over her tear-stained face. "You just can't imagine how scared I was."

"Well, as you can see, we're fine. I was just about to take the kids over to your place." I frown. "Come to think of it, how'd you get over here so fast? I just called Rick fifteen minutes ago."

Darcy swipes at her nose with the back of her hand and gulps back the tears. "What do you mean?"

"Rick? Your husband? Father of my children?"

"I know who he is, but I haven't talked to him. I was grocery shopping when the storm hit and I left my cell phone in the SUV."

"Then what are you, psychic or something? How'd you know about my house?"

Understanding finally registers on her face. "Radio. I was in line at the grocery store when the storm hit. The employees led us all to a storm shelter, but someone had a weather radio and a twister was reported in this part of town. I was nearly frantic." She grins. "Everyone thought I was a nut, because I was pacing back and forth praying for you and the kids out loud. As soon as they gave the all clear and let us out of the shelter, I hurried right over."

Oh, so they finally confirmed what we already knew: a tornado. Good for them.

"Oh, my goodness!" Darcy's eyes grow three sizes in radius. She gasps and covers her mouth.

"What is it? The baby? Do you need to get to the hospital?"

She shakes her head vehemently. "I just remembered I left a whole basketful of groceries in aisle ten."

My relief knows no bounds. I've had this fear ever since she's been pregnant that I'll have to deliver her baby. That's just about the way our relationship has gone and just about my luck to boot. So, excuse me if I'm not concerned about an abandoned basket of groceries on aisle ten. "Good grief. That's no big deal."

"It's a big deal to someone, Claire, especially the person who will have to go all over the store and put everything back that I didn't bother with. You know what Joyce Meyer thinks about that."

Darcy recently discovered Joyce Meyer's books, tapes, TV ministry, conferences. The lady preacher's no-nonsense approach to modern-day Christianity has always struck a chord in me, and I guess Darcy's joined the cause for Joyce's brand of "just do it" Christian living too. Personally, I think it's the best thing for her; maybe now she'll join the rest of us in the real world.

But at this moment, her guilty conscience is really the last thing on my list of priorities. I mean, I've read all of Joyce Meyer's books too, and I've listened to her admonishments about putting things back where you get them and making sure grocery carts are in the proper place instead of left to roll across the parking lot and ding someone's car. When I go to Wal-Mart, she's the voice in my head that keeps me polite no matter how frustrated I get by slow, ignorant people. But despite all these life lessons that are completely relevant 99 percent of the time, I'm sure Joyce doesn't mean a pregnant woman who just lived through a tornado should go back to the store and put away each grocery item one at a time so that she doesn't break some sort of God rule.

Darcy's face is riddled with guilt. And I don't have time to try to convince her. Because I know darned good and well that if I allow this conversation, I'll end up going to that store and putting away all those groceries myself. Tree on house notwithstanding.

I steel myself against her puppy-dog eyes. "Look, if you want to go back and put the stuff away yourself or continue through the checkout line and actually buy the food you need, do it. I'm not going to stop you. But before you go, I need to tell you, I just called Rick and he's already okayed it for the kids to come spend some time with you until the house is livable again. That all right with you?"

She gives me her don't-be-stupid frown of incredulity. "Of course."

I knew it would be, but as the ex-wife, I felt I should give her the option.

"Do they have their things? I could take them with me now."

"We couldn't go upstairs, so they can't get clothes or tooth-brushes or really anything."

"Well they have tons of clothes at my house. And we can pick up anything else they need. Oh, but what about school-books?"

This is one time when waiting until the last minute to do homework paid off. "They all took them downstairs with us to do homework while we waited out the storm. They're in the van with the kids."

She looks toward the driveway. "How are they holding up?"

"Shawn was pretty shaken up during the actual storm. Ari's worried about her things, Jakey seems all right. Who knows with Tommy? I think they're all in a state of shock. But they're tough and at least they have you and Rick."

"And you'll be there too. Can you at least go inside to get your stuff?"

Oh, whoa. No one said a word about me staying there. I'd rather some cowpoke brand my bare behind with a sizzling red-hot iron than spend one night in that pillared, antebellum-wannabe home with my ex-husband and his pregnant wife. I mean, yeah, I'm not so mad at him anymore. But live with him? Not even for one night.

Darcy has apparently zoned into my choking hesitation. "What's wrong? You do plan to stay with us, don't you?"

"Uh, no. I'm making other arrangements."

Think, Claire, think. Who do you know with a guest room or couch where you can crash? Linda, maybe? My best friend just renewed her wedding vows this past December. Her daughter, Trish, is my daughter's best friend. But I hate to impose. Besides, they just bought a home in the newest subdivision in town and are in the middle of unpacking.

Desperately I sling a glance over my shoulder to Greg. Just for a few nights? Should I or shouldn't I even think about it? He gives me a deer-caught-in-headlights look. I dismiss the idea before I give it any real consideration.

Besides, how would it look? And there's also that pesky temptation issue. I'm not sure how strong we could be living under the same roof with only his six-year-old daughter for supervision. I mean, true, we love Jesus, but also true, we've both been married before so we know what we're missing. The Word doesn't say to flee youthful lusts for nothing. I know better than to run into temptation.

I give Greg a shrug and a sheepish grin and the tension in his handsome face relaxes.

Darcy must have picked up on my original thought, because she plants her hands on her newly rounded hips. "Claire Everett, you are absolutely not staying with your boyfriend. What kind of an example would that be to your children, not to mention all the young people in the church? It would ruin Greg's ministry. And what if all your Christian readers found out? They'd stop buying your books."

Did I forget to mention that Greg is a part-time worship leader? Darcy has a point. One that I'd already silently thought of, but that doesn't solve my dilemma. I can*not* stay even one night under my ex-husband's roof. I'd rather sleep in a cardboard box in the middle of January, in a cold, rat-infested alley. And I'm not exaggerating.

"She's staying with my mom." Greg, my darling, my hero, the love of my life, the man with whom I will most likely share the rest of my days, comes to my rescue.

Poor Darcy. Her expression falls, and I swear her lips are trembling. Hormones. Sheesh. "But we have all that room, and you haven't seen the baby's suite yet."

Baby suite. Can you imagine? Rick and I were so poor when our kids were babies, they were lucky they got more than a dresser drawer to sleep in. This midlife-crisis baby of Rick's is definitely getting a grander start than his first four.

"It's really for the best, Darce," I assure her.

"I'm sure it is." She takes one of those gulping breaths as though trying to be brave.

Oh, brother. I hate it when I feel like a jerk. My cynicism combined with Darcy's inherent sweetness always puts me on the guilty side of the equation. Even when I'm the one showing darned good sense.

Which I always am.

Nevertheless, I pat her arm and steer her toward the SUV. "I'll get the kids from the minivan. I just need a minute alone with them to say good-bye. Thank you for being there. I really appreciate the fact that I can leave them with you and know they'll be loved and well cared for."

Darcy's face lights up under the praise. Then she practically tackles me with a fierce hug. "I'm so glad you're all right."

And I'll be *so* glad when you have that baby and your hormones return to normal. Although, to be perfectly frank, normal for Darcy isn't much less neurotic than hormonal. I study her as she waddles to her SUV and climbs into the driver's seat.

I take in a shuddering breath to calm my crazy emotions, fighting back tears as I walk to the minivan. I can't bear the thought of being separated from these children of mine.

I open the sliding side door.

"Told you," Ari says, and I get the feeling she's not talking to me.

"Is Darcy driving us to Dad's?" Shawn's big, sad eyes question me.

"Yes. I need to take care of some things here. Do you mind?"

He gives a little shrug and drops his gaze to his lap. "Are you coming to stay with us at Daddy's?"

I choke back a knee-jerk flippant comment and steady myself. "No, sweetheart."

"Why not?" Jakey pipes in.

Oh, maybe because watching Rick and Darcy cuddle might cause hives to break out all over my body. Because smiling when I want to scream might cause an uncontrollable twitch in my eye. I take a breath. But to find an acceptable excuse for my son . . . that's the task. "Because Darcy is too busy getting ready for the baby to have extra company."

A frown forms between his eyes like he's trying to make the connection. "Are you going to come over later to see us?"

His wide blue eyes are making me feel like a slug. "Not tonight, honey. I have to figure out where I'm staying, and I'll have to go shopping before the stores close." Which I estimate is in about two hours.

Tears well up in his eyes. "Okay." He slides out of the van and wraps his arms around my waist. I gather him close.

"It'll be all right, sweetie. We'll all be back home before you know it." Just before they climb into Darcy's SUV, I hug each of my children long and hard and even Tommy hangs on just a bit longer than he normally would. "I'll see you tomorrow."

Greg stands silently behind me as we watch them drive away. And I think it hits us both at the same time. There is no way I can stay with his mother. I mean sure, she's a lovely lady and she came to Darcy's rescue during the whole Christmas luncheon thing last year. (Darcy wanted to decorate with new decorations including a blasphemous— according to the pastor's aunt—Christmas tree. The entire women's group sided with the ancient woman out of habit until the voice of reason, in the form of Greg's mom, came to Darcy's defense.) So I have a lot of admiration and affection for Mrs. Lewis. But I think we've jumped the gun a bit with our impulsive grasping at straws to get me out of Darcy's clutches.

Judging by Greg's oh-dear-Lord-what-have-I-done silence, I'd say he's thinking the same thing about now.

In theory, it seems like a good plan, but even in the best of circumstances, living with someone can cause a bit of a strain. Problems between his mother and me might dampen my relationship with Greg. And I'm not the easiest person to live with while I'm in writing mode. I don't like to be interrupted even for nice reasons—like supper.

Greg's worried expression adds to his telltale silence, so I decide to put him out of his misery. "It's okay, Greg. I honestly don't need to stay at your mom's. I can probably sleep on my couch downstairs."

"Don't be ridiculous. My mom is going to be delighted to have you." A quick cough into a large tanned fist is the first sign of a man trying to avoid facing the harsh truth.

"No, seriously. It wouldn't work." I give him a little fingertip tap on the arm. "I'm really not very good at being company," I say with what I hope is a quirky I'm-letting-you-off-the-hook grin. "I leave my shoes and clothes thrown around. I never put the lid back on the toothpaste. And I've been known to go through other people's medicine cabinets just to see what kinds of prescription drugs they're taking."

I smile as Greg starts to laugh and slings his arm across my shoulders. I've accomplished my goal: make Greg feel less awkward over his silly flub. Imagine, inviting your girlfriend to stay with your mother. But then, this sort of brings me back to my original problem, which is how to get out of Darcy guilting me into staying at Tara.

Okay, I shouldn't joke about Darcy's home. It's not really Tara. Close, though. But it's lovely. Gorgeous, if a bit pretentious. That's my ex-husband for you. Darcy fits the home well, but then Darcy would fit a trailer or an apartment or a three-bedroom house in the suburbs. That's just the kind of person she is. She's adaptable and attempts to make everyone around her feel special.

Still, that doesn't mean I want to spend two weeks or two months or however long it's going to take for my home to be fixed in her house. Darcy just doesn't get it. To her, we're just one big happy family. Especially since some major healing has taken place between Rick and me during the past few months. But just because I'm no longer considering hiring a hit man for the guy who cheated on me then left me to raise our kids alone, that doesn't mean I want to sit across from him day after day at breakfast and supper and pretend I'm the long-lost sister come to visit. I'd rather max out my credit card on a clean but cheap hotel.

Greg's cell phone chirps out "Here I am to Worship" and he gives me a shrug. "Speak of the devil," he whispers before expelling a cheery "Hello, Mom. We were just talking about you." Hesitates. Frowns a little. "How'd you know?"

My heart stops. How'd she know what?

"Uh, yeah, she's right here." He hands over the phone. "Mom wants to talk to you."

I scowl and take the phone. "Hello, Mrs. Lewis."

"What have I told you about that?" her stern voice asks.

"Sorry. Helen."

Greg chuckles and I punch him in the arm. He clamps his other hand to his arm as though I've mortally wounded him and pantomimes his pain, trying to crack me up. And it's working. I'm forced to turn my back to him or laugh in his mother's ear. And then I'd have to explain it. Better to just look away.

"I hear we're going to be roommates for a while," she says.

"Uh, well . . ." I'm fully aware of the fact that I'm blathering like a dum-dum. But what's the deal with this woman? Radar? "I—what do you mean?"

"I just got a call from Darcy, thanking me for putting you up for a while."

Darcy! That little sneak was checking out my story! I'm insulted, really. She thought I was lying? Well, okay, I guess I sort of was. But actually, Greg's the one who brought it up. All I did was innocently jump on the bandwagon. I can hear my mother's voice in my head, "Oh what tangled webs we weave . . ."

"I didn't mean to put you on the spot, Helen. Greg only mentioned it as a possibility. I'm in the process of making other arrangements."

"Don't be silly. I'd be happy to have you stay. You can sleep in Greg's old room."

She sounds genuine enough, but you never can tell for sure. Helen Lewis is from the school of polite society and unwavering hospitality—the same one my mom attended.

"I don't know. I'm not even sure how long it's going to take to fix."

She skitters away my concern. "I'll be glad to have the

company. There's even plenty of room for you to bring your children with you as well."

"That's kind of you. But they're at their dad's." I can just imagine Darcy's outcry if I try to take the kids to someone else's home. She loves to keep the family close.

"All right, then. Just you."

And just like that, I'm staying with Greg's mom for an indefinite period of time.

Darkness has fallen over my sleepy little south-central Missouri town by the time I reluctantly pull out my emergencies-only credit card and rack up about five hundred dollars' worth of items I can't do without.

Against Greg's wishes, I went upstairs to see if I could make it into my bedroom to grab a few things after all, but he was right. The tree is so enormous it's blocking the hallway to my room. I wanted to crawl over it, but Greg hauled me bodily down the steps when I so much as mentioned it. He was more than likely right. And what a hunk he is when he's being all protective.

Only now I'm homeless and five hundred dollars in the hole—although I did find a great bargain on a pair of size 10 Gap jeans (size 10!)—and have been forced to call Rick and ask him to let me use one of his laptop computers until I can get mine replaced. He doesn't have a problem with it, so we swing by there. Gives me a chance to hug the kids again.

I have to bite back a wicked, nanny-nanny boo-boo grin when Rick just stands there helplessly as Darcy disappears into his office and reappears with his brand-new IBM ThinkPad and tells me to keep it as long as I need it. I know without a doubt he never intended to let me use the new computer. Evidenced by his grunt and jerky nod when I ask him if he has everything backed up.

After being my escort through the mall and over to Rick

and Darcy's, Greg pulls his Avalanche alongside the curb in front of my broken house so I can get my minivan. My heart sinks as I look upon my humble abode with fresh eyes. I can only wonder about the extent of the damage to our things. My throat clogs as I think of my desk. The one Mom gave me when Daddy died. How many nights did I see him studying the Word at that desk? I don't know if I could bear for it to be demolished. And what about Ari's canopy bed she's had since she was six? Or Tommy's Hot Wheels collection?

As if sensing my mood, Greg takes my hand. Such a simple act, but profoundly comforting. I lean my head on his shoulder and allow the tears to fall. Slow, soft. I won't allow myself to sob uncontrollably, but neither can I hold back the pain. We stay there for a long time until finally I remember the time and realize I can't come and go as I please at all hours of the day or night if I'm staying with another person. I sit up and grab a Kleenex out of my purse. "It's going on ten o'clock. I should probably get over to your mom's."

"I'll follow you in my truck and help you carry stuff in."

I nod, grateful that he isn't planning to have me go alone.

"Sadie's still over there anyway, and I need to bring her home. We've got school in the morning."

"Oh." That's right. The world must go on.

He gets out of the truck and opens my door for me. A little ritual we started on our first date and we both like. It's one of those things that stuck. I'm not holding my breath that he might keep it when we get married, but I sort of have a feeling Greg might be the exception to the rule that says once a guy gets married he stops doing all the considerate things that caused you to fall in love in the first place.

I head to the back door and open it, reaching for my bags.

"Claire, wait." He takes my hand.

I give a little embarrassed laugh. "Oh, that's right. You're following me over there. No sense in creating an extra step, is there?" I shut the door.

His smile sparkles beneath the street light. "No. There's not. But listen, I want to talk to you about something else." We walk slowly, hand in hand until we reach my driveway, which is thankfully on the other side of the house from where the tree fell. At least I still have a minivan to drive.

"What is it?" I snicker and nudge him with my elbow. "Cold feet about having me stay with your mom?" I chide. "Afraid she might show me some pictures of you in diapers?"

A deep breath lifts his shoulders. And suddenly the warm, muggy spring night gives me a chill. He looks down into my eyes with such intensity I'm getting a little freaked out.

"What's going on?"

"You know, you don't necessarily have to stay with Mom." He says it like that. Just out of the blue. After two hours of shopping and planning he's changed his mind?

I frown, my heart running a little faster at the seriousness of his tone. He truly doesn't want me to stay with his mom. "Hey, Greg. If this makes you uncomfortable, I can stay at a hotel or a bed and breakfast." I have to admit, I'm a little offended, despite the great Joyce Meyer preaching that warns against a spirit of offense. Still, who is he to suggest it and then take it back? "Just call your mom and tell her I said thanks anyway."

"Wait. Don't fly off the handle." He pulls me close until we each have our arms wrapped around the other's waist and I'm staring into eyes filled with tenderness.

"I never fly off the handle. Besides, you're the one that brought up having me stay with her in the first place. So why'd you change your mind all of a sudden?" I'm pouting like a teenager or a young bride. I'm fully aware of the manipulative properties of this. But something inside of me has digressed in the past few hours ever since Greg started with the whole "Me Tarzan, you Jane" routine. My independence swung away on the vines of a strong alpha male. And I discovered it might be kind of nice to have a guy take charge.

"It's not that I don't want you staying with her." He presses his forehead to mine and I melt at his hero-like action. "It's just that I want you staying with me."

My stomach turns somersaults. "Let's not even consider that possibility. We'll get ourselves in trouble if we do."

"What I mean is . . ." he hesitates. "I mean, what if we just go ahead and get married?"

"What?"

"You know we're headed in that direction, anyway. I wanted to wait until Christmas to give you a ring."

Oh, that's so sweet. I smile and press a kiss to his lips.

"So, what do you say? Tomorrow we can apply for the license and be married in a week."

For one second of fantasy, I consider it. I really do. Even though I've tried not to be the impulsive type lately. The thought of no more lonely nights, having someone to lean on when I need to be weak—those things appeal to me. And let's face it, Greg's perfect. He's the kind of guy any girl would kill for. So what's wrong with me that I can't force a "yes" from my closed-up throat?

Rick, the toad-sucking cheater. It's all his fault. He's ruined me for other guys. And, believe me, it's not because he set the bar so high that other men don't have a chance to measure up. Just the opposite. I expect guys to let me down.

So far Greg's been just a little *too* perfect. Know what I mean? What kind of guy checks the tires on his girlfriend's minivan and takes it in for an oil change? What kind of guy cooks Chinese (because restaurant Chinese is too high in sodium and calories when I'm on a diet) and brings it to me at my desk so I can keep working on my deadline? Oh, and then to top it off, cleans up the kitchen and quietly goes home to spend a Saturday night alone?

Like I said: too perfect. I keep waiting for Hyde to show up and shred my heart into a million and one pieces. I guess it's just that I feel too safe. Come on, even Jesus said, "When they cry peace, safety, then shall sudden destruction come upon them."

Well, all right, that was slightly out of context, and quite possibly misquoted. I don't want to start a new Amazonian, men-hating cult for women scorned. But the fact remains that when a woman has been hurt, it takes a while to trust again. I'm not ready to turn over my heart, soul, and body to someone else just yet. Not even Greg.

"I can't," I say softly. "I'm sorry."

His jaw kind of drops like he can't believe I didn't throw myself into his waiting arms and cry, "Yes, yes, a million times, yes!"

"Wait. You mean not at all? Or not now?"

I smile and snuggle close. "Ask me again another time, and we'll see. Okay?"

"Not exactly what I was hoping to hear."

"I know. I'm sorry. I'm just not ready to make that kind of a promise. Not while everything is so up in the air with my career and now the house. Darcy's baby." Darcy's baby? Since when did my ex-husband's wife's due date factor into things?

"Scratch that last one." I shake my head. "Am I nuts?"

"A little." He drops his hands from my waist and I can sense his irritation. "Let's get you to my mom's before she calls 9-1-1 looking for you."

"Wouldn't it be easier just to call my cell phone? Or yours?"

"Yes, but you don't know my mom that well. Yet." He opens my van door and waits for me to slide under the wheel. "I knew you were going to say no."

Laughter escapes me. "I know. You wouldn't have asked otherwise."

"Not true. If you'd said yes, I would have been the happiest man alive."

Leaning over, I kiss his lips softly and put my hand to his cheek. "And the most afraid."

"Maybe, maybe not." He shrugs and I think he's still stinging a little from my rejection.

"We have time. We haven't been seeing each other that long."

He gives me a serious look, apparently not willing to lighten the mood just yet. "It didn't take me long to know you were the woman I wanted, Claire. I think I knew it from the time you had that crazy panic attack in the physician's clinic last fall."

"The day we met?" To be honest, I fell for him that day, too. I decide to tell him so. It's the least I can do after turning down his proposal. "I'll let you in on a little secret. I was pretty smitten with you that day, too. Thought you had eyes just like Andy Garcia, and you know how I like him."

A smile tips the corners of his mouth. "I'll make you forget all about him." Reaching forward, he brushes my jawline with his thumb. I love it when he does that. "So, it was love at first sight for both of us."

"Apparently so." Andy Garcia who? I move my head to the

side a little and give him a flirty grin. I'm warming to the idea that he can't live another day without me, wants to sweep me into his arms and take me to the cave.

"Then why not just get it over with? Why live down the block from each other when we could join our households? It would be a lot easier all around."

Easier? Hmm. Not exactly what I was looking for. That line of reasoning is more like the practical Greg I know and it effectively douses the flame of spontaneity that had begun to rise from the ashes of my cynical heart. "Maybe I don't want to just 'get it over with,' " I say in a huffy tone. "I was married for all the wrong reasons the first time. If I do it again, I want to do it right. Under God and before my friends and family. I mean, good grief, even Linda and Mark went all out and they were just renewing their vows."

He takes a step back and I see beta male all over him. And that makes me even madder because I was really getting attached to Alpha Greg. "You want to join our households together just to make it easier? Easier for whom? I'll have two more people to cook for, clean for, do laundry for. Sure—it'll be easier on you. But I have a hard enough time keeping up with things now when I'm on a deadline."

Even while I'm spouting the words, I know that's not fair. But golly, does he have to be so cut and dried about the most romantic day of our lives? Of mine anyway. Maybe I'm just a sad substitute for his late wife. If he can't have her, maybe romance isn't important.

The creases between his eyes deepen with a frown and his eyes have grown stormy. "Well, if that's the way you think about being a wife, maybe you shouldn't be one."

"Well, Rick would certainly agree with you there. I guess I just don't have what it takes to keep a man home at night." I slam the door and then realize the window is rolled up and I have one more thing to say. I press the button and the window buzzes down. "Aren't you lucky you dodged that bullet?" I glare and roll the window back up.

From the corner of my eye I see him just standing there. Staring at me through the window. For effect I hit the auto-lock—which is stupid since he has his own set of keys to my house and van, in case of emergencies.

But I know I've gone too far as soon as I hear the locks engage. He spins on his heel. I watch through the rearview mirror as he goes back to his truck with jerky strides. I have nothing else to do but start the van and head off.

By the time I'm halfway to Helen's house, I'm starting to cool off and it hits me how stupid I am. The man of my dreams asked me to marry him tonight. And what did I do? I turned him down, then turned on him completely. Man, I am still carrying much more baggage than I realized.

I find myself watching the headlights on his Avalanche in the rearview mirror. Just to stay connected to him, I guess. Like if I lose sight of him, maybe I'll lose him forever.

We get to his mom's house, and neither of us has much to say as we each grab handfuls of bags and head up the walk. The front door swings open about the time I rally the gumption to apologize. Disappointment slips over me at the missed opportunity. But that's the way life is. Sometimes you have one chance to get it right and you better step up to the plate in the moment, or that's that. My chance came while I was still wallowing in my anger. Now Greg is otherwise engaged. And I'll have to wait until some other time to try to salvage our relationship.

Sadie, his gorgeous, raven-haired daughter, runs out wearing an adorable lacy nightgown and Garfield slippers. The joy on the six-year-old's face as she hurls herself into her daddy's arms effectively overrides my disappointment. I laugh as Greg drops the bags, although not in time to brace himself for impact.

Oomph!

"I missed you, Daddy! There was a tornado, did you know that? Grandma and me went to the basement, and Grandma said no candles because they might blow over and burn the house down. So we had flashlights, but the batteries ran out of mine and we only had Grandma's after that. But then the tornado stopped and besides the lights never actually went out anyway. We were just taking pre-precautious."

"Precautions?"

"Yeah." She glances down at the shopping bags on the ground. "Did you buy me something?"

"Slow down, Miss Jabberbox," Greg says with a chuckle. "Everything in these bags is for Miss Claire. Not you. A big, giant tree fell on her house and she can't go inside to get any of her clothes. So she had to go buy all new clothes and makeup for herself. And all that girlie stuff you women like."

"Can I wear some makeup?" Her eyes, full of mischief, slide sideways and she grins, knowing the answer before her dad even says it.

"Maybe when you're eighty and too old for the boys to chase you."

"Eew!" But she giggles just the same. "Besides, you already promised I can wear it when I turn thirteen."

"Please, baby." He let out a moan. "Don't even start talking about becoming a teenager."

I can't help but laugh at the two. I wonder how Sadie's

going to feel about having to share her dad with a woman and four other kids, eventually.

If I had to place bets, I'd say she's not going to be too happy about it. I've only caught a glimpse of her less-than-angelic side a couple of times during our association, but let me tell you, when she lets loose, it ain't pretty.

Helen appears, face alight with pleasure as she beckons me up the steps and ushers me inside. "It's about time you two showed up. I came close to calling 9-1-1."

In spite of the argument of just a few minutes ago, I look over my shoulder and grin at Greg. He's now carrying Sadie on his back. She's holding on like a spider monkey, and he's retrieved the bags from the ground. He sends me a wink.

Gathering a deep breath, I feel relief wash over me. Though it's obvious we still have some talking to do to clear the air, we've weathered more than one storm tonight. The winds of discontent have calmed and everything has settled back into its proper place.

4

My all-time favorite house in the whole world is the *Father of the Bride* house—the one in the modern remake starring Steve Martin, Diane Keaton, and Kimberly Williams. I adore that house. In my wildest dreams, it's mine. And guess what? Greg's mom owns one almost just like it. I swear. Enormous, white, two-story, shuttered windows. The all-American dream home. So now that I've settled into the idea of being roomies with a seventy-year-old woman, I'm actually getting excited about the prospect of staying in this house for a couple of weeks or so.

"Let me show you to Greg's old room," Helen says. She takes a couple of my bags and my fingers feel the relief in the creases where the plastic handles have been gouging into soft, writer's-hands skin.

"Why not just put her up in a guest room, Mom? You have three of them besides my room and Sadie's room."

That would make this a six-bedroom home? Ooh, I am so coveting. And why doesn't Greg want me in his old room? Does he have something to hide?

"You know good and well I'm turning one of them into an office and the others haven't been dusted in a year. This came up too suddenly and your room was the easiest to fix up on the spur of the moment." She glanced over her shoulder as she ascended the steps.

Now I feel guilty. "I'm sorry for the inconvenience, Helen."

"Huh?" She waves her hand. "Oh, don't be silly. I'm thrilled to have you. Just explaining to my son here why you're using his room." She turns to him. "Besides, what do you have to hide?"

I laugh. Way to go, Helen.

"Daddy?" Sadie tries to turn Greg's face to her. This is a little difficult with her hanging onto his neck. I try not to be irritated with seeing him juggling her while trying not to fall down the stairs. Come, Claire, get it together. You're the adult. Don't get jealous over a little girl. "Do you have a secret in your room?"

"My question exactly," I say, giving him a nudge. It feels good to be close to him, to tease him, and to be on the receiving end of his smile after our argument.

"I have nothing to hide from any of the women in my life." His grin lifts my spirits. "I'm just afraid it still smells like old gym socks."

Helen gives a harrumph. "Over my dead body. Besides, the main reason I want Claire in your room is because it has the best light and a nice view of the duck pond behind the house. I thought that might inspire Claire while she writes."

I'm rendered speechless by her thoughtfulness. I'm truly being treated as an honored guest rather than an imposition.

I think she understands my emotional response, because she gives me a wink and continues to lead the way up the gray carpeted steps and into a hallway that boasts shiny wood floors, an Oriental runner, and a round wooden corner table with a large vase of fake wildflowers. It's just lovely. Like any home you'd see in a movie or on television.

As a child I used to wonder about people who owned houses like this. The beautiful people who seemed to live in a fairy tale. At least to me, growing up in the home my modest-income military parents could afford, the thought of living in the sort of place Greg grew up in was a fantasy.

I suppose it's a shallow thought. But I still want a house like this. I spent the first five years after my divorce working all the time, writing more books than I had time to write, spending less and less time with God and family, and relying heavily on my mother for the hands-on raising of my children. All in pursuit of this ideal.

It took carpal tunnel syndrome and a forced sabbatical to bring me out of my office and help me reconnect with God and my kids. Not to mention I found my best friend, Linda, during that time, and Greg—who is most likely my soul mate.

"Okay, here it is." Greg's mom throws open a mahogany-stained door, and I walk into the most beautiful bedroom I've ever seen. I step onto an Oriental rug spread out over a shining wood floor. My eye is immediately drawn to a rich wood desk with a massive leather chair I could sink into and write in all day. I think I suck all the air from the room with my intake of breath. "It's gorgeous," I manage. I hate to drop all these bags on the bed and clutter it up.

And speaking of the bed, it's a four-poster. The top of the mattress is high. I will not sit down on this bed. I will climb up onto it. The comforter is lovely, a neutral-colored base with tiny roses and bits of green.

I never want to leave this room. It's twice as large as mine at home. And there's a window seat. I imagine myself curled up after a shower, my chenille robe wrapped around me as I read my Beth Moore devotions.

"The bathroom is thataway." Helen's voice pulls me from my fantasy and she waves toward a door I had assumed to be another closet.

I'm marveling at the pretty rose border at the bottom of

the walls when it occurs to me. As much as I love the room, nothing about it speaks of a man like Greg. I toss a glance at Helen. "I can't imagine a teenage boy living in here."

"Believe me, it didn't look like this when I was a kid." He drops his bags on the floor and disengages Sadie's hands from his throat, gently sliding her to the floor. "The day I left home, Mom hired someone to remodel and redecorate."

"Not the very day." Helen gives him a quirky grin, and it's easy to see where he gets his sense of humor. "It took me a month to get a contractor to do the work."

She turns toward me. "The chest of drawers is cleaned out," she says, pointing to the piece of furniture in the corner.

"Thanks. I'm not going to need six drawers just yet. Hopefully I can get some of my own things out of my room as soon as I get in touch with a contractor and get that tree out of my house. Right now I doubt I'd fill up one drawer."

I smile. She smiles back. I think we're going to get along great.

"Well, when you have need, they're all yours. The closet is also empty."

I nod my thanks.

Greg slips his arm around me and pulls me close to his side. "Think you'll be comfortable enough here?"

I look up into his eyes, which are saying so much more than the simple question. He's sorry we argued, too. He cares about me. Wants me to be happy, safe.

Did I ever mention that Greg wears his heart on his sleeve?

Raising my chin, I send him a reassuring smile. "It'll be perfect."

He brushes my lips with his in a feather-light kiss. I'm so shocked I can't even pucker. He's never kissed me in front of Sadie or his mother.

Apparently Sadie's a little rattled by it, too. She grabs her dad's other hand and jumps up and down. "Can we go home now, Daddy?"

"Sadie," Helen admonishes. "It's rude to interrupt."

"Well, I'm tired."

Reluctantly, Greg turns to her and I slip out of the comforting circle of his arm so he can give her his full attention. He lifts the little girl and she wraps her bony legs around his waist, her skinny arms around his neck. Helen gives me a wink. I feel heat spread across my cheeks and know by her chuckle I'm blushing.

"I guess we're leaving," Greg drawls. "Walk us out?"

"Of course." I motion toward the door. "Lead the way."

I'm following. Sadie's chin is resting on Greg's shoulder and she's glaring at me. Staking her claim. Now, I realize I have two choices. I can try to win her over. Smile. Cajole. Ask her about her day. But I have a feeling she'd shoot me down in a millisecond, and that would be embarrassing for Greg and me both, so I opt for door number two. I look away and let her think she's cowered me. I can be the bigger person in the situation. After all, I'm going to get Greg. No matter how much Sadie objects.

To be honest, my heart goes out to her. It's not the kid's fault she lost her mom and is going to have to share her dad. Even if divorce brings up a whole other set of problems for my kids, at least they *do* still have their dad. Lousy husband—great dad. All right, in all fairness, he's not such a lousy husband to Darcy.

Oh, well.

"I'll let you two say good-bye," Helen says when we get downstairs. "Can I make you some tea for when you come back inside?" she asks. "I never go to bed without a cup of chamomile."

I can't help but warm to her sweet smile. "That sounds lovely. Thank you."

She rises up on her socked tiptoes and kisses Greg's cheek, then gives it a maternal pat. " 'Night, son." A look passes between them and I'm not sure how to take it. But Greg's face colors, so I have a feeling it has something to do with me.

I open the door for Greg since his arms are full of his scowling daughter. The cool night air is heavy and smells like another round of rain is on the way. I think of my house. If it rains again, more of my things will be ruined. I don't mean to be materialistic. But I've worked so hard to build a great life for the kids. We've just reached a place where I'm not working as much and we're spending more time together as a family. I don't want to have to go back to such a grueling schedule.

Greg straps Sadie into her booster seat in the backseat of his Avalanche and shuts the door. Then he turns, gathers me into his arms, and leans against the truck. "I'm sorry I made it sound like I don't care about having a nice wedding with family and friends. I know the wedding is important, too. I've envisioned you walking down the aisle to me more times than I can count."

Okay, sometimes this guy just takes my breath away. "You have?"

"Of course. I know my attitude earlier didn't show that. I just wasn't thinking about anything but that tree and how much I'll miss you not being a couple of doors away. A quick marriage seemed to be the solution. In hindsight, I see it wasn't right to just spring it on you like that."

I kiss him briefly to acknowledge my forgiveness. "And I'm

sorry I gave in to my shrewish side and accused you of only wanting a slave."

He laughs and snuggles me close. "Forgiven." We stand there in each other's arms for a while. I figure Sadie must have fallen asleep because she's not kicking the door or calling for Greg to hurry. "I'm sorry about your house, Claire. Do you want me to help you find a contractor? The school janitor's brother-in-law has his own business. I could get his number."

Drowsy, with my cheek pressed against Greg's warm chest, I nod. "Mmm."

"I take that as a yes?" He kisses the top of my head and I get my cue to step back.

"Yes. I'd appreciate the referral. The sooner we're back on the same block the better."

He gives a little growl and pulls me close again. "My thoughts exactly," he says, just before we kiss.

I'm shaking slightly and my heart is about to pump out of my chest by the time he pulls back and brushes my hair from my forehead. "I don't know what you think of this, but . . ."

My suspicious nature creates a dark drama in my head as I wait for the other shoe to drop. "What?"

His eyes soften as a smile tips the corners of his mouth. "Don't look so worried. I've been trying to talk to you for a few days, but we never seemed to find time alone. I hate to spring this on you now, but I need to make some plans and don't want to do it without discussing it with you."

"What kind of plans?" And why do I feel an emotional tornado coming on?

"The church has grown to such a degree that the board and Pastor Devine are considering taking on an associate pastor."

"Good idea." *But what does that have to do with us?* I'm thinking.

He clears his throat nervously. "The fact is, he would like for me to consider the position if it materializes."

Pride that the church leaders see Greg's wonderful potential combines with a little bit of dread. "You want to be an associate pastor?"

"I think so." His eyes are so serious, I feel a lump lodge in my throat. I try not to show my dismay.

"Would you still teach?"

He nods. "I'd only work part-time at the church to take on some of the duties Pastor is getting too busy to do alone. And preach occasionally when he's out of town."

"I see."

"You don't seem happy." He presses his forehead to mine. "Want to tell me what's going through that brain of yours?"

No. I don't. Really. Because what's going through my brain is that I am barely good enough for Greg as it is, and right now he only serves as Wednesday-night worship leader. If he increases his level of ministry, he's going to see pretty quickly how far beneath him I am. Oh, the things that go through my mind sometimes. I feel like Paul all the time: doing the things I don't want to do, not doing the things I know I should.

Sadie picks this moment to bang on the window. Greg drops his arms from my waist and turns to his girl, opening the door. "What, sweetie?"

"Can we go home now?" she asks sleepily. And I could kiss her for getting me out of this conversation.

"You better get her to bed, Greg," I say in my oh-so-sacrificial tone. "She has school tomorrow. You both do."

He nods. "All right, Sadie. We'll go in a sec." Closing the door, he turns back to me and presses a swift kiss to my lips. "We'll talk about this tomorrow."

Associate pastor. That'll make me an associate pastor's wife.

Lord, have mercy.

Helen's kitchen is every woman's dream. An island stove top and grill. All stainless-steel appliances, which just happens to be my favorite kind of kitchen. Gorgeous hand-crafted wood cabinets everywhere. Granite countertops.

She glances up from her perch at the bar and waves me to a seat. "I'll get your tea." By the cinnamony scents wafting from the oven, I think Helen has gone to a little more trouble than merely setting a teakettle on the stove.

Grabbing a potholder, she confirms my suspicion. "I had some cinnamon rolls left over from yesterday's baking. I have them warming in the oven. I hope you like them."

Is she kidding? I can feel my hips spreading just thinking about gooey, warm, iced cinnamon rolls.

"Yum. You're not trying to fatten me up so Greg will lose interest, are you?"

Her brown eyes, so like Greg's, twinkle as she sets a cup and saucer in front of me and a little plate with an enormous roll next to it. "Not a chance. I'm tickled pink that he's found you."

Taken aback by her sincerity, I'm embarrassed into silence, so I bite and chew quick-like to avoid the necessity of a reply. "Delifshush," I say with my mouth full.

I'd rather snuggle up in one of the branches of my house tree than have to engage Helen in a conversation about my relationship with Greg. But Helen, it seems, is settling in for a nice long chat.

She sets a serving plate between us with at least six warm cinnamon rolls and my palms start to sweat. Nervousness hits me on two levels. One, like I said, I don't want to talk to her about Greg. I have a bad habit of saying too much. Two, I could easily eat every one of those soft, yeasty, calorie-and-fat-laden treats of comfort and delight.

My heart is beating as though I've been pushed into a corner. I know there's only one way out of this. I fake a big, wide yawn, complete with an over-the-head arm stretch. I may have overdone it, because the expression on Helen's face is anything but clueless.

"You've had an exhausting evening," she says, totally letting me off the hook even though I know darn well she has my number. "I'll put these away for breakfast."

Relieved beyond words, I swallow my last bite while nodding my approval as she grabs plastic wrap from a drawer and proceeds to cover the baked goods. My nerves are beginning to calm. I'm halfway to escape. And honestly, I'm beginning to feel the effects of the stressful evening. I'm more than ready to take a shower and lose myself in that enormous bed.

The tea presents another challenge, though. It's steaming hot. No gulping for a hasty exit. And after I said I wanted some, I can't really leave the cup full without making a valiant effort to drink it down.

Again, Helen comes to the rescue. "You look about ready to drop, dear. Why don't you take your tea up to your room with you?"

"You don't mind?"

"Not at all." She swipes at the countertop with a damp cloth. "We'll have plenty of chances for girl talk. And I promise not to pry into your relationship with my son."

I slide off the stool and snatch my cup and saucer from the counter. "I'm that obvious, huh?"

"Never try to play poker, Claire. You'll lose your shirt." She laughs.

Amusement slips through me. She's right about that. I couldn't bluff my way out of a paper bag. I mull this over as I climb the steps, carefully hanging onto the saucer so that I don't drop it or spill the contents of the cup. Isn't it better to be a straight shooter? To be honest at all costs? At least no one ever has to wonder where they stand with me. That's a quality I admire in the people I keep close to me. I want to know truth above all else. Even my children know that they'll get in a lot less trouble if they own up to whatever it is they've done. And there's always something. Believe me.

I enter the amazing bedroom and go to work immediately emptying bags of underwear, bras, shirts, jeans, all things I could find on sale. I didn't venture too far from Sears. Other than the size 10 Gap jeans and to Dillards for Clinique skin care and makeup. Still, five hundred dollars doesn't go that far when you have to buy a little bit of everything, so it doesn't take long to put everything away.

I grab my new SpongeBob pj bottoms and a black undershirt I bought to sleep in. (I really wanted to get a silky nightgown, but Greg was hovering. I had to order him out of the lingerie section when I picked out new bras and underwear.)

I enter the bathroom and have to bite back a cry of ecstasy. A Jacuzzi tub. Okay, all thoughts of a shower are firmly removed from my mind. Now I have to go borrow a book from Helen so I can soak and read.

I pad barefoot out to the hallway. I notice a light glowing from the bedroom at the other end of the hall and assume that's where Helen's at.

I tap on the door.

"Come in," Helen calls. I enter the master bedroom and my

jaw drops. I'm pathetic. It's downright elegant. "Is something wrong?" Helen is sitting up in bed, reading by the light of a beautiful brass lamp sitting on her nightstand.

"I wondered if you might have a book I can read." Too late I remember I faked a yawn to get out of our conversation. But considering she wasn't fooled in the first place, I'm not surprised by her warm smile.

She nods toward a nook in the corner of the room. "Help yourself."

Wide-eyed, I step across to a little built-in library. "Wow. This is amazing."

"Jim built it for me as a surprise on our tenth anniversary," she says from the other room. "That used to be the nursery. When we bought the house, I dreamed of keeping it full. But it took us seven years to have Greg and I couldn't have any more after him. I suppose nowadays we could find a way. But doctors didn't know then what they do now about fertility."

My heart goes out to her. I can't imagine life without my brood. Just thinking about it, the loneliness squeezes my heart. How will I survive without my kids for what could be weeks? I'm trying to find the proper response when she apparently takes my silence for what it is: me not knowing what to say.

"Anyway, Jim knew the nursery made me sad, so he shipped Greg and me off to my mother's for a week and while I was gone, he did this as a surprise."

I pull on the top of a book to bring it close enough to read the spine. "That's sweet. It's easy to see where Greg gets his nurturing."

"Yes. He was close to his father until Jim passed away during Greg's senior year of high school. He went a little wild. I don't think he would have married Kimberly if she hadn't gotten pregnant."

Startled, I drop the book back into place and step out of the library. "What?"

Her face goes white and I get the distinct feeling Greg's mom has just let the cat out of the proverbial bag. "Greg hasn't told you about Kimberly?"

Well, he definitely hasn't said anything about getting her pregnant before marriage. The thing is I am not one to throw stones. I wasn't a paragon of virtue before my wedding night to Rick. My shock has nothing to do with judgment, but rather the fact that he's never bothered to tell me such an important detail. I try to hide my rising irritation. "Other than the fact that he loved her and she died three years ago, no."

"Well, I probably shouldn't go into it."

Come on, sure you should. I mean, you've already spilled more than I knew.

I think the lady must be a mind reader, because she echoes my thoughts. "Well, I suppose I've already opened my mouth, I can't really leave you hanging, can I?"

"I'll sleep better if you don't."

She pats her mattress and I pad across the soft, rose-colored carpet and climb up into her bed. "I don't understand. If Kimberly was pregnant that long ago, shouldn't Greg have a teenager?"

Her face clouds and she nods. "They were married a week after Greg found out about the baby. By a judge, of all people. I wanted them to at least have a minister do the service, but Kim wasn't much on church."

I've rarely seen Greg's mom with anything but a smile on her face, but now there's definitely a scowl, and I'm tempted to assure her that when I marry Greg, we will definitely do it at the altar, complete with a communion service and our pastor presiding over the whole thing.

I'm relieved when she continues without awaiting a response from me. "She lost the baby within a month of their marriage. Greg never actually said anything, but I knew he felt cheated out of so much in life. He had planned to go to college on a basketball scholarship." She gives me a sad little smile. "He really was good enough, I think, to have gone on to play professional basketball. But he couldn't go off and play college ball with a wife at home. Kim still had one year of high school.

"Not long after the marriage, Kim's mother left her father and moved to Arizona. Kim cried until Greg felt he had no choice but to try to make her happy." She expels a soft sigh. "She was so young. Too young to be separated from her mother. She didn't even wait to graduate. They moved to Tucson at the end of the summer. Kim finished her last year of high school and Greg went to college and got his teaching degree."

"That shows a lot of character. How many guys would have had such a sense of responsibility?"

She nods, but her eyes are staring at the comforter as though she's reliving the past. "Greg grew to love Kim in his own way. They began attending church and she eventually found the Lord. I think that helped his feelings toward her. At any rate, he chose to make the best out of his life. I think he would have had children sooner, but Kimberly was afraid after the miscarriage."

"No wonder he's so close to Sadie."

"They have a bond that's even stronger than most little girls and their daddies." Her gaze pierces me. "But it's not a substitute for the bond between a man and a woman. I thank God for bringing you into my son's life." Her eyes get a little misty and I'm feeling like a big jerk for turning him down earlier. "I think he's really in love for the first time in his life, Claire. He's happy."

"I'm glad. He makes me happy, too." A lame response, but I'm at a loss for words, so it's the best I can do. "Well, I better get that book and let you get some sleep. Thank you for telling me all of this. I guess if Greg had wanted me to know, he would have told me. So I feel a little guilty knowing." I send her a grin. "But I'm still glad you told me."

"Well, he should have told you months ago. I think he just wants to let it go."

"I guess so." Back in the library, I grab the first book I come across that looks even remotely engaging. When I come out, Helen still seems to be deep in thought. "Good night," I say.

"Good night, dear. I hope you won't be angry with Greg about all of this."

"Naw. I'm sure he would have told me eventually."

But on the way back to my room, it rankles me a little that Greg hasn't been very forthcoming about his first wife. I never really thought to ask too much. I guess I just thought he loved her too much to talk about her. Now I know it was just that he didn't want to rehash all of his past mistakes. I guess I can appreciate that, but it still doesn't help my suspicious side cope with one nagging question: What else has he kept from me?

5

The next afternoon Greg has made good on his promise to find me a contractor. I'm more than a little worried that the guy is so readily available on such short notice in the spring—the beginning of a busy season for most contractors. Nevertheless, Milton Travis is standing upstairs in my house, wearing a ratty red cap, looking over the damage so he can give me an estimate. His presence helps me to push aside the whole "associate pastor" situation. It's a welcome relief, and I can't help but breathe a little easier that I'm moving forward on my house so quickly.

Milt, the contractor, lets off a long, low whistle. "That is some big tree."

His uncanny penchant for understatement just fills me with raw emotion. And not in a good way. To make matters worse, the guy has that bend-over butt-crack syndrome that guys with beer bellies and tool belts tend to get. And every time he bends over to look at the tree from another angle, I'm forced to avert my gaze. We may have to work out some sort of warning system if he's going to be a permanent fixture around here for the next few weeks.

"So, what do you think?" I ask.

"Well, hon," he says, and this is my second indication I'm not going to like this guy (the aforementioned butt-crack syndrome being the first). I don't have any patience with "hon"-calling men. "First thing you're gonna have to do is get yourself a tree-removal service."

I assumed he would just take care of it all. Take off the tree, fix the roof. This is going to be a step-by-step process involving more people to hire? I feel my stomach sinking down to my toes. The more people involved in anything, the more complicated things become.

"Oh, sure. Mostly they take care of trees that folks want yanked out of the ground and moved. But most of 'em take care of storm damage kind of stuff, too."

Well, this one is already yanked out of the ground, compliments of Mother Nature, so there's one step eliminated. "Okay, so first we have to move the tree."

"Yep."

"Then what? How much and how long will it take to get you to fix my roof and the inside of the rooms?"

"Well, I cain't be for sure until I get a good look. But more than likely it'll run you in the ballpark of thirty or forty thousand. And I'll need a third of that up front."

I do a mental assessment of my bank account. Thanks to years of saving every extra penny, I could just come up with the money, and then replace it when the insurance check comes through. But gee whiz, if the guy makes that kind of money on one job, surely he can afford a pair of pants that fit.

"All right. Can you recommend someone to do the tree removal?"

He scratches his nearly bald head through six strands of hair, strategically combed over to the side and held there with some kind of goop. Either that or it's just greasy. Ew. "Have you tried the yellow pages?"

Okay. Big help, buddy.

"Uh, no. But I'll do that today and get back with you as soon as I can."

Milt grabs his belt loops and jerks his ripped jeans back up over his behind like it's no big deal that he's mooning the world. He works his way back down the steps as his pants make their way back down his body. I follow him to the door, keeping my eyes firmly focused on his neck, and bid him good-bye at the door, watching for a sec as he meanders to his work truck, a beat up 1980-something Chevy with "MIL 'S C NTRA TING" painted on the side. Not someone who takes a lot of pride in the little things, I see.

Totally lacking confidence in my new "c ntra tor," I shake my head and turn back to the kitchen to grab my phone book. I sit at the table, praying the ceiling doesn't cave in while I thumb through the yellow pages.

The phones must be ringing off the hook for these people because the first three companies I call have their answering machines turned on. Finally I find a guy who answers.

"Yello," he says.

"Hello?"

"Yello."

Okay, that's what I thought he said.

"Um, Roy's Tree Removal Service?"

"Yep."

"I have a tree on my roof. Any chance you could come and take it away?"

"You say you got a tree on your roof?"

"Yes. The tornado last night yanked it out of the ground and dropped it there."

"That's tough luck."

Tell me something I don't know.

"Got a permit?"

"A what?"

"A permit from the county. Got to have a permit before I can move it."

"I need a permit to remove a tree from my own yard?"

"Yep. Some of 'em are protected under law."

"Good grief."

"Well, now, hold on. You say the tree was pulled up out of the ground?"

"Yes, by the tornado last night."

"That right? My wife and I didn't hear a thing. Didn't even know about a tornado until we started getting calls this mornin'. Must've come whilst we was watchin' *Jeopardy*. The wife has bad ears, don't ya know, and we have to turn the dern thing up so high, it ain't no wonder we couldn't hear no tornado."

Fascinating story. I fight to squelch my impatience. "Mr. uh-Roy. Who do I have to contact about a permit?"

"Oh, I don't think you're gonna need one."

"What do you mean? I thought you just told me the law requires—"

"That was before I found out it was pulled up. Ain't much chance it's alive anymore. Is there?"

"I wouldn't think so. Do you think you can come over any time soon to do this? I really should get started on repairs."

"Oh, sure. I need to round up my boys and we can be over there first thing in the morning. Probably take the better part of two days to get it all gone."

I press my forehead into my palm. "All right. I'll be here in the morning." I give him the address and hang up the phone, not feeling extremely confident in my chances of ever actually moving back into my house.

No, Mom. For the tenth time, no one was hurt." Except now my head hurts from incessantly slapping it with my palm for the last five minutes. What in the world induced me to give her a call? I've refrained from telling her about the house until now because I knew she'd freak out and ask a bunch of questions that I have no answer for.

"I think I'd better come stay with you for a while until you sort this out."

Hasn't she been listening? "I don't even have a house for you to stay with me *in*."

"Where are you living? Not with Greg, I hope."

"Of course not." I almost tell her that I'd thought about it, but decide there's no sense in opening a can of worms. "The kids are at Rick and Darcy's, I'm staying with Greg's mom."

"How long until you get back into your own house?"

"I'm not sure. I'm working on getting some estimates for now. The guys are coming tomorrow to get the tree out of the house."

Okay, saying that just doesn't seem right.

"I just wish I were there to help out."

"Now, Mom. Remember, you moved to Texas so you could live your own life. The way you want. You have to stop feeling guilty."

"I know. I just miss you and those kids so much."

"We'll get you here for a good long visit as soon as I'm back in my house. Okay?" I search for a topic to divert her attention to my situation. "Hey, how's Bob?"

Mom's shaky sigh reaches my ears, causing a frown and raising my concerns. "Mom? What's wrong?"

"Bob and I broke up last night."

Now, I was never big on my mom seeing the Texas Cowboy college president in the first place, but how dare he break my mom's heart? Loser.

"What happened?"

"It was just one of those things. He wanted to marry me and I wasn't ready to take that step."

Stunned déjà vu kicks me in the teeth. For years I've been fighting gravity, gray hair, and annoying mom-type sayings like "As long as you live in my house, young lady, you'll do as I say," so people can't compare me to her. Only, as I think back to Greg's proposal in light of her own reason for breaking up with Bob, I realize something: I really am becoming my mother. There's just no escaping the inevitable. No matter how hard we fight it, girls grow up to be their mothers. Someone just shoot me and put me out of my misery, will ya?

I'm telling you, Linda. I think I'm being punished for some unconfessed sin I committed in my youth," I say an hour later, sitting in Churchill's, a local coffee shop, with my best friend and pouring out the details of my sad, storm-ravaged story.

Linda looks like Ginger from *Gilligan's Island*, only without the sleazy Marilyn Monroe imitation. With red hair and luminous green eyes, my friend has "romance heroine" written all over her. I usually eat light when I'm with her so I don't feel so bad about myself, but today I forego the "skinny" and go straight for the creamy, whole-milk mocha latte with sugar and whipped cream. I add to my calorie/fat-laden binge an apple turnover. Total comfort food, but I don't care. After all, if anyone needs comforting, it's me.

Linda chuckles at my theory of God-correction. "More likely the tornado just hit the wrong house. It was probably headed for John Wells. Isn't he an atheist?" She's talking with her mouth full and still looks classy. I hate my life. She swallows down her bite with a mouthful of chai tea. Then she gives me a quirky smile. "Seems like if God was going to teach anyone a lesson it'd be him. Know what I mean?"

In spite of myself, I can't help but find the humor. I give a sideways grin. "Yeah. That's probably it. Lack of communication between heaven and the natural disaster. I wonder who I contact to file a complaint."

My new neighbor—in the English-cottage-looking house to the right of my house—moved in during a late February storm that dumped six inches of snow on us and knocked out the power for twelve hours. (I should have seen it coming then.) Every house on the block participated in helping the seventy-year-old bachelor move in. Being that he's elderly and single, we naturally assumed he was a widower, but no. He's recently retired from the stage, where he's worked in New York, London, Paris. He decided to move here to be closer to his daughter—who he unashamedly revealed was the product of an illicit affair during his forties. And I get the feeling from his man-of-the-world attitude that "illicit affair" is John's middle name.

He made no apologies for his life or his beliefs. And after we had him all moved in he thanked us for the help, then informed us that he is staunchly atheist, but will respect our antiquated, outdated, and downright ignorant beliefs if we will please not inundate him with our proselytizing efforts. That's how he said it, too. (Except for "ignorant." That was only implied.)

He's pleasant enough. But how much better it would be if he weren't headed for hell. You know?

"Hey, speak of the atheist," Linda says, all hush-hush as the bell above the door dings.

I look up at the same time John Wells sees me. He strides my way.

Knowing I will now have to be a good example, I nix my sullen, God-blaming attitude and force a smile. "Hello, Mr. Wells."

"My dear girl. I couldn't help but notice the tree on your house." Okay, if anyone else had said those particular words, I'd have thought they were making fun of my predicament, but John is so cool, he could recite "Little Miss Muffet" and get a standing ovation and cries for an encore. His expression is one of genuine concern and I warm to the sympathy.

"Yeah. I guess you can't predict the weather."

He lifts the ticket from our table. "I insist upon treating you both."

I'm about to turn him down, but Linda speaks up first. "Thanks! That's so sweet of you." She beams and blushes a little like a giggling girl. Hello? Remember your newly re-vowed husband, Mark?

"My pleasure." His gray moustache twitches as he passes along a distinguished, white-toothed smile and heads off to find a seat.

"Do you suppose those are his own teeth?" I ask.

"They don't look fake," Linda says and I swear she's watching the old geezer saunter, all full of himself, to his seat. "Don't you think he sort of looks like Sean Connery?"

I take a quick glance at him. "Not really. I think it's the hat. And the fact that he walks straight and sure, which is unusual for a man his age."

"Too bad he's not a Christian. Greg's mom is single, isn't she?"

Having recently renewed her wedding vows, Linda is oh-so-in-love (barring the occasional ogling of attractive older men).

"I'm not fixing up my boyfriend's mom with my atheist neighbor."

"I know. I said *if* he were a Christian."

A buxom blonde enters the coffee shop and we watch wordlessly as she heads over to Mr. Wells's table. He stands, kisses her cheek, and holds her chair for her.

"Looks like she's not his type anyway."

"'Guess not," Linda says, sounding a little offended for older women everywhere. She grabs her purse. "I have to be going. Listen, if your contractor doesn't work out, let me know. My brother, Van, is starting up his own business. He works cheap for now while he's building up a résumé. He's got a couple of pretty good references." She fishes into the purse and draws out a business card.

Not that I'd let business and friendship mix, but I take the card anyway. "Okay. I'll keep him in mind."

My eyes land on another business card that has fallen from her purse and onto the table. I pick up the champagne-colored card, and in true, nosy-best-friend fashion, turn it over and read it: "Emma Carrington, Life Coach. One free thirty-minute telephone session."

"What's this?"

Her face has suddenly gone scarlet. "I took it last year when I thought Mark and I were getting a divorce."

"Did you ever call her?"

She shakes her head. "I met you instead. Talking it over with you helped. And then I found out Mark wanted to re-marry me."

I rack my brain trying to remember how helpful I could

have been, jaded as I was over my own bad divorce. I give a mental shrug and offer her the card.

"Throw it away," she says. "I don't need it anymore."

With a wink, she turns and sashays out of the coffee shop. I turn the card over a couple of times, then drop it into my purse just as the server appears to take away Linda's dishes.

"I'll be staying to do some work," I say. "Could you bring me a cup of regular coffee and just keep it coming?"

Thankfully, she's the pleasant sort. She smiles and agrees. I pull out Rick's laptop and plug in my headphones and jump drive. I have no desire to work on this proposal for a new romance novel. But now more than ever I know I have to keep the checks rolling in.

Ignoring the angst on the inside of me, I set to work on a synopsis. It's pretty basic. Boy meets girl. Boy falls in love with girl. Boy loses girl. Girl has crisis. Boy wins girl back. Boy and girl live happily ever after. Yada yada. Oh, and boy and girl are Christians.

Three hours later, feeling more depressed than ever, I stand up to leave. But when I gather my things and head for the door, I notice a crowd has gathered. I stop short as that once-familiar anxiety shoots through my stomach. My head begins to swarm and my heart picks up speed like a mustang on the open highway. I drop back into my chair, knowing there's no way I'm wading through that group. Tears well up. I thought I was done with anxiety attacks for good. God! Where are you?

"Miss Everett?" I turn to the sound of John Wells's voice. "May I be of assistance?"

"John," I gasp, fighting for air. "I think I'm having a panic attack."

"It's all right, my dear. Try to take slow breaths. I'll be right back."

He strides across the room and returns with a paper bag. "Breathe into this." He strokes my wrists as I do as I'm told. Within just a few minutes, my pulse slows.

"Thank you." I take a glass of water from the server.

"Anxiety attacks. How familiar I am with them," John says. "I've had my share. Trust me."

I'm losing it and he wants to take a trip down memory lane? Besides, I'm not buying it from Mr. Calm-cool-and-collected. "You've never had an anxiety attack," I accuse. "You know you're just trying to make me feel better."

He smiles with affectionate tolerance and presses his hand to his chest. "I vow to you that I wouldn't lie to a lady."

I snort. "Give me a break. A man does not reach senior citizen status as a bachelor without having perfected the art of lying to ladies."

A nod of acknowledgment answers my observation. "All right. Because I feel I can trust you, I will admit to exaggerating a time or two, when I had no choice. But in this case, I give you my word that I too have suffered with panic attacks. Talent isn't a guarantee against a case of nerves. Thirty minutes before curtain and for the first ten minutes into any performance I had to fight panic."

I give him a lopsided grin. "You don't seem the type to give in to nerves. You're way too suave and *debonair*." (I say this last with a swanky French accent.)

"Ah, how little you know me." With a wink, he stands and extends his hand to me. "Let me walk you out."

"Thank you."

We are at my van before it occurs to me to wonder why he

has just spent three hours in a coffee shop. I resort to back-door prying. "I hope I didn't interrupt your lunch date."

His faded blue eyes twinkle with merriment. "Curious, are you?"

Heat spreads across my cheeks. I nod. "A little. Sorry."

"Not at all." He opens my door for me as one would expect from a man like John Wells. "Mrs. Jensen would like to pursue acting as a profession and considering that I have been looking into opening a coaching studio in my attic, I agreed to an appointment with her."

"A three-hour appointment?" What a nosy girl I am! Like Jessica Fletcher. I'm sleuthing.

He chuckles. "She's very enthusiastic about her prospects."

I just bet she is.

"Thanks for coming to the rescue, John. If I didn't know better I'd think you were an angel unaware."

He lifts my hand and his moustache tickles the soft skin on the inside of my wrist as he presses a kiss there. "But you do know better and are fully *aware* that I am no angel. Nor do I believe in such things."

"You're nothing but a flirt, John Wells. And I'm half your age."

He chuckles. "At least."

I drive away with a thought: Wouldn't it be incredible if God used me to lead an atheist to Jesus?

I sit cross-legged and stare at the card laying on the comforter in front of me. Emma Carrington, Life Coach. Should I or shouldn't I? It's just so obvious that I need help. Or at least someone I can talk to who might have some sage advice to offer. I glance at the clock. Greg will be here in about an hour to pick me up for dinner at Rick and Darcy's. I showered and dressed early just in case I had the guts to go through with the call.

Now I'm getting cold feet. But I really should call. I think I should. The anxiety attacks alone . . . Mom, Greg, I don't know. What's it going to hurt just to give it one shot? The first consultation is free. Right?

Okay, I've talked myself into it. Without further hesitation, I dial the number. My heart pounds as I wait for her to pick up.

"Hello, this is Emma Carrington."

I gather a long breath and am about to respond when I hear "I'm so sorry I missed your call." Her recorded voice is soft, gentle, relaxing. As, I suppose, it should be. "I sincerely wish to speak with you. Please leave your name and phone number and I will call you at the earliest opportunity."

I blow out my breath. Doggone. I figure there's no way she's ever going to call me back. But for some reason—desperation?—I leave my name and number anyway.

Now I still have an hour to kill. Make that fifty-five minutes. I pad over to the window seat. The moon shining off the duck pond brings tears to my eyes. I lean my head against the window, not sure just why the picture brings on such melancholy. Probably PMS. But I let the tears fall anyway. Wouldn't the kids love this view?

The phone rings a moment later when I'm in the middle of a really great cry. At first glance, I don't recognize the caller-ID number. Still, I snatch it up and a Kleenex at the same time. "Hang on," I say, and set the phone down long enough to blow my nose. Then I pick the phone back up. "This is Claire."

"Hello. Emma Carrington, returning your call."

She sounds a bit put out, this woman who is supposed to be dedicated to helping people. My defenses alerted, I sniff. I suppose she'd have preferred I let my nose run?

Politeness dictates I stuff my irritation and force a pleasant conversation long enough to blow this Emma person off and go back to my window seat and uncontrollable sobbing. "Thank you for calling, Emma." Only Emma sounds more like Emba because of my stuffy nose. "I really don't need to talk."

"May I ask what has changed in the past ten minutes since you called my number?" Her tone is even. Practiced steadiness? No way am I getting sucked into a conversation with a woman who can't even be patient long enough for me to blow my nose.

"Oh, I shouldn't have called in the first place. I was just feeling a bit overwhelmed."

"And now you're not?"

"Well, I . . ." I sigh. "I suppose I still am."

"Claire. You have one free session. How about giving me a chance to help you?" Her voice is pleasant, seems to be genuinely interested. I suppose it's not going to hurt anything to just share.

Thirty minutes later, Emma has my credit card number and I have a commitment to one thirty-minute session per week for the next twelve weeks. Funny thing, ten minutes into our conversation I started feeling better. Maybe this is going to help after all.

Dinner at Darcy's table is one of those affairs. I'd have to describe the entire experience as overcompensation. To explain: Darcy was raised on the wrong side of the tracks by a mother who conceived and bore her out of wedlock—the product of an affair with a married man. They both paid for it socially during Darcy's growing-up years.

But those beginnings motivated her to make something better of her life. She took etiquette classes, decorating classes, any kind of class that might help her better fit into Rick's social lifestyle. The lifestyle I resented every single day we were married. But Darcy is happy with it. She's happy hanging on his arm and gracing his home with style and class. It suits her. It definitely did *not* suit me.

Now as I sit at her gorgeous dining room table with my children, Rick and Darcy, of course, and Greg and Sadie, I wonder who these children are. They are dressed appropriately, neat, clean, and using the proper silverware. They are polite and are displaying exemplary table manners. I'm baffled.

"So, Claire," Rick says as he passes a platter of roast tenderloin to the left. "What did you find out today from the contractor?"

I fill them in on the details. Tree-removal guy coming in the morning. Should only take one day. Contractor guy will be coming back the following day to give an estimate and will hopefully begin the actual work on the rooms and roof soon thereafter.

"I've never heard of Milton Travis," Rick says. "Did you check him out?"

"Don't worry about it, Rick. He had an excellent referral."

I ignore the way his eyes cloud at my flippant response. Even five years after our divorce, I still can't help but push his buttons. In my defense, though, he knows I'm going to do it, so why does he set himself up by asking annoying questions?

"Who gave him a referral?" he asks.

I grin at Greg and jab my thumb in his direction.

Greg grins back. "Milt's cousins with the janitor at the school. He's been in business around here for a lot of years."

"I see." Rick's frowning that I-don't-know-if-this-is-such-a-good-idea frown that I know all too well, and quite frankly, I want to slug him. It's none of his business who I get to fix my house. He doesn't pay the mortgage. Not one penny of child support has ever gone to support me. I worked three jobs to make sure I could take care of myself. His child-support money was split between four bank accounts: Ari, Tommy, Shawn, and Jake. Not to be a martyr or anything, but blood, sweat, and tears keep my head above water. Not my ex-husband. I'm just about to remind him of these facts when Greg speaks up. "I didn't really check him out, so maybe we should do that."

"No," I say firmly. "We don't need to check him out. He's the janitor's brother-in-law and Greg recommended him, and that's good enough for me."

"Claire . . ." Rick starts to argue, but Darcy breaks in.

"Let's eat. I know the kids are starving. Aren't you, kids?"

It is so like Darcy to remind us that our kids are listening to every word we say and that the last thing they need right now is to hear their parents arguing.

"Tell me about school, guys," I say.

"Track meet tomorrow, Mom," Ari says. "Don't forget. Right after school at our field."

"I'll be there."

"Me too," Rick says.

Ari shrugs. "Okay."

I cast a look between them, but both have their heads down staring at their plates. I switch my glance to Darcy, who gives me one of those "we'll talk about it later" stares.

The two little boys have little to say about school. Jakey just wants the next month to hurry up and get over with so that summer vacation can start.

"I have a note for you to sign," Shawn says, and I feel dread rising. Last fall Shawn got into trouble for writing not-so-nice notes to a busty school secretary. He's been in counseling.

Greg winks at me. "He's not in trouble."

"What is it, Shawn?" I ask.

"There's a children's theater starting this summer. And I want to join."

"That's a fantastic idea, Shawny," I say, and his face brightens. I toss a glance to Greg. "The school is sponsoring a children's theater?"

Greg shakes his head. "John Wells got the okay from the school board to provide flyers and permission slips. Kind of like little league does."

"So I can do it?" Shawn breaks in.

His excitement is catching. "Of course. Bring me the form after dinner and I'll sign it for you."

"You know, I could do that, bud," Rick pipes in.

"I know. But Mom already said she would."

Tommy shifts in his seat and leans forward on his elbows. "I got something you can sign, Dad."

I have to restrain myself from telling him to get his long hair out of his food.

Rick gives him a suspicious, raised-brow look. "What's that?"

"Pastor Shane wants to sponsor me. But I need permission from both parents since you're divorced."

Nice the way he played on our feelings of guilt over the split-up. I've got to hand it to him. Brilliant tactic.

Shane Vale is our young skateboarding youth pastor. He's spent the last year hanging out at The Board, a skateboarding hangout. Recently he convinced the church to purchase the building and the equipment when the owners put it up for sale. He runs it. I admire the heart he has for these kids, even if I'm not crazy about the fact that my kid likes to hang out with them.

"I don't know, Toms, I want to look into it first."

"Claire, I think we can trust the youth pastor, don't you?" Rick says, and I swear I'd like to knock him out of his chair. "Bring it to me after dinner, Tommy. I'll sign."

I'm furious at his utter disregard for my opinion. "Wait. I said we need to see." I glare and mentally begin making my list of topics for my next conversation with Emma.

"And as his father—you do remember I'm their father, right?—I say it'll be good for him."

"Uh, hey, you two. It's no big deal." Tommy breaks in before I can reply. "It's a stupid idea anyway. I'm really not good enough to be in the competition circuit."

I know darned well that's not true. Tommy burned up a competition last fall. Won a great new professional-quality skateboard in the process. Of course we couldn't let him keep it because we caught him smoking behind the building after he competed, but the point is, he's good. Very good. And if anyone has the talent to enter skateboarding competitions it's this kid.

"Hey, you know what, Tommy? Your dad's right. You should get this chance. I'll sign it too—since divorced parents *both* have to sign." I give him my I-know-you're-full-of-bull look about that and he grins.

"Well, only one of you actually has to sign it."

"That's what I thought. Let your dad do it. That way if you break any bones, there's no record that I actually agreed to this."

It's not until I'm back at Helen's and Greg has already said his good-byes and kissed me good night that I remember I never actually spoke with Darcy about Ari's attitude toward her dad. I know my daughter has times when she's upset with him over his infidelity. She forgives, but it comes back. She's just a kid, after all. And he broke up our home. I think more than anyone, she feels the loss of that family unit. I resolve to have a good talk with her tomorrow after the track meet. Maybe we need a trip to Dairy Queen for a banana split.

But first things first. I fill my amazing bathtub with water and sink into a steaming tub of jasmine-scented bubbles. An hour later I emerge feeling all warm and relaxed. I towel off and slip into my SpongeBob pajamas. It's comforting to crawl into bed with my Bible and Beth Moore devotional and re-member that no matter how out of control and overwhelmed I'm feeling, God is always looking out for me. He's just there, you know? Being God and being good and loving me with His incredible, unfathomable love.

I'm just dozing off when my cell phone rings on the nightstand next to me. Who would call this late? My first thought as I sit up is that one of the kids is hurt or sick. With my heart pounding against my chest, I answer.

Linda's voice on the other line relieves me until she starts talking. "You aren't going to believe what I'm looking at."

"What?"

"Your daughter and mine going into Barney's with a couple of guys I've never seen."

Barney's is a local pizza hangout where they serve wheat crust pizza and play live music every night. High-school kids frequent the place until about ten, when the college students take over. The music gets a little louder, more beers flow around the place. I take a glance at my clock. After midnight.

"You sure you saw right?"

"I know I did." Linda's voice radiates with the same anger that's starting to rise inside of me. "I heard Trish sneaking out, so I decided rather than stop her, I'd follow to see where she was going. She picked Ari up at the end of that ridiculously long driveway of Rick and Darcy's. Then they met these guys at Barney's. You coming? I'll wait if you are."

"You better believe it. Don't let the front door out of your sight. I don't want them escaping before I get there." I already have the covers pushed back and I'm rummaging for a pair of jeans. "It'll just take me a sec to get dressed."

"What are you wearing right now?"

I confide to having on the SpongeBob jammie bottoms and an undershirt. And my leopard-spotted slippers I wore downstairs that fateful tornado day.

"Claire, don't change. Wear that. I've got my pajamas on, too. It'll serve them right."

Oh, yeah. It's so obvious why we're best friends.

Helen is coming toward the stairs with a cup of tea obviously headed up to her room to read when I come downstairs.

"Oh, Claire, I thought you'd already gone to bed. Your light was off when I decided to come down for some tea, or I'd have offered you some."

"You're up awfully late." I pull my keys from my purse.

"New book. I can't put it down." She smiles fondly. "What's your excuse?"

"I have a slight kid problem." I give her the digest version and her eyes widen. "Oh, dear."

"Yeah."

Ten minutes later, I swing in behind Linda's little red Miata parked in the nearly empty lot across the street. She is standing beside her car by the time I unbuckle and get over to her. I give her a quick once-over and grin at the ladybug pajamas and matching slippers. Perfect. "Are you ready for this?" she asks.

"You have no idea how ready I am."

So off we go. We jaywalk across the street and through the glass storefront I see Ari, Trish, and their two dates sitting in a little booth about halfway through the dining room. "What a cozy little foursome," I say.

"Yeah, let's go make their lives miserable."

We walk through the door and head toward the table. Heads are definitely turning at the sight of two moms, no makeup, both wearing pajamas and fuzzy slippers—Linda even wore her robe for effect. Ari glances up and her eyes go wide with horror like she's a child on Elm Street and I'm Freddy Krueger. She nudges the young man next to her to let her out, but I hurry over to her. "Hi, honey, mind if we join you?" I give her date a sweet smile. "Scoot over, cutie."

Blond-headed, blue-eyed, he looks like the all-American boy. "Uh, excuse me, ma'am. But I think there's a table just over there." Gotta give the kid credit. At least he's polite.

"Oh, don't mind us," Linda says, pushing her way into the other seat next to Trish's date. I'm sure we make quite the picture with the two young girls pressed against the inside of the booth, Linda and me sort of hanging over the edge of the seats, and the two clueless guys squeezed between us and our daughters.

"Doesn't that pizza look good?" I ask Linda.

She grins and nods and reaches for a slice. "Mmm, tastes good, too."

"Mom," Trish says, leaning around her date. "What are you two doing?"

"What do you mean?" Linda asks. "Oh, you mean coming here after midnight on a school night? Funny. We were just wondering the same thing about you two."

Ari is used to our mother/daughter back and forth, so she knows better than to start anything. But I can't help myself. "Ari, honey. Aren't you going to introduce us?"

"No."

The young man gives her a puzzled look and reaches out his hand to me. "Clyde Frederickson."

I shake his hand. "Clyde. You seem like a really nice guy. And I notice you're not drinking beer like your friend there." I point to the mug in front of Trish's date. Trish and her guy both blush.

"Never touch the stuff," Clyde says. "Dad's a pastor. He'd kill me."

"See?" I say, looking around him to my daughter, whose face shows no contrition. "I knew he was a good guy."

"Yeah, Mom. He's a regular Billy Graham. Now can we just go?"

"Go? But I haven't finished my pizza yet," Linda jumps on the bandwagon. She glances at Trish. "And you know how cranky I get when I don't get to finish my pizza."

"All right. Enough." Ari slaps her hand flat on the table. "I get it, okay? I'm grounded for the rest of my life." She turns to Clyde. "I lied. I'm sixteen—"

"And a half, honey." Sometimes I just can't help it.

"Yeah, right," she mutters. "And a half."

Clyde gives her a little frown. "Oh, wow. You lied to me."

"Very astute," I say, just because I'm in an acerbic-remark mood. I suppose it's not his fault Ari lied to him. "How old are you, Clyde?"

"Eighteen."

In theory, he's not too old for my Ari, but she's just a junior in high school. And with senior year still ahead of her, I'm not prepared for her to date college boys.

"Let's just go, Mom. All right?" Ari says through clenched teeth.

I glance at Linda to see if she thinks Trish has had enough. She winks and nods.

"All right, then." I slide out of the booth and lean one hand on the table while I plant the other on my hip. "Slide out of there, will you, Clyde? It's past my daughter's bedtime."

"Yes, ma'am." He steps back and doesn't look at Ari as she scoots out. Linda follows suit.

"Sorry for lying to you, Clyde," Ari says, and to be honest, I'm a little proud of the way she handles the whole thing. "You're a nice guy and didn't deserve this." She waves toward me.

"Are you kidding me?" Indignation shoots through me. "I'm

the 'this' he doesn't deserve? How about he doesn't deserve to be lied to by a little girl playing grown-up?" I'm so mad I can hardly stand to look at her. "Get your behind out to the van."

Darcy's mouth is wide with shock when I get to their porch fifteen minutes later. I have, of course, called ahead to let Rick know that I am bringing our wayward daughter back to his house.

"I just can't believe you snuck out." There's a tremor in Darcy's voice like she's taking it personally. As though *she's* the one who's been betrayed.

"Sorry, Darce." Ari slips past her stepmother and it occurs to me that this little apology is more than I've gotten.

Rick is standing beside Darcy wearing blue pajama bottoms and a T-shirt. His face is red and scowling. "What are we going to do about her?"

I give a shrug. "I don't know, Rick. She's never done anything like this before."

"That you know of."

I hate it when he acts smug. Especially when our daughter turned into a liar and a sneak on his watch.

"I do know it, buster."

"All right, you two. It's one in the morning." Little Miss Voice-of-reason sounds weary. "Let's hash all of this out in the morning. Claire, do you want to crash here? We have plenty of room."

Not even if the only thing between me and sure frostbite was the warmth of Rick's hearth. "No thanks. Helen is waiting up for me." I toss a glance back to Rick. "Don't punish her without me."

I start to turn toward the door when Jakey's sleepy little

voice reaches my ears. "Mommy?" I glance up the steps and my heart melts at the sight of my youngest child rubbing his eyes. His race-car pj's are crumpled from sleep.

"What are you doing up, sweetie?"

"I'm thirsty."

Darcy heads towards the kitchen. "I'll get you some water, Jakey. Do you want to come down here and kiss your mom good night?"

My heart clenches as his little legs negotiate the enormous steps. I smile and open my arms. He clasps me so tightly around the waist, I feel the blood rushing to my head. "You okay, bud?"

"Can I come home with you?"

Rick steps forward. "Remember, Jake, your house has to be fixed? Your mom is staying over at Mrs. Lewis's house."

As though his dad hadn't spoken, Jake bends his neck back and looks up at me. "Can't I stay with you?"

"Not tonight, sweetheart." What's a mom to say at a time like this? He's always loved coming to his dad's house, but I guess it's not the same when you factor in the uncertainty of not knowing how long you'll be staying. It's obviously messing with his sense of security. "How about I tuck you back in bed?"

His little head bobs. I lift my gaze to Rick's just to make sure. I resent his nod. I mean, since when does a mom have to ask permission to tuck in her baby? Darcy returns with Jake's water and he takes just a sip then gives it back.

She holds out her hand. "Want me to tuck you in, Jakey?"

A frown creases his perfect young skin. "No. Mommy's going to."

Surprise lifts her equally flawless skin. Hurt flashes across her eyes. "All right."

My heart goes out to her a little, but come on. He *is* mine. "He just misses me." I pat her arm as Jake grabs mine and pulls me toward the steps.

From the corner of my eye I notice Rick move next to Darcy and slip an arm about her shoulders. They're waiting for me at the bottom of the steps fifteen minutes later after I've read Jakey a story, sung him a song, and kissed him ten times.

"Hey, you two. Sorry to keep you up. Well, actually, blame Ari. She's the one who caused all this."

Rick walks me to the door. "What are we going to do about her?" He gives me a preemptive look. "And let's don't start fighting about which of us is more lenient, please?"

"I wasn't going to." I wish I had the guts to stick out my tongue. "I've been thinking about her punishment. We should definitely take away all driving privileges for at least a month. And ground her from going anywhere with any of her friends who drive."

He nods in uncommon cooperation. "I agree. And maybe she should have to volunteer at the homeless shelter?"

I feel the blood drain from my face to Lord knows where. "I don't want her to do that!"

"Why not?"

"Because she's too young to be exposed to that sort of life."

He folds his arms across his chest. When Rick folds his arms across his chest it can only mean one thing: he's making a stand. I don't feel all that intimidating in SpongeBob jammies and leopard-spotted slippers. Nevertheless I pull myself up to my full height and dig in my fuzzy heels.

"If she keeps sneaking out at night that might be the sort of life she's headed for." He towers over me and I fight the urge to place my palms on his middle-aged, letting-himself-go, squishy pecs (and who says I'm gloating just 'cause I've been working out?) and shove him backward to get him out of my personal space. I'm not about to let him make this decision about punishment if he's going to be so ignorant about it. My daughter is far from a homeless runaway just because she snuck out to meet a nice guy at a pizza place. "Don't you think that's overreacting a bit?"

"No, as a matter of fact, I don't think I'm overreacting. That girl has been getting away with entirely too much. Better to nip it in the bud right off the bat, if you ask me."

"Well, I didn't ask you, buster."

"Yes, as a matter of fact, you did."

"No. I said don't punish her without me. But since you put your spin on my meaning, let me be blunt. I'll deal with my daughter in my own way."

"Your daughter? Since when did she stop being our daughter and start being just yours, Claire? What, do you just make up the rules that suit you as you go along?" His face is red with anger and his blue eyes are flashing.

I fold my arms across my chest and plant my feet hip-distance apart. "Argue all you want. But the fact is, Ari has been in my primary custody since you left." I gather in a sharp breath for control. I refuse to turn this into a "woman scorned" conversation. "For the last time, my child will *not* be volunteering down there. Unless you want to volunteer with her to keep her safe."

His face is still red, and I notice beads of sweat on his brow. "You know I work sixty hours a week already. When do you suppose I should do that?"

Darcy lays her hand on his arm and her soft voice lifts into the air between us. "Careful of your blood pressure, sweetheart."

That explains the red face and sweating forehead. But Rick is only thirty-eight years old. He's not in *that* bad of shape. "Blood pressure? What's wrong with it?"

"It's just a little high, that's all," he says, totally blowing me off. "My doctor just wants me to lose twenty pounds and exercise. Now back to Ari."

I was afraid he was going to say that. How am I supposed to argue with a man this close to a stroke? "All right. One time. She can volunteer once just to make your point. I'll go with her, since you're too busy." And obviously don't need the added stress.

"I have another idea," he says.

Miffed that I gave in against my better judgment only to have him change his mind, I give an impatient huff. "What idea?"

"I volunteer my services at Hope House once a month. What if I have Ari come with me next time? It's the day after tomorrow."

"What good is that as a punishment?"

His eyebrow goes up, and he looks through hooded eyes. "What do you think, Claire?" Rick is an ob-gyn. And reading his suggestion from that perspective I see his meaning all too clearly. Hope House is a multi-church-funded house for unwed teen mothers. They're allowed to stay for the duration of their pregnancy and for six months thereafter if they've nowhere to go. And you'd be surprised how many have been kicked out or have run away from home.

Suddenly the image of Ari all big-bellied and swollen-ankled comes to mind. I shove the offending thought aside. "That's just about all you know about your daughter, Rick Frank." I turn to Darcy. "Tell him, Darce. Ari is a good girl."

Darcy's about to open her mouth, but Rick interrupts. "But

how long will she be a good girl if she's sneaking out to meet college guys?"

"Sneaking out for *pizza*."

"But what if you hadn't stopped her?"

"I wasn't going to sleep with him, if that's what you're implying, Dad." Ari stomps down the stairs, wearing men's boxers and a spaghetti-strap undershirt. "Thanks for the support, Ma. At least one of my parents believes in me."

Her nose is about a mile in the air and she has an Angelina Jolie–sized chip on her shoulder. The implication scares me to death. And despite the fact that she's somehow allied herself with me, I know I have to be on Rick's side if we're going to have any effect on this new side of her. "Watch your tone with your dad, Ari. He's looking out for you, and if you had an ounce of common sense, you'd appreciate it."

She stops short midway down the steps. Her face registers her shock since she knows darned well that her father and I usually don't agree on much. And unfortunately the kids have seen and heard way too much of our opposing opinions. But even if I don't fully agree with Rick, I'm starting to understand why he feels the way he does. Especially in light of this attitude she's displaying. I mean, come on. The kid just got caught red-handed sneaking out. I take in the haughty expression on my daughter's face and suddenly I know he's got a point. We have to nip this in the bud—pronto.

"Since you're here, we might as well let you in on our decision about your punishment."

"No need." She continues her descent with jerky, twisty, I-don't-give-a-rip movements. "I heard everything from the landing. I lose my license for a month, can't hang out with my friends, and I have to go sit with all the knocked-up teenagers at Hope House."

Ticked off! That's me. Totally. And sleepy to boot. A lethal combination. I look at Rick. "Silly girl. She thinks she lost her license for a month."

He grins. It's sort of goofy, considering he hasn't the faintest idea what I'm getting at, but he does know me well enough to play along. "Can you believe her?"

Darcy is wearing a confused frown. Totally not catching our drift.

"What do you mean?" Ari has reached the bottom of the steps now. "I heard you both agree to one month."

I snag her with a firm, don't-mess-with-me look and tone. "Well, that was before I saw how sorry you *aren't*."

Rick's head inclines in approval just as Darcy's eyes go wide with understanding.

The Angelina wannabe drops the 'tude. "Mom, I'm sorry I lied and snuck out."

"Lied, too? This is worse than I thought. I didn't know anything about a lie. Well, I mean I know you lied to that poor guy who wasted his money on the pizza."

She mumbles something.

Rick chuckles. Darcy covers her mouth to hide a smirk. Apparently I'm the only one who didn't make out what Ari said.

"What was that, honey?"

Laughter rumbles in Rick's chest. "She said she paid for the pizza."

My lips twist into a grin. "Oh, good. Then I don't feel so bad about eating some of it."

Red-faced, she tries to regain her composure. "So how long are we talking, Mom?"

Behind her back, Rick holds up three fingers.

"Three months." The instant I relay the message, a groan

shoots from my daughter and she drops to the bottom step with a dramatic flair that would make John Wells most proud.

"Look on the bright side, Ari." I give a twisted grin, feeling slightly guilty for rubbing it in. But the fact that she is so un-sorry grates on me.

"There is no bright side." She pins me with a glare hereto-fore reserved for her little brothers and any remaining compassion flees my heart.

"Sure there is, honey. Now's your chance to dive into *War and Peace*. If you get started right away, you ought to have just enough time to finish before you get behind the wheel again."

7

This looks like a good one." I draw a red circle around the classified ad and pass it across the seat to Linda. "What do you think? Three bedrooms and a finished basement. Tommy can sleep downstairs."

"Not bad, but five hundred dollars a month. Can you swing that?"

I shrug. I know in some areas five hundred dollars a month would rent a dive, but in south-central Missouri, you can actually get a pretty decent place to live for that.

"I don't see that I really have a choice. Between that stunt the girls pulled last night, Shawn needing me, and Jakey wanting to come home . . ." I don't mention Tommy because I think he'd handle it no matter where he was staying as long as we didn't take away his skateboard. But the honest fact of the matter is that I miss them all desperately. "I just can't leave them for weeks or months."

We're sitting in front of my house waiting for the tree-removal guys to show up. Linda and I must have our morning latte after the ordeal with our daughters the night before. Then she's going to help me look over rental properties.

"Didn't Helen say you can keep the kids with you there?"

I give her a look. "Sure, like that would really work."

"Yeah, I guess you have point." She frowns.

"What's wrong?"

"Shh, listen."

I cock my head and hear something very big and machine-sounding coming down the road. With all the noise, it's a *War of the Worlds* sort of moment and I'm ashamed to say that my heart picks up rhythm.

"What the heck is that?"

"I think it's a crane." I look around and see an enormous piece of machinery driving noisily down the street. "Think that's for me?" I ask, without taking my eyes off the giant piece of metal.

Linda gives a short laugh. "I think that's a fairly safe bet."

"Well, that's good, I guess. Since they're charging by the hour."

"I don't follow."

"Using a machine that size means they know what they're doing, right? And surely it'll be faster. I mean they don't let just anyone operate those things."

By the look Linda shoots me, I think she's finally figured out I'm not playing with a full deck.

As predicted, the machine pulls into the yard. A pickup truck pulls alongside the curb. I let out a sigh. The thought of dealing with men who find me three fries short of a Happy Meal (and face it, all mechanically inclined men consider us the "little ladies") is about the last thing I'm in the mood for. But better to give them directions and get it over with.

The guy getting out of the driver's side of the pickup is sliding into a harness and securing it around his hips. The other man is elderly. He regards me with frank assessment. "You the little lady I talked with on the phone yesterday?" See what I mean?

He extends a work-roughened hand and I slip mine into his for a second. "You surely do have one big tree in your yard, girlie."

"Yes, sir. I take it you're Roy?"

He nods and waves toward the guy getting all decked out in work gear. "That's my boy, Roy Jr. He's the arborist." Whatever that is. I don't ask, because I don't really care. All I care about is getting the tree gone so the contractor can come and do his job.

He points toward the machine. "My nephew Orson's the crane operator."

I nod. "All right then. I don't want to keep you."

"Yep. We best get to work. Clock starts now."

Then by all means get to work. If his estimate is correct, I can expect to shell out close to fifteen hundred dollars by the end of the day. I will get reimbursed, of course, by the insurance company. But the initial investment is enough to make me sweat.

Roy Jr. heads over to the tree as the crane makes dirt trails through my yard. Thinking about the yard repair I'm going to have to deal with, I shake my head as I climb back inside my van. "Well, I guess they know what they're doing," I say.

"Surely a guy wouldn't start climbing a half-uprooted tree if he didn't know what he was doing, right?"

"Presumably."

I pull the van out of my driveway without a lot of confidence. But by the time I get back around four that afternoon, I'm pleasantly surprised to find that they are all but gone. I've already dropped Linda off at home so I don't have my moral support, but it appears as if all is going according to plan. Another truck has been added to the mix and is removing the tree from the street, where the crane has placed all the branches.

I'm careful of the crane as I walk toward the truck, where Roy is still watching the entire process. "How's it going?" I ask when he sees me and meets me across the yard.

"Good. We're just about done."

Fantastic. I go back to the van and grab my checkbook as the crane pulls away from the yard and chugs down the road. "Soon as Ralph there has the branches all picked up, we'll be ready to leave."

We stand, silently watching the grapple truck picking up branches. "So, who you hiring to fix the roof and walls?" He slugs down a mouthful of coffee from a to-go cup.

"Milton Travis."

The coffee goes flying across my yard.

"What?" I ask.

"You already hired Milt, have ya?"

"Pretty much. My boyfriend recommended him. I agreed to hire him as soon as the tree was removed."

"That right?" He shakes his head, and I don't find this comforting in the least.

"Why do you ask, Roy? Isn't Milt any good?"

"Well, now. It's not Christian of me to speak poorly of someone. But if I was you, I wouldn't let him get started on this. I'd hire someone more reliable." He lifts the bill of his cap and swipes at the sweat on his brow with the back of his hand. "My boy Edgar never was much one for tree moving, but he's done right good for himself at construction."

"I see." Perfectly clearly. Roy wants me to keep all the money for this job in his family. Yeah, okay. Thanks but no thanks, Roy.

I dazzle him with my brightest smile. "Well, like I said, I've already verbally agreed to hire Milt. I wouldn't feel right going back on my word. I hope you understand."

"Suit yourself."

I try to ignore my growing sense of dread about Milt, but sheesh.

I open the door of the new place and watch the kids' faces as one by one they step through ahead of me. I don't know what I was hoping for, but these looks of confusion and dread aren't even close to how I thought they'd react.

Jake slides into home plate right in front of the entertainment center and opens the bottom drawers. "Where's my Nintendo?" Well, okay. That actually *is* how I expected Jakey to react. He's predictably one-track minded. About once every six weeks to two months, I restrict him from all electronic games for a week or so. Breaks the addiction for a while. After a tough first day of withdrawal, he always seems to find other occupiers.

"Come on, Jake," I say, walking in behind everyone and shutting the door. "Don't you want to see your new room?"

"Temporary room," Ari says. "Right?"

"Yes." I turn my attention to Tommy. He's leaning against a bare wall holding his skateboard like a security blanket. "Listen, Toms, you won't be able to do your skateboard out here on the sidewalks or parking lots."

Horror narrows his eyes. "What do you mean? I have to practice."

"I'm sorry. The complex has rules against skateboarders."

"That bites!" he grinds out. "I might as well tell Shane to find someone else to sponsor, Mom. If I can't practice, I'm going to lose all my form."

"Can't you practice over at The Board?" I ask, thinking it's an excellent question. "It's only for a few weeks at the most."

"I guess. If you'll drive me over there."

"I don't mind driving him when you're busy, Mom." Ari's generosity as usual astounds me. Not.

She gets what she deserves: a wide, knowing grin from me

and a pat on the head as though she's a six-year-old. "Nice try. If only you weren't grounded from the keys."

"Even in an emergency?" Her wide-eyed innocence is truly moving.

"I seriously doubt you're going to have to deal with any emergencies when I won't be around to do the driving." I turn to my middle boy. "What do you think of our temporary place, Shawn?"

Relief washes over his face and I know instantly what's in my boy's heart. I wrap my arms around him. "I'm glad we're all together again," I say.

"Yeah, I guess it's okay," Tommy concedes. "As long as we don't have to do it for very long."

Jakey's plugging in all the cords to hook up his game. "What do you say, Jakey? This place going to work for you?"

"Yeah, I like it."

I can't help but smile. I turn to Ari. "How about you? Can you live with it for a couple of months?"

"I don't mind it," Ari says graciously. Then she gives me an impish grin. "This is the apartment complex most of the college kids live in."

Too bad I didn't check into that before I signed the three-month lease. Suddenly that makes sense, too. A three-month lease isn't real common. But if a student—or a group of students, most likely, for a three-bedroom townhouse like this one—were going home for summer break, it would make sense to allow a short lease.

I have a feeling I'm going to be busy all summer keeping a close eye on my girl. Oy.

I settle in that evening, more than ready for my call with Emma. I can't wait to open up about Ari and Rick. And this dinky apartment with vibrating walls from the loud music next door.

She picks up on the third ring, sounding a little breathless. "Hello?"

"Emma? This is Claire Everett. Did I get our appointment time wrong?"

"Oh, Claire! No. No, you're right on time. I'm sorry to sound so frazzled. I was just finishing up with another client." Her voice cracks a little.

"Is everything okay?"

"Of course." She pauses a minute and I hear her swallow as though she's just gulped a mouthful of water or something. "Tell me about your week."

She seems normal now. Or as normal as I know her to be, and at a hundred and thirty dollars per session, there aren't too many minutes to waste. I lie back on my couch and begin by spilling out my discontent over my dinner at Rick's. "I'm feeling undermined," I complain. "As though I was being usurped just because I've been temporarily displaced."

"It sounds as though you made the right choice in finding an apartment and moving your children back in with you."

Okay, it's good that she said that, because I was starting to have second thoughts. Guilty thoughts about how I was self-ish to bring my kids to an apartment complex when they could be living in a nice home in an upscale neighborhood.

I force myself back to the one-hundred-thirty-dollars-per-session giver of advice. She's rambling whether I'm listening or not, so I best keep my attention focused. "You should see a bit of normalcy return soon. Everyone will revert back to their roles. Rick will again be their father but not their primary caregiver, and the kids will settle into their new environment.

And I suspect you will be able to relax now that you have your children around you again."

I could swear I hear her voice crack again. "Emma, you okay?"

She clears her throat in a manner I can only assume is an effort to regain composure and that doesn't exactly reassure me. "If you need me to reschedule, I'd be happy to call back some other time. Or just add the last ten minutes to my next session if you want."

"I assure you, everything is fine. How about talking about Greg?"

It doesn't take much for me to open up here. I give her the history of my relationship with Greg. When I get to the part where he proposed the night of the storm, I'm certain I can hear her sigh. Or is she yawning?

"He sounds like a great guy. What do you think is holding you back from committing to him?"

"Oh, I'm committed. I just feel like I need to have some structure back in my life before I agree to marriage."

"I see."

Oh, I hate that. I hate it when people think they see things about me that they don't.

"Look, I'm not afraid to commit, okay? I am committed to a relationship with him."

"I believe you."

"No, you don't. Look, he wants to be an associate pastor."

"And how do you feel about that?" Oh man, what is she, a shrink or a life coach? Still, I force myself to calm down and just try to answer the question. After all, isn't this what the sessions are all about? I gather a deep breath. "I think Greg will be amazing as an associate pastor. He's warm and wise, and God has truly gifted him for ministry."

She stays silent. Am I supposed to keep talking without a response, or did she fall asleep? "Emma?"

"I'm still here, Claire. I don't think you're finished. What do you think about his becoming an associate pastor?"

I let out a breath. "I'm not sure what my place is going to be in that part of his life."

I hear a ding in the background and I know my time is up.

"Claire, this week I want you to concentrate on how you are feeling. Journal each night and be very honest."

"All right."

"Remember, if you should need to talk through the week, I'm available for more sessions."

"Thanks." At a hundred and thirty bucks a pop, I think I'll just hold it all in and unload once a week.

Greg's face lights up when he sees me walk into Red Lobster for our dinner date. This is the first time we've been out in the two weeks since the tornado, and not only do I need some time to de-stress, I just need to spend the evening alone with him. He's sitting in the waiting area, but stands as soon as I wade through the other customers waiting for a table.

My heart does a loop-de-loop when he bends forward and brushes his warm lips against my cheek. "Our table should be ready soon." He leads me to a couch, where we sit shoulder to shoulder. I relish the scent of his cologne (Polo, which I love as long as it's not overdone).

Our hands are laced and resting on my crossed knee. He runs his thumb along the back of my hand and leans closer. "So, what have you heard from the contractor?" His voice is soft and his lips are next to my ear. The room is buzzing, but I think he does it to be closer to me. And I'm not complaining. Believe me!

"Not a word since a week ago." I hate to admit it, but I'm starting to worry.

"And you gave him how much up front?"

"Ten thousand dollars." A third of the estimate. "He said it was standard."

"Could be. But I think we need to start making some phone calls if you don't hear from him by Monday."

"I agree."

The hostess calls for us, and Greg and I exchange a smile as we stand. Funny how the smallest things mean so much. A touch here. A smile there. Just that sense of belonging to someone. I've been thinking a lot about my relationship with Greg lately, and I've come to the conclusion that he's worth giving up the remote control for. And if I have to do laundry for two extra people, that's worth it, too. After all, I'll have someone to take care of the cars and make sure the garbage is on the curb for the trash collectors each week.

I don't know. I'm starting to think it would be really great to have a partner in life.

We sit in a quiet little booth out of the way of traffic, for which I'm grateful. I hate getting seated close to the kitchen doors. After we give our drink orders, Greg takes my hands across the table. "It's nice to have you all to myself for a while." He's not kidding! I feel the same way. "I have something important to tell you."

My heart picks up because I've decided if he asks me to marry him again, I'm going to say yes. No more lack of commitment for this chick. I'm ready to take that plunge.

"Look, Claire, you know how much I love you . . ."

Yes, yes.

"Diet Coke?"

Huh? Stupid waitress. Leave the Coke and go. I sit back and

force a smile as she sets down my soda and Greg's iced tea. "Thank you," I say in my polite voice.

"Are you ready to order?" she asks, her smile looking a bit stretched. I know how she feels.

"Uh, we haven't looked at the menu yet."

I've been a waitress so I know she's just doing her job. But doggone it. Leave already.

Greg smiles at her, and I see her melt a little. I know some women get jealous when other women flirt with their guys, but not me. I figure as long as he's not flirting back (and Greg's never done that), then it's really a compliment to me that other women find him attractive. Right? Or is that weird?

"We don't want to throw you behind schedule," he says, "but we haven't had a chance to spend time together in a couple of weeks and we have a lot of catching up to do. Would you mind coming back in about fifteen minutes? By then we should be ready. I promise we won't complain about slow service."

She giggles, and a blush spreads across her face. "I'll hold you to that." She gives him a light tap on the shoulder. Okay, that raises an involuntary eyebrow. Flirting is one thing. Touching is quite another. I'm about to hop out of the booth and slam her to the ground when she sends me a "keep this one" wink and walks away.

I sip my Diet Coke and then slip my hands back in Greg's.

"As I was saying," he says with a smile, "you know how much I love you."

"Yes. I love you, too."

He raises my hands and brushes a kiss across my knuckles—first the left hand, then the right. "I've been thinking a lot about your reasoning for not wanting to marry me yet."

Reasons? What reasons? I know of no reasons why we shouldn't be wed.

"Yeah, about that, Greg—"

"Let me finish, okay? I just need to say this while I have the courage."

I know how hard it is for a man to propose when he isn't sure what the answer will be, so I admire him. I zip my lip, determined that I'm not going to interrupt him until it's time for me sit trembling ever so slightly while a single tear of joy slips down my alabaster cheek (okay, it's *my* fantasy moment—I can have an alabaster cheek if I want to) and falls onto the teardrop-shaped solitaire he's just placed on the third finger of my left hand.

He pauses to take a sip. Poor guy. He's about as nervous as a pig at a sausage factory. "It's all right, Greg. Just say it."

A smile curves his lips. "You were right. Now isn't the time for us to marry."

I don't have one of those stupid moments where I answer the question I thought he was going to ask. I'm not one of those people who say something dumb like, "Of course I'll marry you, darling," when he never proposed. I heard him loud and clear.

Greg just keeps on talking, oblivious to the fact that I'm wishing the earth would open and swallow me in a big hole.

"Your desire to make sure your life is in order and your career on track before you settle down inspired me to want to do the same." He thumbs my knuckles and I have to force myself to keep from yanking my hands away. How dare he use my former words against me when he knows it's a woman's prerogative to change her mind?

"I thought your life was already on track, Greg," I say quietly. I'm trying to force a little *oomph* behind the words, but they fall flat. I'm totally depressed. Can't help but wish I'd stayed home in my apartment and listened to the loud music coming from the students on either side of me, all of whom have decided to take summer classes in order to graduate early.

"I thought it was, too. I mean, I teach a great class of students, I lead worship on Wednesday nights, I have a great girlfriend and a wonderful daughter and a mother who encourages me to follow my dreams. Life is great."

"So, what's the problem?" Hey, if the guy's having a midlife crisis, I'd just as soon he gets it out of his system before bringing it into a marriage anyway.

"I realize that God has called me to something more."

"More like what? How could you possibly fit anything else into your schedule?" *And still have time for me.* I slide one hand out of his and reach for my glass.

"I'm going to Bible school. I'm enrolling full-time next year. It's only a two-year program. But I can receive full ordination upon graduation."

"Ordination to do what?" I look at him over the rim of my soda glass as I sip from the straw.

"Pastor my own church."

I shouldn't have taken the drink. Because it goes down the wrong pipe, and I spend a few seconds coughing my head off.

"Are you okay, Claire?" I'm fighting for air as he slides around to my side of the booth. I know people are starting to stare, but I can't nix the coughing fit. Greg pounds my back with a little more force than I personally think is necessary. I wonder if he's letting out his frustration over the fact that I didn't *ooh* and *ahh* over his dumb decision to leave me to go to Bible college—which I happen to know is in Tulsa. He nudges me over and I scoot.

"What about associate pastor? Whatever happened to that plan?" Suddenly that looks extremely inviting.

"The board offered it to me. But to be honest, I didn't feel like I was supposed to do it. I feel like some day I'll want to become a pastor, and I want some training before that day comes. For now, I can attend school and when I graduate, Pastor's already committed to giving me the associate position."

"Let me get this straight. You can either take the associate position now or you can go away for two years, get schooling, come home, and take the same position you could have anyway?" Without having to go away. What is he thinking?

"I know it seems crazy when you spell it out like that."

"You got that right."

He smiles as though indulging a small child. "Honey, if I were interested in becoming an associate and staying in that position, I'd take it and not think about school. But that's not what I feel God is telling me to do."

I harrumph a little and fold my arms across my chest. Totally pouting. I mean, gee whiz. I was planning to tell him how wrong I was for hesitating when he brought up the associate position to begin with. I was going to tell him the heck with a big wedding, let's just get married. Instead, I look him in the eye and frown. "What do you plan to live on while you're in school?"

"My dad left a large insurance policy. Mom put a lot of it aside for me. Not to mention my inheritance in general. That's the good thing about being an only child to late-in-life parents. They're already established before you ever come into the world. The house is paid for. I have a pretty big savings of my own, but I'd have to exhaust it over the two years." He gives me an apologetic look. "We wouldn't have a nest egg when we get married."

Believe me, bucko, nest eggs are the least of my worries at the moment.

There is an excitement flashing in his eyes that I've never seen before, and I know there's no talking him out of this. Someone he loves a lot more than he does me has apparently spoken loud and clear. And as depressed as what he's saying makes me, who am I to tell him God's got the wrong idea?

"I'll be coming home on weekends. Mom and I both think it's best for Sadie if she stays here rather than uprooting her from school and home. And it's only a four-hour drive. With your writing schedule, you could come see me through the week at least once a month."

"Greg," I say, my stomach sinking so low I'm afraid I'll step on it if I stand up. Associate pastor was one thing. This is way bigger than what he originally suggested. "Do you realize what this will mean?"

"It will be an adjustment." He stretches his arm along the top of the booth. "But it's only for two years, then we can get married and all of this will be behind us. It'll go by fast."

Okay, focus, preacher boy, and listen to what Claire's got to tell you. I turn my body to face him. "That's not what I'm talking about."

He frowns. "What then?"

"Greg, I can't be a pastor's wife."

T his is Milton. I'm out of the office right now, but if ya leave your name, number, and a brief message explaining your problem, I'll return your call as soon as I can."

Fury burns on the inside of me. I've had a rotten weekend as it is, what with Greg's big announcement Friday night at dinner, and I'm in no mood for this stupid message for the millionth time.

"Milt, this is Claire Everett. There are three rooms in my house that still look like a tree caved in on them. You were supposed to be in touch with me no later than one week ago today and—" *Beep*.

Shoot.

Milt needs to buy a better answering machine.

I jam my finger on the redial button and wait.

"This is Milton . . ." Yada yada.

"Claire Everett again. You took ten thousand dollars of my hard-earned money, and I expect one of two things to happen within twenty-four hours. One, you return my money. Two—" *Beep*.

Grrr. I re-redial.

"This is Milton . . ." Yeah, yeah, just give me the beep already.

"Okay, Milt. Claire Everett *again*. Number two, you come to my house in the morning with the materials that were only supposed to take three days—tops—to order. Or three, I will be calling the police."

I slam the phone down and head to the kitchen table—my office for the next two months (or longer if my contractor never shows up). Before sitting down I grab a mug from the dishwasher and fill it with freshly-brewed vanilla coffee, shake two packets of Sweet'n Low into the dark liquid, then finish off the preparation with a tablespoon of half-and-half.

Only it doesn't look creamy enough, so I throw caution to the wind and just pour and stir at the same time until it looks right. I sit in front of my borrowed laptop.

Instead of focusing on the romance proposal I'm finally getting around to working on again for Stu, my thoughts sprint over to my great office in my great house where at this minute, there's not much in the way of progress taking shape.

My fears about the destruction of most of my equipment in my office were correct. But by some miracle my dad's old desk made it through the storm damage with only a few scratches, and actually I'm not a hundred percent certain they weren't already there. I haven't had the heart to refinish the desk since Dad died, so it's pretty scarred up.

Ari's computer is okay. The tree only damaged a little bit of her room, so she's happy to know she'll be able to salvage ninety percent of her personal things.

Tommy's room, however, looks like a . . . well, like a tornado hit it. Which isn't too far off from how it always looked anyway, with the exception of all the breakage. Of course, it was hard on him losing some of the things he prized, including a couple of pretty expensive skateboards, his computer, and some video games.

The little boys' room got it about as bad as Tommy's did. But they didn't have a TV or computer to demolish as I had to take all video games from Jakey's room or he'd be on them day and night. Ditto with Shawn and TV.

My office only got clipped, but like I said, the tree took out my computer and squished my file boxes, but I'm pretty sure the files themselves will be salvageable. So far, I haven't had the guts to step into my office because there's a big hole in the wall, and I'm afraid of heights. I can barely look out the two-story window without getting dizzy.

The contractor could have been a week into the repairs by now. *Where is he, Lord? Where?*

I have a sinking feeling that Milt never intended to fix my house. I know if I took a peek in the mirror, right now, there'd be an enormous *L* on my forehead. *Loser.*

I *have* to force my attention back to this proposal. As much as I resent every breathy sigh, every passionate kiss, every tender marriage proposal, I know this is where my bread is buttered, and I need to make the most of the name I've made for myself.

And like Stu said, romance readers got me where I am. Right? So I owe it to my readers to write my very best and not allow my resentment over not being able to write the book I truly feel God put on my heart to overshadow my pleasure in the simple act of creating a new story.

I open my file and pull up the synopsis I wrote the day I met John Wells and his new protégé at Churchill's. I need to write up a couple of chapters since we're having to target a new publisher; my former publisher would have taken it with just a synopsis. Stu's called me three times this week to ask me about the doggone thing. He's pushing me—something Stu never does. Apparently a publisher—and he's not telling me which one, so that makes me a little nervous—wrote to him asking specifically for a certain type of romance book. I can deliver. I'm a pro at this.

Don't get me wrong. I appreciate every romance book God has graciously allowed me to write. I'm humbled and awed by the letters I receive from women of all ages telling me how much the books have meant to them. But good grief. Am I chained to a certain type of book just because that's what people expect from me? What about creative integrity? What about obeying the voice of God deep on the inside of me when He says, "This is the way to go, walk in it"?

My practical nature is at war with that part of me that wants to throw caution to the wind and see if I could succeed with something else. But now is the time to play by the rules. The proverbial safety net. I have kids to feed. Rent and a mortgage to pay. And I might possibly have to admit to losing ten grand. Drat that Milt.

Just like that, my fingers start to tingle. Dread engulfs me. My heart begins to speed up and I press my fist against my chest. Fighting for breath. These panic attacks are coming with more and more frequency. I know I should go see a doctor. But how embarrassing to admit life is overwhelming me.

Remembering John Wells's paper bag trick that day in the coffee shop, I look for one. Nothing. My head is beginning to swim, but I find a plastic Wal-Mart bag and start to breathe deeply inside. I stumble to the living room and stretch out on the couch. I'm lying there, eyes closed, breathing into a plastic bag and hoping that I'm not sucking in carcinogens, when someone knocks on my door. A moan stirs up from the bottom of my throat. The last thing I want to do is get up.

"I know you're in there, Claire. I saw your van."

Linda?

My friend isn't normally aggressive, so I know her visit is

important. But I can't move. I just can't bear the thought of opening that door. "Go away, please," I groan, knowing full well there's no way she heard me.

When my cell phone chimes out "Going to the Chapel" I know Linda's really, really serious.

I feel around for my phone on the coffee table. "Hello?" I say in a pitiful voice.

"I know you're in the apartment. I heard that ring. Are you going to open up, or do I go get the manager to let me in?"

"Use the emergency key."

She lets out a little gasp. "I can't believe you do that when you're living in an apartment. It's dangerous."

The lock rattles and the door opens. My head stays on the couch pillow and I flip the phone down.

"Claire. You can't put your spare key under the welcome mat. Are you nuts? You're in the college section of town."

I hear the key clink on my coffee table and I open one eye to look up at my friend. "What's up?"

She extends her hands palm up to take in my position on the couch. "This! This is what's up. You've been ignoring your phone all weekend. Where were you Sunday? You missed an awesome service."

"They're all awesome," I say glumly, not the least bit interested in hearing about the service I had to miss. "So it doesn't really matter which ones you miss."

She plants her hands on her hips. "Since when have you been having panic attacks again?" She snatches the plastic bag away from me and plops down on the coffee table. "Stop breathing that garbage. Don't you have a paper bag?"

I dissolve into tears. Not because she's being a little tough-lovish with me, but because I'm fed up. First my career, then a tornado, then dumb Greg wants to preach, and I can't get my contractor to work on my house. I blubber pitifully while I confide all of this to my friend. At not one red cent per hour. Maybe I'm paying too much for Emma.

She hands me back the plastic bag as I fight for air. I breathe deeply of the man-made material.

"Listen, Claire, you're going to have to calm down."

Oh, gee. I need this advice? I glare at her over the bag.

"Okay, sorry. I know." She sits on my coffee table, rubbing my arm, and it's helping me to relax. "So, Greg wants to be a preacher?"

I nod and suck in a mouthful of plastic.

"Well, that sort of makes sense. He's pretty awesome on Wednesdays and when Pastor's gone."

So not the response I'm looking for.

"You didn't tell him how you feel about it, did you?" Her voice is filled with that say-it-isn't-so tone.

I look at her without committing.

"Oh, Claire. Good grief. Poor Greg." She snatches a Kleenex from the table and hands it to me.

"Poor Greg? *Poor Greg?*" I sit up, stuff the bag between the couch cushions, and swipe at my nose. "Greg misrepresented himself in this relationship."

Her mouth drops open. But she closes it with a nod. "Okay, I can see how you might think that. He never told you he wanted to be a pastor. But Claire, the signs were all there. You know they were."

My head swims as I shake it so hard I think I might have to lie back down. "No. No, I don't see that at all." And even if I do, I'm not saying it out loud. I sit back as my head starts to spin again. "The truth is, I've known Greg was happiest doing ministry work. Really, I do know that. I just thought he'd be happy doing it part time. He's such a great teacher. Why would he want to drop everything and go to Bible school?"

Linda raises a silky eyebrow and pins me with a pointed stare. "Maybe for the same reason you want to stop writing romance novels and move to another type of book?"

Ooh, that's just not fair, using me against me.

"But if he does this, I'm out of his life, Linda. How can that be God? I really thought Greg was the one for me."

She gives a short laugh. "Why can't it be God for him to marry you *and* become a pastor?"

Oh, come on. Is she kidding? Okay, maybe not. Her face goes expressionless as she waits for me to enlighten her. Nothing to do but oblige. "I can't be a pastor's wife, for the love of pete."

"Why?"

"Oh, it's so obvious!"

She gives me that I'm-not-following-you look.

"For one thing, I don't socialize well. Darcy had to beg and plead just to get me to start coming to Ladies' Bible Study."

"And look how well that's going."

"Yes, but only because I don't talk to very many of the women." Oh, man, I'm starting to sweat again just thinking about it. I grab the bag.

Linda pats my knee. "Take it easy," she soothes. "Don't get upset."

"Oh, sure, easy for you to say. Everyone likes you. I work at home to avoid socialization. Do you know what pastors' wives have to do?"

"Sleep with the pastor?" She gives me a cheeky grin and waggles her eyebrows. "You know there are women in the church who would run off with Pastor in a heartbeat if he wasn't so in love with God and his own wife."

I sort of give a huff. "Why is that, anyway? Why do women always fall for the pastor?" I'm waxing philosophical. "He can be fat, bald, old, skinny, with bad breath and half his teeth, but if he's the pastor, someone wants to take him away from his family."

She shrugs. "I think it's the anointing of God. You know, like the light that surrounded Moses when he came down from the mountain?"

"I guess." Now I'm thinking of Greg. He has plenty of glory surrounding him when he's ministering. "So women can't resist that, huh?"

"It would appear so. Sad thing is that for the Jezebels who actually succeed, that glory lifts and all that's left is a fat, bald, old man with bad breath and half his teeth." Linda gives a chuckle. "Serves them right."

"Greg doesn't even have bad breath," I mutter. Even without the anointing, Greg's a major catch.

"You don't have to worry about him looking twice at anyone." She gets up from the coffee table and heads to the kitchen. "Unless he doesn't have a woman of his own, that is."

"You're not going to jealous me into agreeing to this," I call into the kitchen.

"Who says I'm trying to make you jealous?" she calls back.

I stand on trembly legs, glad the attack is wearing off. I meet her next to the coffee pot, where she's dumping grounds into the filter basket for a fresh pot. "Do you think you're really serious about not marrying him?" She asks as though the thought is just now occurring to her.

Seeing that she has everything under control, I drop into a kitchen chair. "I can't be a pastor's wife."

"Even if it means losing him?"

Tears spring to my eyes. "I guess so."

She takes the chair across from me. "But why, Claire? Don't you think God knew He was going to be calling Greg to go train for the ministry? Even before the two of you started dating?"

You'd think He would have. True. But apparently someone read the signs all wrong. And most likely it was me. "Trust me, God never intended for me to marry a pastor. He knows I'm not wired for it. As I just said, do you know what pastors' wives do?" I grin. "Besides sleep with the pastor."

"What?"

"Social stuff. They have to cook dinners and arrange bake sales and teach Ladies' Bible Study. And work in the nursery."

"You can't do those things?"

"I don't want to. I like my life, Linda. I was never called to work in the church. I mean, I shop for extra food items to donate to the food pantry that feeds the lower-income families. I always pay my tithe and give in special offerings. Not everybody who goes to church has to work it. I love our church, but my ministry is geared toward the women I can reach with my books."

There, let her try to deny that. After all, it was through reading my book *Tobey's Choice* that she was able to forgive her unfaithful husband. God used the book to heal their marriage.

I flash her an I-so-have-your-number grin.

She gets up and goes to the cabinet to pull out a couple of coffee mugs, then fills them and sets them on the table. "Okay, your books have broad ministry value. But maybe God wants you to stretch your wings a little more. Take the lessons He teaches you through your own books and give them practical application for women who need your brand of ministry."

"My brand of ministry?" I stiffen. "What's that supposed to mean?"

"The simplicity with which you love and serve God."

"Some people call that immaturity."

Lifting her cup to her mouth, she shakes her head a bit and sips. "I give up. Now, about this contractor."

"Ugh. Don't remind me. I think I've been swindled."

"I thought Greg recommended him."

"See? No discernment. See why he shouldn't be a pastor?" I'm only kidding, of course, but I am a little miffed that he didn't check into Milton's credentials before giving me the old contractor's number.

"My brother's still available."

"Well, I'm going to give Milt one more day, and then I might have no choice but to call your brother. Only I won't have much to put down."

"I'm sure he'll work something out with you until the insurance check comes."

She downs her coffee and sets the cup on the table with a thud. "Now, go upstairs and shower and change your clothes. We're going out."

My heart pounds at the very thought. "I can't. I have to work."

"No, you don't. Not for the next couple of hours."

"Really, Linda."

"Don't 'really' me. We're getting you out of the house. Into the fresh air and sunshine." She gives me a quick hug. "Don't worry. There's nothing to feel anxiety about. I'll be there."

Turns out the walk in the park and a bucket of chicken eaten next to the pond did me a world of good. By the time the kids get home from school, I'm ready to cook them a decent meal that even Ari declares edible. Then we settle down to watch our Monday-night movie together. It's my turn to pick, so I force the little munchkins to sit through *The Wizard of Oz.* They groan but manage to stay glued to it and even sing along to "Follow the Yellow Brick Road." Tommy does a hilarious imitation of the Cowardly Lion, and Shawn impresses us all with "If I Only Had a Brain," dance moves and all. Ari and Tommy are so stunned by his talent, as am I, that they forget to taunt him about not having a brain.

Jakey just wants to know how long the dumb movie is because he left his Nintendo paused long enough to do his duty. Family movie night is nonnegotiable. Oh, well, three out of four interactive kids is better than it has been at times.

"Where are Greg and Sadie tonight, anyway?" Ari asks. One Monday night of the month, Greg and Sadie come over and join us. Tonight is the first Monday of the month, and they should be here.

"Oh, they couldn't make it."

Her brow scrunches. "Did he break up with you?"

Now that stings. Why would she automatically assume I'm the dumpee? What if I'm the dumper, which is actually the case.

Tommy walks back into the room with a can of Pepsi. "No way! Lewis broke up with Mom? Did he find someone else?"

Shawn stops short and his expressive eyes relay his sorrow to me. "Do you think he asked Ms. Clark out?"

Ms. Clark, the school secretary, school floozy, and the woman who inspired Shawn's descent into perverted poetry last fall. Any principal worth the paper his check is printed on would have let her go a long time ago. I mean, she dresses inappropriately in short, tight skirts (vinyl—ew!) and tight, low-cut blouses. But this principal keeps her around for eye candy and all the little boys are learning about the birds and bees by pure male instinct.

She had a thing for Greg back in the fall and early winter, but I thought Greg had nipped that in the bud. Maybe now that he's free of me, he's decided to take a little detour before officially starting Bible school.

Jealousy shoots through me like a flaming arrow and lodges right into my heart.

Tommy thumps Shawn on the head. "Ms. Clark isn't Greg's type, dweeb. He likes Christian women like Mom." Tommy's officially on my good list again, even if he did just thump Shawn and call him a name. "Only, well, maybe he doesn't anymore since he dumped Mom."

Okay, he's back on the bad list. That didn't last long. "Keep your hands off your brother and don't call him names."

"So, did you break up, Mom?" Ari asks, obviously not willing to let it go until I answer.

I give a shaky breath and try to be brave. "I guess so."

Jakey, who hasn't really been paying attention, jumps to his feet and comes to stand inches from my face. He's glaring, anger reddening his face. "What did you do? I don't want to break up with Sadie!"

My first instinct is to send him to his room for yelling at his mother. Well, no, my first instinct is to paddle his behind. But considering I'd like to stomp and pitch a little fit of my own, I cut him a little slack.

"I didn't do anything, honey. And listen, just because I'm not going to be dating Greg doesn't mean you and Sadie can't still be buds."

"But Mom, why did he break up with you?" Ari was a lot cuter when she was six and not so curious. "He always seemed so happy anytime you two were together."

Bless her for saying that last. "Listen, kids. Sometimes adults just realize for whatever reason that they aren't right for each other. That's sort of what happened with us. And for your information, he didn't break up with me. If anything, I broke up with him."

A grin splits Ari's face. "All right, Mom!"

Her praise is implication that I'm a heartbreaking "hip" mom who could have any man I want. It took breaking my own heart to gain my daughter's approval at last. Life is not fair.

Two days later, I'm waiting in front of my house—
waiting, as a matter of fact, for Linda's contractor
brother. Even after my blatant threat to call the police,
Milt still didn't show up or call.

Turns out, the police have him listed as deceased. Poor Milt
had a heart attack and keeled right over during a steak dinner
at Western Sizzlin'. Now I feel bad for leaving all the threatening messages on his machine. I haven't heard back from any
of his family members, so I assume my money is gone. I don't
have the heart to try to collect now. At least not until a little
bit of time has eased his family's grief somewhat.

Anyway, I was forced to get in touch with Linda's brother.

Only he's late. I glance impatiently at my watch. Fifteen
minutes late. What is it with contractors? Is there an unwrit-
ten code that demands a lack of punctuality? Sort of like the
Hippocratic oath of contractors? *Be thou never on time.*

I open the van door and slide out. I desperately need to find
a research book in my office. There are a couple of questions
I have about eighteenth-century London for the proposal
Stu's about to have a stroke over. I own the perfect book to
give me the information. I can get the book as long as I don't
look out the hole in my wall and roof. Fear of heights and
Milt's warning to stay out have kept me away from the room
thus far. But the need to get Stu off my back and maybe get a
paying gig is stronger than my fear.

I ignore my gut, which is crying, *No, no, don't do it! It's not worth it for a stupid book. Just order another copy from Amazon.com or the local bookstore. No need to risk your life!* Rather dramatic.

In theory, my gut is right. But I'm stubborn. I want what I want. I don't want to wait four days for a book to arrive. I need this information now. I need to finish up this proposal for Stu to send out to whoever might be interested in buying my Christian romance novels.

I have enough unease in my life; unfinished business seems to be my middle name. This gnawing sense that I'm doing something wrong won't stop clutching and clawing at me. I wake up during the night knowing I've had a bad dream, but unable to remember what exactly woke me up. Then I remember, I'm living a real-life nightmare—Greg is gone from my life, my house is in pieces, and my career is not fulfilling me.

I don't know. Maybe I just want too much. Or do I? Surely there's love out there for me, even if it's not Greg. As much as that thought seems foreign and just plain wrong, I would never try to keep him from following the road that he truly feels God is leading him down.

I walk up the steps to my porch. My house feels eerily empty, like a haunted house or something, when I enter. No one has been here for two weeks, and it has that unoccupied musty smell. I open all the downstairs windows and leave the front door open, including the storm door. I figure any flies that want in have already come through the gaping holes in the ceiling. We tarped it, but in the words of Michael Crichton in *Jurassic Park*, "Nature finds a way."

Okay, enough stalling now. It's time to go up those stairs and carefully walk along the hallway. It'll just take a minute for me to snag my book and get out of there. Not even enough time, really, to fall through the floor and kill or maim myself.

I'm standing at the end of the hall. According to Milt Travis, the hallway shouldn't be dangerous, but going inside the rooms could be because the boards aren't structurally sound. We should assume any of them could be dangerous.

But I know from Milt's original look-see of the house that my office hasn't really had that much damage, so I'm not concerned. Much.

I gather a breath designed to make me brave. The technique is an abysmal failure. I take a tentative step in the hallway, then another. Okay, so far so good. The hallway floor feels no different than it always has. No suspicious creaks, no gaps beneath the carpet to indicate a sinkhole. So I'm reasonably confident. With all the bedroom doors closed, I almost feel as though nothing had happened, except for the thick sawdust layering every visible surface. A parting gift from the tree guys. I'd have gladly paid another hundred bucks if they'd included vacuuming with the estimate.

Standing outside my office, I give the knob a tentative twist and shove. The door swings open. I can't help the sob that catches in my throat, nor the quick tears that appear in my eyes. Aside from the sawdust covering all my beautiful books—without regard to my first-edition copy of *Gone With the Wind* displayed on a cheesy picture-frame easel or my treasured copy of John Bunyan's *Pilgrim's Progress* given to me by my dad when I graduated from high school—there's not a lot of damage to this room. I'm pretty confident as I walk over to the wall where my research bookshelf is leaning slightly askew but is otherwise untouched by nature's fury.

There's a hole in my wall about the size of a window, where a branch must have speared through as it crashed. And above me, a skylight I never asked for. Although I'm seriously thinking about asking the contractor what it would set me back just to add one since there's a hole for it already. I keep thinking how neat it would be to work at night under the stars and a big, bright moon.

My bookshelf is right next to the hole in the wall. I'm not stupid. I know I need to be extra careful. Cautiously, I approach. I scan the shelf where I last saw my book. It's not there. I tell myself "Don't panic." There are several missing editions, so it stands to reason they were knocked off by the force of the invading tree. I scan the dusty floor around the bookcase and wall.

A sigh pushes from my lips as I locate the treasure I'm after. It's on the floor right below the hole in the wall. I hesitate as fear grips me in a flash of heat and butterflies. But I know I can't get this close to what I came to find only to leave it behind because of a little irrational fear of heights.

I tiptoe (like being quiet is going to spare me a brutal death should I fall out that hole) until I'm close enough to bend over. My fingers curl around the book and I feel a surge of accomplishment. Task completed. Something has finally gone right in my twisted life.

From the corner of my eye, I catch movement.

Okay, let me just admit that I'm jumpy. I wish I weren't. But the fact is that I am. So when I'm alone in a creepy, musty house, and I catch movement, the first thing I'm going to do is scream. And that's what I do. An ear-piercing screech that leaves the windows and mirrors in serious jeopardy of major crackage.

Simultaneously, I jump—only there is debris on the floor and I stumble. Horrified, I lose my footing and start to fall backward, toward the window-sized hole in my wall. And let me tell you, a flimsy tarp isn't going to keep a size 12 butt (size 10 before my list of crises over the past two weeks sent me to Pizza Hut more times than I care to admit) from scooting on through the hole. I'm picturing myself falling backwards to my death.

Suddenly, the movement I detected materializes in the form of a hero. He zips across the room like Tom Welling (aka Clark Kent from *Smallville*) and before I know it, strong arms have encircled me and I'm upright and in the arms of a strange man. Even in my crazy mind-set, I deduce, judging from the auburn hair and green eyes—identical to Linda's— that my best friend's brother has finally arrived.

His face is mere centimeters from mine and suddenly he smiles. A dazzling toothpaste-commercial smile. And just like that, I'm finding renewed inspiration to write romance. Stu's going to be so happy.

The good thing about having an over-the-phone life coach is the anonymity it offers. I feel like I can be completely honest—not that I'm a big liar in general, but I might have trouble opening up if we were face to face or trying to explain to a friend (as opposed to a paid professional) how rotten I feel over losing Greg. How every single day I'm tempted to pick up the phone and beg him to stop thinking about being a pastor.

All of my friends would say, "Stop being so dumb and call him. Be a pastor's wife. You can do all things through Christ . . ." Yada yada. I know better than to talk to Mom about it, or Linda, or even Darcy, because they all think Greg is the best thing to come along since the value meal at McDonald's.

But this life coach is here for me. I pay her a lot of money to be.

"I just don't think I can be a pastor's wife," I'm telling her.

"Why not?"

"Pastor's wives are amazing." I'm thinking of Tina Devine, my pastor's wife. She really is fantastic. Organized, put together, sings beautifully. Deals with people in the proper way (I'd probably be losing my religion every day if I had to put up with criticism and stupidity from people who probably don't have the biblical knowledge to find the book of Genesis).

"Aren't you amazing?"

I snort. And really, I think that pretty much answers the question.

I wait for her to respond. Finally I realize that she isn't going to pipe in with anything resembling reassurance that I am, in fact, amazing like one of my friends would have done.

What does she know anyway? I think, miffed. I'm tempted to just keep quiet and make her come up with some brilliant life-coachy thing to say, but I figure, hey, it's my dime. Better to suck it up and explain why I'm not amazing enough to be a pastor's wife.

"Okay, here's the thing," I say, but as long as it's been since she's uttered a word I have a feeling that she's either dozed off or is watching TV by reading the closed captioning. Still, I'm sort of committed to the process by now. "Well, I'm divorced for one thing."

"A lot of people are divorced." Ah, so she is listening.

"Yes, but some Christians believe a divorced person shouldn't remarry."

Now it's her turn to snort. I feel my hackles rising in defense of all my Christian brothers and sisters who hold to this

belief. Hey, whatever happened to being the objective ob-
server? She finally speaks a full sentence. "I suppose that's
something you have to decide for yourself." I'm proud of her.
I really am. She could have given some really opinionated
philosophies, but she didn't go there.

"Considering how some folks feel, I'm afraid I might hurt
Greg's ministry if I'm his wife."

"And yet he asked you to marry him?"

"Yes."

"Then he must not be too worried about it."

"I am though."

"Claire, I feel you need to consider that fear of ruining his
ministry isn't the only thing holding you back from marriage
to a man you clearly love."

Tears pop into my eyes because she is so right. I adore
Greg. I love, love, love him with a mushy capital L. But as
much as I want to spend my life with him, I know I can't be
the kind of wife he needs. I know I probably don't want to put
myself out there. I mean, pastors' wives work hard and have
to be nice to morons who think they know better than the
pastor the direction God is leading the church. I'd be hard-
pressed not to just show those people to the door and point
to the street corner, where the next church sits in our church-
on-every-corner section of the Bible Belt. "I guess I'm not
willing to step into that position with him." Oh wow. I just
went from *I can't* to *I don't want to.*

"Very good insight."

"Is it?" I ask in a shuddering voice.

"Your inner desires are speaking more loudly than even
your strong emotions. You must give them some consideration. Often our inner desires, those feelings at the core, are
what lead us into our destiny."

See, it sounds all right when she says it like that. So how come I have this little niggling of unease about Emma? The very first time I called her, I asked her if she believes in God, to which she responded that she believes in a higher power and is a deeply spiritual person. She would call that higher power God, but many people don't see God in the same way evangelical Christians do. She prefers the term *higher power* so that she doesn't offend. I let it be known that she was free to use the word *God* with me any time, but so far she hasn't taken me up on my generous offer. I focus back on what she's saying, which is costing me by the minute.

"Claire, there is nothing wrong with discovering that you don't have the same ideas about the future as the man you love. In no way does it trivialize your feelings for him."

"Then why do I feel so guilty?" I can hear the despair in my own voice, the tremor I get sometimes just before I let loose with a flood of tears.

"Guilt is nothing but a lie. Don't give in to it." Her voice is determined, not the gentle monotone I've become accustomed to. This is more aggression than I've heard from my even-keeled life coach since I started talking to her.

How do I not feel guilty when I'm not sure I've made the right decision?

As if in answer to my unspoken question, Emma continues her advice. "If I were you, I'd get back into the dating ring as soon as possible."

As soon as possible? Doesn't she realize that it took me five years to get back into the dating ring after my divorce? I may never get over losing Greg. "I just don't think I'll be ready for that anytime soon. Besides, where would I find anyone who wants to date me?"

"You have as much responsibility as the guy to show availability. What about your new contractor? You said he was pretty cute."

And if by "pretty cute" she means hunk-a-rama, then yeah, I guess he is.

The children's theater is putting on *Peter Pan*. I'm thinking it's a little ambitious for the first play performed by the new theater group. But since no one bothered to ask my opinion, let alone take it into consideration, auditions begin today. I pull my minivan alongside the curb and turn to look at Shawn. Sitting in the passenger seat, the kid looks like he's about to throw up.

"You okay, bud?" I need to distract him so I don't end up with a mess in my van.

He nods.

"Look, you know you don't have to do this. If you get in there and you don't want to stay, it's no big deal to me. We'll do something else."

I think that snaps him out of it, because he looks at me askance and scowls. "I don't want to back out. I just have to push through my fear and be professional."

This from an eleven-year-old?

My jaw drops a little at the new, grown-up version of my little boy. The thing is, I know he has the talent to be an actor, singer, musician, anything he wants. He and Tommy are even in a "band." They're horrible, but that's mostly because poor Tommy needs to stick to what he's good at: skateboarding. But this mom is *not* going to discourage him for however long he wants to think he's a singer.

Shawn is still trying to screw up enough courage to open the door. "Do you want me to come in with you?"

He seems to consider it, then shakes his head. "You'll make me more nervous."

Now, a lesser woman would definitely be hurt by this. But I know Shawn didn't mean anything by it. He just meant he'd be trying to impress me and might do just the opposite. Nothing to feel rejection over. Besides, I happen to know I can park around back, sneak in through the side door, and hide in the balcony to watch every move he makes. Duplicitous, perhaps, and I'm not recommending it to anyone necessarily, but come on, I *have* to watch.

"Come back in two hours," he says like he's a teenager (his sister, for instance, who has been blowing me off on a regular basis for the last four years).

I try to take it in stride. "Okay, I'll be here by three o'clock." I lean over to kiss him good-bye, only to be greeted by his back.

"Bye, Mom!"

Okay, then. Bye-bye.

I wait for him to be swallowed up by two massive theater doors, not at all sure I'm ready to let this one go. As a matter of fact, I know I'm not.

A few minutes later, I've parked around back and slipped inside and into the balcony. The theater is dim except for the stage lights and the muted lights along the aisles and walls to keep people from running into anything on their way to the bathroom.

The kids must be sitting in the seats as they wait their turn to audition, because I can't see Shawn. I do, however, see a familiar regal figure striding across the stage. John Wells, the atheist, almost-Broadway, world-traveling actor. Reduced to children's theater. How the mighty have fallen.

Unwittingly, I let out pretty loud snort. Doggone it. I step back into the shadows, but of course my paranoia is misplaced. No one is going to see me this far up. John begins to speak, and even without a microphone his voice projects throughout the empty theater.

The children don't make a move. I mean no whispering, no shuffling of little Nikes on the concrete floor, nothing. Not a peep, not a finger wiggle. Nothing.

Not that I blame them. Sheesh, John Wells is obviously in charge. His ramrod-straight spine looks as though it were fused that way. And for some reason, he's holding a gold-handled walking stick I've never seen before. I suspect John's only carrying it for effect. To tell you the truth, it's working. He looks suave, debonair, and not a day over sixty.

Still, that's from a woman's perspective. If I were a little boy like Shawn, I'd be looking for the nearest exit and forget the whole thing. I mean, it's one thing to be an adult and engage in a little friendly back-and-forth with the heathenistic actor, quite another to audition for him. The very thought renders me weak with compassion over the ordeal upon which my son is about to embark.

"Good afternoon, children." John's studied gaze slides from one side to the other of the front row of the middle section of seats. "Welcome to the first audition for *Peter Pan*. Before we proceed, you will be divided into sections according to the part for which you wish to audition. Please stand."

The children do as they are instructed. Again, with very little noise and no shuffling about once they are standing.

"All right. I want all Peter Pans to move to the left, filling the six seats in the front and second rows," John said.

The non–Peter Pans move aside and allow the immortal child hopefuls to fill their seats.

"Next, all those auditioning for Wendy. Please leave two

seats between you and the Peter Pans. Fill the eight seats on the front row and seven on the second directly behind."

These, too, do as they are asked. "Fine, fine. Now I would like the rest of you to leave two seats on the front row, and three on the second, and fill in the next four seats on the front and second rows. We'll begin with auditions for the Lost Boys. Mrs. Jensen will call two names. You will go to those steps"— he points to the stairs by the stage door—"Through the door. The second name called will stay backstage while the first is auditioning. When the first is finished, he or she will then exit on the opposite side of the stage through that door." He points to the other door. "Mrs. Jensen will then call the next name, and you will come up and remain backstage while number two comes to center stage."

He pauses and looks over what I'm sure are thirty blank faces. "Any questions?"

Not even one.

"Fine, then. I shall take a seat behind all of you. Please do not fidget and distract me from the auditions. If you cannot be still or quiet, you will be asked to leave. Once more, any questions?"

Again, not a one. I bite back a laugh. No way these kids got all that on the first time through. I just know someone is going to get lost, go to the wrong door, leave the stage on the same side they came in on.

But after four Lost Boys and two Tinker Bells, I realize I've been proven wrong. Knowing children like I do (mother of four here), I'm amazed at the ease with which John's instructions have been received and followed.

Note to self: Ask John Wells his secret for commanding the respect and/or obedience of children. I'm thinking hypnosis has occurred and I somehow missed it.

I sit through the auditions of at least thirty kids from ages six years old (the minimum) to fifteen (the maximum—I think they want the older boys for Hook and the other pirates). Most of the acting is passable for amateur children's theater. The singing is positively painful with the exception of four or five kids—all of whom are girls except the fifteen-year-old boy who, as I suspected, wants to be the infamous Captain Hook. Judging by his performance and the fact that no one else tried out, I'm guessing he'll get a callback.

Over an hour later, I'm waiting impatiently as the Peter Pans finally begin their auditions. By the fourth Peter Pan audition, I feel a sinful sense of glee that not only can't any of them act their way out of a paper bag, but they can't sing either. And to be honest, most of them just aren't all that cute.

If all the kids are like this, I think with smug assurance, Shawn's got this in the bag.

A little frown creases my brow, and I don't even bother to smooth it out (thereby avoiding permanent creases between my eyes—a wretched sign of aging). A blonde girl walks onto the stage, and I recognize her as Jenny Devine. She has a little round face and rosy cheeks. I know from memory that the pastor's daughter has enormous blue eyes. The child could have been sent straight from heaven. Her soul is as beautiful as her outward appearance. Only there must be some mistake because these are the auditions for Peter Pan, not Wendy. The Wendy auditions ended fifteen minutes ago.

John's voice creeps from the fourth row back. "Begin when you're ready, Miss Devine."

The music begins, and my stomach plummets. There's no mistaking that Jenny is following the footsteps of Mary Martin. And Sandy Duncan. She's taking the traditional route and auditioning to play the role of Peter Pan.

Oh, Lord. Don't let her get it. Please. She would be just as good as Wendy.

"Ms. Everett? Is that you?"

I nearly jump out of my skin as I turn and see Patrick coming into the balcony.

"Shh," I say with a frown.

He nods and makes his way down the steps to stand next to me. "Don't worry," he whispers, "Jen doesn't know I'm here, either. I guess I'm early picking her up. But I'm glad I get to see her audition."

I just wish he'd shut up before he gets us busted. "Sonar Ears" Wells is glancing up here.

Jennifer has a beautiful voice. When her song is over, she does a short scene with one of the Wendy wannabes, gives an adorable little curtsey that might have charmed me if I didn't want to bump her off to eliminate my son's only real competition.

"Isn't she great?" The proud brother is nearly bursting.

"Yeah." Trying to muster a little good-sportsmanlike enthusiasm, but failing miserably.

Finally, the moment I've been waiting for. Shawn walks slowly across the stage, his hands stuffed into the front pockets of his Tommy Hilfiger jean shorts, passed down from his brother Tommy, who begged his dad for them two years ago. I wouldn't pay forty bucks for a pair of shorts if I had the Queen's cash flow. But lucky for my champagne-taste son, his dad's an overcompensating-for-abandoning-his-kids sucker.

I lean forward in my chair so that I'm resting my elbows on the railing—the only thing separating me from certain death should an earthquake suddenly tilt the balcony a few degrees and send me sliding downward.

Patrick's tensing up next to me. He knows my Shawn is probably Jenny's only real competition.

Shawn starts to sing "I Can Fly," and suddenly my heart is soaring on the wings of a mother's pride. I watch my son, remembering his struggle last year, his insecurity, the anger, the notes he wrote Ms. Clark. Those things fade away as rapturous joy beams from his precious face.

When the song ends, he acts a scene with the same Wendy wannabe that has read lines with all of the Peter Pans so far. (I figure John must be seriously considering the little girl lead if he's auditioning her opposite all of the Peter Pan hopefuls.) As Shawn says his lines, he's calm, in control, and convincing. Not like most child stars, who are more cutesy than talent.

"That's fine, Mr. Everett," John says.

I cringe a little on the inside at the mistake. I use my maiden name, "Everett," but the kids have their dad's last name, "Frank." I wait for Shawn to correct him, but he doesn't. He simply nods, says "Thank you, sir," and moves backstage. I see him coming out the stage door a second later. He descends the four steps and takes his seat on the front row next to Jenny. She leans over, and I wish I had a mike hooked up.

Two things I know for sure. One, my son has found his place in this world. Two, I'll be darned if Jenny Devine is taking it away from him.

10

After Shawn's audition ends, I say a swift good-bye to Patrick and sneak out of the balcony. I get back in the van and drive around to a deceptive parking space in front of the theater, where it will look to Shawn as though I've just arrived and have been waiting. My cell phone rings just as I shut off the van.

"Hello?"

"Hello, Claire," a sexy male voice says. "This is Van."

My heart does a little lilt. Funny how I might not have thought about him as a prospective date before Emma put in her two cents' worth. Now, however, my palms are sweating. "Hi, Van." I imagine the contractor standing all grinning and heroic in my house just after he saved my life.

I check my appearance in the rearview mirror—a knee-jerk reaction when a great-looking guy calls. I feel a little guilty at the way my heart picks up. I mean, sure, Greg and I parted amicably and we weren't married, so why do I feel like a cheating toad-sucker?

"Good news," Van says. "The damage isn't as extensive as the previous contractor quoted."

Sigh. My hero. "So how much are we talking?"

He quotes his price.

A thrill shoots through me and is mingled with big, huge relief. But before I can gush with gratitude, I hesitate and allow good common sense to take over. That's going to be ten thousand below the original estimate. That can't be right.

"Come on," I say. "How can it be that much cheaper?"

"Trust me, will you? I'm just starting out. The way I get contracts is to underbid the guys who've been around a long time." Amusement is thick in his Matthew McConaughey voice. "The real question is, why does it surprise you that my estimate is that much cheaper?"

I blush like a sixteen-year-old. Sitting up straighter in my seat, I do my best to pull myself together. "When can you start?"

"I can go to the lumberyard right now and see if they have everything we need. If not, I'll put in an order and can probably get started on Monday, if the weather holds."

"Sounds great." My nerves make a stop in my stomach and form all kinds of jumpy creatures. I hate to even ask the next question in light of my rapidly depleting savings. "How much do you need for a down payment?"

"You don't pay me a dime until I finish the job to your satisfaction."

Okay, that's not what I expected to hear. I pause, embarrassed a little, because I figure Linda must have given him my sob story. I can just hear her: *"And to top it all off she just broke up with her boyfriend because she's too much of a disappointment in general for anyone to possibly think she's pastor's-wife material."*

My defenses shoot up, incinerating the floating nerve creatures in my stomach. I'm no longer feeling like a schoolgirl. "Listen, Van. I appreciate the thought. But I want to be treated like any other customer. I planned for a down payment equal to the one I paid Milt." The thieving jerk. "I don't want any favors just because I'm friends with Linda."

He gives a short laugh. "Trust me, I don't hand out favors based on a person's relationship with my sister. Just ask her how much I charged Mark and her to add a deck to their new house."

My neck feels hot, and I know it's splotchy, like it gets when I'm humiliated. "Well, I'm not a charity case, either."

"I agree," he says, without a second of hesitation. "I have an account at the lumberyard. I prefer to put what I need on account and pay it when I get paid—after the job is done. It's easier for me to keep my receipts straight that way."

"Okay, that makes absolutely no sense to me. What difference does it make?"

"I knew you were going to ask that." His tone is so light and friendly that I can't help but warm to him. Even if I couldn't picture his gorgeous auburn hair and sea-green eyes—which I can.

"Oh, you did?" I say, flirting like a coed and not really caring if he knows it.

"Yep. Always anticipate the next question and prepare the answer in advance."

"So, what is it?"

"What is what?"

I giggle, knowing that he's teasing me.

"The answer to my question. Or are you stalling so that you can try to think of something?" I still sort of think he's just taking pity on me with the whole not-taking-a-down-payment thing.

"I like to put all my supplies per job on one receipt. While I work on your house, I'm sure I'll have to go back for nails or whatever. When it's all over, I'll just pay it off, get one receipt, and that way I don't have tons of little papers to sort through by April fifteenth."

Hmm. Not all that romantic. In view of that explanation, I'm not really in the mood to flirt anymore. And while I'm at it, let's just get a dose of reality. Why would this guy, who has to be at least five years my junior (maybe more), be interested in an overweight, middle-aged woman with four kids and a broken house? I'm a real catch. Like a turtle on a hook.

Whack! The sound of me getting hit upside the head with a reality stick.

From the corner of my eye, I see the glass theater doors open. Kids start pouring out.

"Thanks for calling, Van. Let me know when you get started." I scan for Shawn, but I'm not seeing him. I picture my sweet boy huddled in a corner somewhere crying bitter tears because a girl beat him out of the role of Peter Pan.

"Will do," Van says. "I'll see you at church tonight."

"Church?" He has my attention again. But he better make it quick, because Shawn still hasn't shown up and I'm about to go inside and find him.

"Don't you go where my sister goes?"

"Oh, yeah. You're going with her?"

"Yes. I hate to give up my home church, but since I'm finally moved into town, the ninety-minute drive home is a little too far when there's a great church right here."

The doors open again. Finally, Shawn appears. John follows, his hand on my son's shoulder. Like he's letting him down easy.

"Okay, Van. I'll talk to you later."

"Uh—okay, sure. Bye, Claire."

I close my phone and beep the horn. I wave and smile.

To my surprise, John accompanies Shawn to the van. I think I might be about to get scolded for hiding in the balcony.

He walks around to my side and I roll down the window. John tips his hat. I can't help it that I melt a little. Who doesn't secretly wish they'd had a date with Dean Martin or Frank Sinatra in their young days? Okay, maybe I'm the only thirty-six-year-old who thinks about it. And gee whiz, how nuts am I, anyway? Ten minutes ago, I'm robbing the cradle, now I'm robbing the nursing home? I shove aside all thoughts of the Rat Pack.

"So, what's the verdict? Is my kid going to be the boy who loses his shadow, or what?"

His eye slides closed and open in a wink. "That, my dear lady, remains to be seen. Mrs. Jensen will do callbacks this week. So, if he doesn't get a call, you'll know. If he does, well, then he's made it to the next round."

"Mr. Wells is giving acting lessons, Mom," Shawn's voice interrupts. Something he knows better than to do. "Isn't that cool?"

I turn to my son. He's nearly exploding with excitement. A little theater is one thing. Handing my son over to this hedonistic Sean Connery wannabe is quite another. I turn back to John with a frown.

He presses his hat to his chest, where a deep rumble begins and ends with a chuckle. "I won't corrupt the boy, Miss Everett."

"Ms.," I correct. "And I know you won't because it's not going to happen."

"Mom!" Shawn seems horrified by this news, as though he had built it up in his mind that I would have no objections.

"We'll talk about it later," I say firmly.

"Think it over, *Ms*. Everett." John's mustache twitches over his full lips.

I don't want to be the bad guy, so I take the easy way out.

"We appreciate it, John. Really, it would be an honor." Did I sound convincing enough? Maybe I should make my voice crack as though I'm about to cry as I say the next words. No, I'm a lousy actress. I can't even read my own manuscripts out loud because I sound so fake. I stick with a straight, even tone. "I'm afraid acting lessons aren't in our budget right now. My first contractor swindled me and I'm having to hire another one. And there's this suspicious rattle under the van hood. I think I'm going to have to start looking for a new vehicle soon."

Why is John looking at me and grinning smugly?

"You've misunderstood entirely. I'm offering to coach the lad free of charge."

"Why would you do that?" John's an okay guy. I like him. I really do—quite a lot, actually. But, come on, the man's an atheist. Not exactly the type I'd have suspected of having a generous spirit. On the other hand, basic disbelief in God isn't necessarily proof of low morals or a cold heart. Guilt nips at me for the second time today. I shouldn't generalize people. He did buy lunch for Linda and me that day. And he helped me outside. Got me a paper bag for breathing.

I know how much his lessons go for. Sharon Greene signed her daughter up and bragged about how much she paid. I learned from another source no more than two weeks later that John had given her back her money and told her not to bother. Little Kayla didn't have an ounce of acting ability and even less singing ability. I laughed out loud when I heard he'd suggested if Sharon really loved her daughter, she'd show some mercy and stop pushing her toward something that's only going to cause her humiliation and pain.

But that's far from John's opinion of my son. And he's telling me that now. "The boy's got some of the most natural talent I've ever seen. He's expressed an interest in acting as a profession. I thought it prudent that he have the best acting coach possible."

John Wells is nothing if not humble.

"Sorry, John. You know it's not just about the money."

"I do. I must say, I'm rather disappointed to realize that you're so narrow-minded."

"Not narrow-minded." You never can tell with someone so guarded, but I think my refusal of his amazingly generous offer has hurt him. I place my hand on his arm and offer him a smile to let him know I love him even if I won't allow him to be a bad example to my son. I've never really tried to witness to John before, but somehow, I have this urge to say the next thing that comes to mind. "I'm just on a narrow road, and planning to keep my children on that same road until they're safely at their final destination—after they've lived to ripe old ages, of course."

"This narrow road leads to heaven, I presume?"

"It does. And happiness and peace of mind during the journey."

He pins me with that know-it-all gaze and I get the urge to fidget in my seat. I'm just about to tell him I have to go when he reaches through the window and gives my cheek a fatherly pat. "Happiness and peace?" He lowers his voice so that Shawn can't hear, and leans closer. "You, my dear Ms. Everett, are neither happy nor at peace. Are you positive you're going in the right direction?"

He waves at Shawn. "You did a fine job today, son. Remember that, no matter what happens."

We sit watching him swinging his walking stick as he strides away with regal demeanor.

"Please, Mom. He has contacts. Mr. Wells thinks with a year

or so of training I might be able to get an agent and maybe get some real stage work."

Stage work? Hello? Who is this kid?

"Sorry, kiddo." I pull away from the curb and merge carefully into traffic.

"Why, Mom? Why? Please. I'll do anything you want me to do, if you'll just let me have this opportunity. I have to do this."

"Shawn, I know you don't understand. But you're just going to have to trust me."

Not the least bit impressed or moved by my calm words of wisdom, Shawn continues to plead. "Please! I'll clean out the garage and do all my chores without having to be told. I'll keep my room clean. Anything."

I gather a steadying breath. Although his last argument almost did me in (ammunition for chores and a clean room— what parent wouldn't at least give it some serious consideration?). Still, I have to be strong at least until I can have another little talk with John and reassure myself that he can be trusted not to turn my son. "The discussion is over," I say with firm resolve, just a notch below raising my voice.

My son folds his arms across his chest and stares silently out the window for the rest of the trip home. My heart goes out to him. Hope deferred makes the heart sick, according to the Word. I'll allow him time to get over having his hopes smashed to smithereens. After all, I'm dealing with my own dashed hopes right now.

I haven't seen or spoken with Greg since his over-dinner revelation.

Shawn sniffs. Ah, he's crying. My heart clenches at his tears. I feel like a slug. But I have to be firm.

"There's Kleenex in the glove box," I say quietly.

He swipes his nose with the back of his arm and I swear he only does it to spite me. I fight back revulsion but refuse to dignify his action with acknowledgment. I won't be bullied into changing my mind. And that's just all there is to it. Let him sit there with snot on his arm.

Oh man. With one eye on the road, I reach over him—careful to avoid his arm—and grab the tissue from the glove box myself. "Wipe it off," I say in my most commanding tone.

Whew. He does it.

My kids know I don't change my mind too easily. When I say no, that's that. For the most part.

And judging from the fact that Greg hasn't attempted to make contact since Friday night, I guess he's figured that out about me, too.

My heart sinks to an all-time low at the thought. It's one thing to appreciate the attentions of a good-looking contractor. It's another to feel secure and loved in the arms of a man who wants to spend his life making you happy.

I shake my head bitterly. No. He doesn't want me to be happy. Well, I suppose he does. But he wants me to be happy on his terms.

John Wells's words suddenly shoot through me once more. *"You are neither happy nor at peace. Are you sure you are heading in the right direction?"*

That night I force myself to get ready and drive the kids to church when what I really want to do is crawl into bed and pretend the last three weeks haven't occurred. No tornado, no stupid apartment where partying is keeping me up all night. Not to mention how worried I am about my daughter being so close to that environment.

As soon as I walk through the church doors, I'm able to set

all of that aside. I'm glad I came. The band is warming up, and the atmosphere is charged with energy. Just what I need.

Shawn moves ahead of me to find a friend to sit with in the section of the church designated for kids his age. He's still sulking, and hasn't spoken more than two words to me all afternoon, but he'll get over it.

Ari and Tommy head off in their own directions, as does Jakey. I find myself alone and glancing about trying to find a place to sit. And okay, I admit I'm not only looking for a seat. I'm hoping for a glimpse of Greg.

"Claire?"

Not Greg, but definitely a man's voice. I look up into the handsome face of Van Collins.

I gulp. In the few hours since I've seen the man, I've forgotten how gorgeous he is. He flashes that Matthew McConaughey grin and all I can think to say is "Oh, hi!" Like I'm pretending I don't remember he said he'd be here. "Where's Linda?"

"Trish is sick, so she stayed home to play Florence Nightingale." I'm trying to feel sorry for Trish, but my head is a little woozy from watching his pullover Polo shirt strain against his carpenter-muscled pecs and biceps. Hmmm, Trish who?

Someone brushes past me and I jerk to my senses. I've had enough experience with guys talking to my chest that I force my gaze to meet his amazing green eyes. "So, um, Linda's sick? I'll have to give her a call." Man, I'd give anything to just slide my gaze back to those sleek, tanned arms. Stop it!

"Trish."

"I'm sorry?"

"Trish is the one who is sick. Not Linda."

Ohh, that's right. The daughter.

"So, where are you sitting?" He flashes a boyish grin and I know doggone well he's fully aware of his effect on me. Probably on every female of any age. He knows how to handle himself in this situation.

I scan the seats and find an empty row. "Over there."

"Let's go." His warm palm cups my elbow as he leads me to my seat. Then he just stands there. It suddenly dawns on me that he has every intention of sitting *with* me.

Horror clutches my heart as the music begins, signaling the start of the service. I jerk around to the front and lock onto Greg. I want to die. He's holding his mike and standing, frozen at center stage. Staring at me. And I know he just missed his cue to start the song. I try to convey my deepest apology by my silent gaze. Folks will assume I'm already dating. Humiliation burns my cheeks.

"Claire, can you move over and let me in?"

Oh, good grief. Van is still standing in the middle aisle.

"Sorry," I mutter, and scooch over.

I don't know how I'm going to get through the service. Even more so, I wonder how Greg is able to muster the dignity to be amazing, talented, and anointed. His voice breaks a few times during "I Surrender All." I should be worshipping, but I can hardly take my eyes off of him. He stands with his face lifted heavenward, tears streaming down his cheeks as he sings. His face shines with an otherworldly glow (which in all likelihood is a result of the bright, hot stage lights overhead). Still, when he drops to his knees, a sign of the deepest humility and yieldedness (and half the church follows his example), I can't help but wonder: Is he surrendering his love for me in order to follow the Lord? And as I look around, I don't think I'm the only one thinking it, because even Eddie Cain gives me a pointed look as he passes me on the way to the men's room. I guess he's getting his revenge for my little laughing fit last month.

I feel like a total Jezebel. Potiphar's wife. Mary Magdalene in her "before" shot—not to mention that bad girl of bad girls, Delilah.

I know I'm not good enough for Greg. Not worthy to be the wife of a man devoted to ministry. But suddenly I feel like not only am I not good enough for Greg, but maybe I'm just not good enough, period. Even God knows I'm not the one for Greg and that's why Greg has to let me go. I know it was my decision, but I feel betrayed, all the same. Like God is one of those parents on the right side of the tracks, convincing his son that the girl from the other side just isn't "their kind of people."

In that moment, as I watch Greg give me up, I feel utterly abandoned. Van shifts next to me and I turn. He's looking down at me and gives me a wink. "Neat church," he whispers. "I'm glad I came."

I slide a glance to Greg, who is still singing and kneeling. Then back to hunk-a-rama. I guess I'm yesterday's news to Greg. Pushing aside the sudden ache, I allow my lips to soften into a smile. "I'm glad you did, too."

11

Saturday afternoon, I face an empty nest while the kids are with Rick and Darcy for the weekend. After a quick cleanup of the apartment, I sort out a couple of loads of laundry, grab a book, and off I go to the laundry room. I'm puffing a little by the time I get there, a reminder I've been neglecting my running for the past three and a half weeks. Man, I don't want to gain back all twenty-five pounds I've lost since last September. Or even five of it—although I'm sort of thinking it might be a little late for that. I'd better find a place to run and get back with the program. I have another ten to lose, but you know how those last ten are . . .

The laundry room is empty when I walk inside. Mercifully empty. Or, I should say, the room itself is unoccupied. When I open the washer, I find it has a full load finished and needing to be put in the dryer.

I expel a big, martyrish sigh. I have two choices, wait for the owner of these clothes (which are undies and bras—just my luck) to come and claim them. Or be a Good Samaritan and put them in the dryer (and, for the record, use my own money to dry them).

Since there's no way I'm walking all the way back to my apartment with two loads of dirty laundry, I grudgingly divest the washer of its soggy contents and load the dryer.

My clothes are halfway through the cycle when a fresh-faced African American woman bursts into the room. She stops short when she sees me, looks to the washer, the dryer, then puts two and two together.

"Oh, man. I'm sorry." She fishes out a dollar twenty-five and hands it over.

I take it because I figure a stranger's not going to want me paying to dry her panties. She's glancing over the settings, a worried little frown creasing her otherwise smooth brow.

"Don't worry," I say, tucking the money into my pocket. "I set the dryer on delicate and cool so your things wouldn't get messed up."

"Thanks. I appreciate it. Last time I got here a little late, someone put my cashmere sweater in the dryer." She gives me a disgusted, "Uh, uh, uh. Can you believe that?"

"No kidding?" Anyone who knows me would take the remark for what it is: total sarcasm. I don't know how intuitive this girl is, but if she's reading between the lines, she'll realize I wasn't crazy about getting her things out, either.

In this day and age, folks just aren't very tolerant. I wouldn't be surprised if someday we didn't see laundry-room rage.

Anyway, I think she gets it, because she's wearing a sheepish smile as she sits next to me on one of the four metal chairs available. She holds out her hand. "Penny Krueger."

"Nice to meet you." Her palm is cool to the touch as I clasp her hand.

"My older brother's name is Freddy. Can you believe that?"
"Really?"

"I swear it." She shakes her head. "I don't know what my mama was thinking."

A real, genuine shot of laughter leaves my throat. The first in quite a few days and it feels great.

"So, what's your name?" She pulls out a pack of cigarettes from her mini backpack.

"Claire Everett." I'm tracking her every movement with my eyes. Nervous. Defensive. All I can think of is that I really hope she's not going to light up in this closed-in room. Cigarette smoke grosses me out because—okay, confession time—I was a smoker before I got pregnant with Ari. They say ex-smokers are much more sensitive to it than those who have never taken that first drag.

Instead of pulling out a cigarette, she glances at her watch, wrinkles her nose, and sets the pack down in the chair next to her. When she catches my gaze, she gives me a shrug. "Trying to quit. I'm forcing myself to taper off to one per hour."

A for effort. Got to give her that.

"How long has it been?"

The arm twists around again so she can see her watch. "Fifteen minutes."

Good grief.

My silence prompts her to fill the emptiness with new conversation. I've never been around anyone so antsy, and it's starting to trigger my anxiety.

"What did you say your name is?" She's fishing through her backpack again.

"Claire Everett." Penny Krueger is really starting to scare me.

"Ah, there it is." Triumphantly, she withdraws a stick of spearmint gum. "I knew I had some," she says with a wide smile. "That name sounds familiar."

"Huh?"

"Your name. Claire Everett. Sounds familiar."

"Oh. Well, it's just one of those names." I quirk an eyebrow. "You haven't been getting my mail, have you?" I wish now that I'd never had it forwarded. "The post office can't seem to find the right apartment. There's no telling what I've missed."

She grins. "I'll keep an eye out."

"Thanks."

"Which apartment are you in?"

I tell her and she nods brightly. "I'm in the building catty-corner to yours. I'm getting pretty tired of all that partying in the townhouse next to you."

"Girlfriend," I say, and then feel stupid, because that's not a word I'd ever use. And wouldn't now if this pretty young college student weren't black. Inwardly I cringe, but I look past her raised eyebrows and forge ahead. "I've been tired of that loud music since the day we moved in. Aren't there rules against that kind of thing?"

"There sure are, but no one will complain." She passes me the clipboard she's been holding, and I see a list of names. A petition.

> We the tenants of Olive Street Apartments demand an immediate stop to all loud music coming from Building 4, Apartment A after eight o'clock at night.
>
> This demand is in compliance with rule 10 of the regulations set forth by the management of these apartments.

There are at least twenty names on the list. I'm not sure that's enough to do much good. Still, I add my name and then the names of all four of my children.

She frowns.

I wink and can't help myself. "Multiple personality disorder. It can only help."

Her eyes go wide and a shot of fear flashes in the chocolate-brown depths.

I laugh and give her a wave. "Oh, girl. Don't be all nervous." Good grief, there I go again.

Full lips widen into a slow smile, showing white, white teeth. "You messing with me?"

"I'm afraid so," I say. "Actually those are my kids' names."

She frowns and glances at the clipboard. "Is that legal?"

"I don't see why not. I own them until they're eighteen."

She gives a shrug. "Works for me."

The dryer stops, and she sets the clipboard down on the laundry table. "You in college?" she asks, as she lifts her un-mentionables out of the dryer. I feel my cheeks warm a little, and I avert my gaze. It's not like I haven't seen her itty-bitty thongs already when I put them in the dryer. Still . . . know-ing that she's probably thinking about the fact that I took them out. I don't know her well enough to feel comfortable in this situation. As a matter of fact, there's not a person alive I know well enough to be comfortable in this situation.

Before I can answer her question, she emits a heavy groan. "Would you look at that?"

With a sense of dread I glance up to find her holding a lacy pink bra. "It's stretched out three times its size," she com-plains. "I swear, I'd have to be Quasimodo to ever wear it again."

I giggle. Can't help myself. "Looks like it got caught on the agitator in the washing machine."

"I wonder if I could get the manager to replace it."

We sort of share a look. Then she shakes her head. "No, probably not." She gathers a breath and repeats her previous question. "So, you in college?"

"No, I'm not in college." I look down at my book and pre-tend to concentrate on the book cover. "Just temporarily dis-placed since the tornado a few weeks ago."

"No kidding? Was your house blown away?"

"No. A tree fell on my roof and ruined some rooms."

"Anyone get hurt?"

"No, thank the Lord."

"You got that right."

I don't know, but something about the way she said "You got that right" makes me think she's been around the gospel block. "You a Christian, Penny?"

"Not the best one in the world. But my mama raised me in church."

I don't know what to say to this. I always feel a little stupid. No one wants to be preached at, but it's apparent that Penny is either backslidden or just complacent. I can identify with both from my own past struggles. And I feel that nudge.

Oh, sure. Not good enough to marry a pastor, but good enough to witness in a laundry room.

Guiltily, I push aside the rebellious thought and smile at the back of Penny's head, just in case she turns around. "You go to church anywhere?"

She looks over her shoulder, and I'm glad I have a pleasant look on my face as she gives me a guarded glance. "Not since I moved here to go to school last semester."

Okay, here's the opening I need. "If you ever want to go, just let me know. Ours is really the best church around."

A smug smile lifts her lips. "I've heard that from at least six people since I've been in town."

"Then they must all go to mine." I send her a cheeky grin. "See? It's unanimous. We all want you to come visit our church."

"I like you, Claire Everett." She folds a silky camisole and lays it on top of the pile of folded clothes in her basket. "Dryer's all yours."

"Thanks."

"Nice meeting you." She heads for the door. "Thanks for signing my petition."

"No problem. I hope it helps."

"Me too, girl." See, it sounds so much better coming from her.

When the washer and dryer are both full of my clothes, I pause at the soda machine and treat myself to a Diet Coke. I bend over to pull it out of the plastic drop-down thingie, and when I straighten back up my eye catches on a sign tacked to the bulletin board.

STRESSED?

Uh—yeah.

LACKING FOCUS?

Hmm. Sort of.

HAVING DIFFICULTY IN RELATIONSHIPS?

You could say that.

WONDERING IF YOU SHOULD MAKE A CAREER CHANGE?

Definitely.

EVER THOUGHT ABOUT TALKING TO A LIFE COACH?

Been there, done that.

Graduate student looking for clinical studies for thesis. Bachelor's degree in psychology with a focus on counseling. Offering free sessions upon acceptance, in return for your agreement to allow documentation of our work together. If interested, please contact Ina at 555-4197.

Ina's a little late. I should stick with Emma, but I take down the number anyway. A little backup can't hurt.

I settle back on the chair and open my book to wait out the dryer cycle. I really want to believe I can have a bright future. But things are not looking great. I rake my fingers through my hair and end up staring out the window at the gathering clouds.

The day is lonely without my kids. You'd think after six years of being a single mom I'd be used to these weekends. But I'm not. It's not so bad during the summer, like now, when the kids are home with me during the day. But during the school year, I barely have any free time with them. They go to school, come home and do homework, or stay after for extracurriculars. We have supper, chores, devotions, and *poof*, the day is all gone and it's bedtime. Not a lot of quality togetherness.

Summer's a whole other thing. But I still miss them on the weekends. Unless I'm on a deadline. Or if they've been fighting all week. Then I figure I need and deserve the break.

Today, however, all the laundry is washed and put away, the house is uncharacteristically clean, and I'm ready to climb the walls. It's not even quite noon. I try to work a little, but even that's not helping.

Finally, I slip into a pair of white capri jeans and a pink pullover top, apply some necessary cosmetics, slide into a pair of flip-flops, and head for the parking lot.

Van found enough of the materials he needed at the local lumberyard to get a good start on the house. He has a crew of about five guys and is estimating three to four months at least to complete the work. If the weather holds. It's noon and I take a chance the guys haven't eaten, stop at the local sub-sandwich shop, and order enough food for an army.

When I pull up a few minutes later, the workers are gone.

Disappointment rips through me. That's what I get for assuming, I suppose. Should have called ahead and let them know I was buying lunch.

I decide I'll go for a drive. Bennett Springs State Park is only ten miles or so outside of town. The highway leading there is curvy and hilly and really a lot of fun to drive. Slowly, I back up and head for the open road. Once I hit the highway, I open it up, pretending I'm driving a cherry red '67 Mustang, top down.

Twenty minutes later, I'm stuck at a little roadside barbecue place, reminded that I am driving the van, am a middle-aged woman, and was not born to be wild. Now that I'm back to a little state of mind called reality, I am thanking God that the dumb thing didn't die on the side of the dangerous highway where there's a good chance I would have ended up getting hit.

Using directory assistance, I begin dialing numbers. Frustration is building as every service station and towing company I call is either backed up for hours or closes at noon on Saturday.

Finally, in desperation I make one last call. Close to tears, I wait for Greg to pick up. The cell phone rings four times. I know on five his voice mail kicks in. "Greg, this is Claire. I'm sorry to call, considering everything, but I'm stuck at the side of the road on Highway 64 at Ellie's Barbecue. My van died and I can't get anyone to come out here." I hear the desperation in my voice, and I sort of feel like the woman in *Fatal Attraction* who won't let go once the relationship is over.

I hope Greg doesn't start worrying about dead bunnies. But he's my last chance before I'm forced to call in the last resort. Rick. I'd rather walk all eight miles back to town than call him. But I'm sure the owner of this barbecue joint wouldn't stand for a used, non-working van loitering in her parking lot. Of course, it's not like she could get anyone to tow it anyway.

I click off the phone. Only it's already off. Oh, shoot. It's dead. Tears prick my eyes. I won't even be able to answer if Greg does call me back. In this hopeless situation, I grab my purse and head inside Ellie's. My stomach begins to rumble the second I smell the tangy barbecue sauce.

The place is practically empty. I settle into a booth. In seconds a heavyset waitress appears. She smiles, showing braces and dimples. Bristly black lashes frame a pair of the prettiest violet-colored eyes I've ever seen. She's wearing a black T-shirt with white lettering that reads (appropriately) "Ellie's BBQ." It's a bit too snug across her chest and arms.

She sets a frosty glass on the table in front of me. "Hi, I'm Brandi," she says all bubbly, like she lives to bring me water.

"Hi, Brandi. How fresh is the coffee?"

"Just made a pot." She motions out the window to my van, which is just off the highway—as far as it made it before the thing died. "I saw you barely make it into the parking lot. I figured you'd have to call for a tow."

Very perceptive. I think a nice tip is in this girl's future.

"Do you want to see a lunch menu? Or are you just drinking coffee today?"

Mindful of the hollow spot in my gut from lack of breakfast or lunch, I push aside visions of the sandwiches still in my van and give her a nod. "Bring me one."

She flashes her braces again. "Okay, be back in a jif."

And she's not kidding. Less than two minutes later I'm staring at a menu and there's a cup of freshly brewed coffee just begging to fill my veins with much-needed caffeine.

"What do you recommend, Brandi?"

"There are no bad choices on that menu, ma'am." She stands patiently waiting for me to make up my mind. "I can honestly say that."

"Ah, but is that under threat of termination?" I tease.

A short laugh leaves her throat. "I can't be fired; I'm the granddaughter of the owner and next in line to take over."

"Don't be so sure of that, young lady," an elderly woman calls from a barstool across the room. "You don't mind your p's and q's and I'll let you go." She snaps her crooked fingers. "Just like that."

I have to smile at the amused affection in the old woman's voice. "Grandma, I presume?" I take a sip of my coffee, keeping my eyes fixed on the waitress over the rim of my cup.

"Yep, that's her, all right. Eighty-four years old and won't retire because she's afraid I'll run the place into the ground without her."

"You probably would. Standing there chatting with the customers when there's work to do."

I order a barbecued beef sandwich and give Brandi my menu. As I sip my coffee and wait, my gaze ventures to the window and I take note of the dark western horizon. The clouds from this morning have returned and it looks like there might be a thunderstorm anytime. Flashes of light glimmer high in the clouds.

Brandi returns and sets my plate in front of me. My eyes go

big. That has to be the most enormous sandwich I've ever seen in my life, and while I might eat it all if I were alone, there's no way I'm going to do so in public.

"Wow."

"I know." Brandi gives a chuckle. "I'll bring you a box and a knife to cut it in half."

"Thanks."

She returns momentarily. "Looks like we're about to get a gully washer."

I nod. "Looks that way."

Ripping my ticket from her book, she slides it on the table. "I'll go ahead and leave this so I don't get too busy and forget about it. This place is about to fill up."

"How do you know that?"

"Always does when it rains. Campers from the park, travelers on the highway."

"That makes sense. Sorry I have to take up space when you're about to be busy. If you want me to sit in my van until help comes I'd be happy to."

A laugh and a wave. "Don't even think about it. You sit there as long as you like."

Thunder crashes overhead, and the sky opens, sending a sudden hard rain—the prophesied gully washer.

As the place starts to fill, I can't take my eyes off Brandi. For a large, thirtysomething woman, she moves with the grace and speed of a supermodel. The only difference besides her weight is that she is always smiling, laughing, pleasant. The more I watch her, the more fascinated I become as every customer who enters the restaurant immediately falls under the spell of her grace and charm.

Suddenly a new heroine comes to life in my mind. A new book plot. My heart begins to pound. The thought I'm having isn't a romance. It also isn't the "Everywoman" stuff Stu basically mocked (jerk). This is different. This feels . . . like God set all this up.

My eyes fill with immediate tears. I'm still on God's radar after all.

I snatch a napkin from the holder and a pen from my purse and I start to sketch. The characters are demanding to be heard; everyone is talking at once, telling me their stories, interacting with each other until the plot begins to form. My pile of napkins keeps rising. Brandi slides by with the coffee pot and fills my cup I don't know how many times, but she seems to know not to bother me.

Finally, I look up. The sky has quieted. The rain has stopped, the sun is shining through the window once more. I arch my aching back and lean against the booth. The restaurant is empty except for Brandi. She seems to sense my perusal and glances up from counting receipts and smiles. "You run out of napkins?"

My cheeks warm. "Sorry about that. I'll pay for them."

"Don't be silly. We get a good deal on napkins. We're a barbecue place."

She reaches under the counter and pulls out a half-empty package of napkins and walks to my table. "You a writer?"

"How'd you guess?" I smirk.

She dimples, and I make a mental note to add those to my heroine's characterization. "Got anything published?"

This situation always makes me feel awkward. The average reader doesn't have a clue who I am. Christian readers might, but not secular readers. So to say yes always leaves me feeling like apologizing for not being more well known.

Still, there's only one answer. "A few things."

"Impressive," she says, wiping off the table next to mine. "What type of book?"

"Christian romance, mostly."

Her face brightens. "I love those! Hang on." She walks across the room and takes a book out from under the counter.

"Just so you know I'm telling the truth about loving Christian romance."

I can hardly believe it when I see the cover. My newest novel, *Esmeralda's Heart*. I finished it just before my sabbatical last fall. I was a bit late, so they rushed it into publication. It's been out less than a month.

Again I'm faced with an awkward situation. Do I say "I wrote that book"?

Turns out my indecision is moot because Brandi gives a little frown. "Wait a sec." She turns the book over to the back cover copy, where I happen to know there's a picture of me.

"You're Claire Everett?" Amazingly, Brandi's voice is calm. Not the silly, giggly response I usually get from fans who meet me in regular life situations as opposed to conferences or book-signing events where you'd expect to see an author. This young woman is most definitely the right model for my new character.

"That's me," I say.

"It's an honor to have you in the place," she says, still in a very calm voice as she leaves the book on the table (like it's mine since it's got my name on it).

From the corner of my eye, I happen to notice a vehicle pull into the parking lot. Greg's Avalanche. I fish out my money and a generous tip that is actually three times the price of the sandwich and drop it to the table. I smile at my new character. "The honor has been all mine, Brandi."

"Would you mind signing my book?"

"Sure."

"Here." She hands me her pen, since I've already thrown mine back into my purse.

"To Brandi . . ." I glanced up at her with my eyebrows raised. "Brandi what?"

"Wells."

"Wells? You wouldn't happen to be related to John Wells, the actor, would you?"

Her face loses its pleasant expression for the first time since I walked into Ellie's, and I know I've hit the jackpot.

"Sore topic?"

"Only for him."

John? He only moved here to be near her. Doesn't she know that?

"You sure about that?"

She gives a humorless smile and grabs the book in one hand and my coffee cup in the other. "Trust me."

"My son is in his children's theater group."

A cynical smile tips one corner of her mouth. "Small world."

"Yes." My gaze drifts over her shoulder and out the window. The driver's side door is open and the hood popped. Greg's trying to figure out what's wrong.

Brandi follows my gaze. "He belong to you?"

Okay, I know she didn't mean to twist the knife, but the pain is so harsh. "Not anymore."

Silky dark eyebrows go up as she jerks her head toward the window. "Doesn't look like he knows that."

I smile. "He does. He's just a nice guy and I needed help." I stuff my new book idea into my purse and slip the strap over my shoulder.

"A nice guy?" She gives a snort. "How old is he? Because if you don't want him . . ."

Okay, I know she's kidding. But my claws start to unsheathe.

Her dimples wink as she notes my back stiffening. "You are so not over that guy. Take my advice, Claire Everett: go to him and work out whatever is between you. There just aren't that many choices out there."

"Thanks for the advice," I say, just as Greg drops the hood and starts to head this way. My heart does a little flip at the sight of his long, tanned legs in a pair of denim shorts. A loose T-shirt with the church logo hangs from his shoulders.

"Nice meeting you, Brandi," I say, as the bell above the door clangs. "Give your dad the benefit of the doubt. I know he loves you."

This gorgeous girl isn't so pretty with a curled lip. She expels an expletive that I never would have pictured coming from the mouth of someone who reads my books.

But then I guess you just never can tell. Maybe she's more her father's daughter than she thinks.

At any rate, I shrug it off for now, knowing I'll be seeing this young woman again.

Turning, I paste on a smile and force my trembling legs forward to speak with Greg for the first time since his "nonproposal."

Greg's Avalanche smells so good. Like him. His aftershave lingers subtly in the closed air and I feel like I'm home again.

I flatly refuse the tears of loss that are trying to make me look bad. I push them aside. I'm a mature woman who made the only possible decision, given the choices available.

We drive the curvy highway that is wet from the latest round of sprinkles. Polite silence permeates the Greg-scented air. Come on, Claire, small talk. You can do small talk.

"So, how is your mother?"

"Fine."

"Good. Sadie?"

"Also fine."

Alrighty. So much for small talk.

"Look, Claire. I need to tell you something before you hear it tomorrow at church."

"You're marrying someone else?"

Good grief. Why do I blurt the first thing that comes to mind?

Greg takes his eyes off the road long enough to give me an incredulous, eyebrow-raised look. "No."

"I was kidding," I mumble.

"I'm leaving for Oklahoma next week."

Suddenly I feel as though all the air in the cab has somehow been sucked out and I can't breathe. "What do you mean? I . . . I thought you were waiting until fall."

"They're offering summer classes for the first time. It'll knock off a full year if I take a full load this summer, fall, spring, and next summer. It'll be better for Sadie."

"Wow."

That's me—the last of the great conversationalists. Always ready with just the right response. But how am I supposed to respond to this with grace or class? He's leaving me!

" 'Wow' is all you have to say?"

"I don't know how to respond. I'll miss you."

He gives one of those "sure you will" nods.

He's making me feel so bad that I do what I promised myself I wouldn't do—rehash. "I'm so sorry things turned out this way." My voice breaks, and I take a second to pull myself together before I go on. "I guess it's better that we found this out now rather than after the wedding, huh?" I give a smile I'm so far from feeling. But I'm trying to keep things light. Crying in front of him won't do either of us any good.

"I suppose you're right," he says quietly. I frown a little. I mean, sure we've discovered we are going different places in life. I can't be a pastor's wife, and he has to follow God's plan. But does he have to accept it so easily? Come on. Just a little begging? What would it hurt?

His comment leaves nowhere to take the conversation. I offered a reasonable comment and he agreed. Darn him.

At this point, a smart woman would just sit in silence. Keep her big fat trap shut. But then, no one has ever accused me of being Einstein, have they?

"I've heard lots of women attend Bible school to find a pastor for a husband." Oh, no, I didn't! Did I? "Well, I mean, if you're wanting a wife who could support you in the ministry,

Bible school is a great place to . . ." Deep breath. Just shut up, Claire, would you?

He gives me the kind of look Ari gives me when I try to help her pick out clothes. Like I don't have a clue. Although I actually do have better taste in clothes than she does. Much better. But that's not the point right now.

"Just the kind of woman I'm hoping to find." He doesn't even bother to hide his annoyance.

I fold into myself, wishing I'd opted for awkward silence as a riding companion rather than idiot ramblings. "Sorry."

His chest rises with a sigh and he reaches across the seat to take my hand. I want to pull away. I know I should, considering that there is no way either of us are changing our minds. But it feels so good. So familiar. Like finding a lost treasure. I turn my hand over and our fingers naturally intertwine.

"I don't want to find another woman, Claire. I'm not looking for a wife. I fell in love with you and want to spend my life with you. But just because you won't marry me doesn't mean I'm going to run off and find a replacement. You came into my life when I wasn't looking for love. I can be a pastor without a wife, and I have no plans to look for one at Bible school."

It's not really fair to him how relieved I am to hear this. I just don't know what else to say. And I've learned my lesson.

"Thank you for picking me up. I don't know what I'd have done without you. Especially since the towing guys can't pick up the van until Monday."

"Don't thank me for doing what I want to do," he practically growls. "Don't you know how badly I want to take care of you?"

Okay, do you know how sexy that is? How come every woman in the world wants to nab a pastor except me? And how come of all the men in the world I had to go fall in love with a jerk who wants to be a pastor? I give myself one fleeting second to reconsider my position and beg him to take me back. Then I get an image of me standing in front of women's group trying to smile when all I want to do is go home and curl up with a good book—or a good man—and I go cold.

"I'm sorry, Greg." It's all I can think to say.

Silence is the name of the game for the last ten minutes of our drive. But when we pull into the parking lot of my apartment complex, Greg's face darkens into a scowl. "Look, how long is that guy going to take fixing your house?"

The way he says "that guy" leaves no doubt in my mind that Greg's not a bit happy about Van.

"He says a couple of months."

"You don't want to live here a couple of months, do you?"

Not sure what he's getting at, I shrug. "I really don't have a choice. I wouldn't want to stay much longer than that, but until then I can put up with it." Hopefully Penny's petition will do some good, and the party guys will cut it out. Judging from the noise coming from my building, though, I highly doubt if anything short of eviction is going to convince those guys.

"You could stay at my house."

"Come on, Greg. I know you want to look out for me, but you don't have to worry about it anymore. I can take care of myself."

"I know." He looks at my building. The redbrick apartment building holds two townhouses. But they were built at least twenty years ago, and the wear and tear is more than apparent. But at least they're clean and bug-free. "I don't want to leave the house empty for a whole year. You could stay there free just to keep it lived in."

"But it's not practical. The kids and I are going to be back in our house in two months. Leave me a key and we'll keep an eye on it. Make sure it doesn't look empty so no one will break in."

"My things are going into storage anyway."

So, he *was* just offering for my sake. Something inside of me shrivels. I swallow hard before I reiterate my refusal. "Thanks anyway. But it's not necessary."

"All right."

I take the silence that follows as my cue to get out of the truck. I open the door. "Thanks again." I turn just before sliding out. "I'm really happy for you. It's gutsy to give up a career and someone you love to do what you're doing. I hope . . ."

For the record, I was going to say "I hope you find someone to make you happy." But that's not true. I mean, I want him to be happy. But happiness doesn't necessarily mean *married* and I'm not going to bring that up again. Ignoring the inner voice reminding me that "it is not good for man to be alone," I look into his expectant eyes. "I hope you have a safe trip."

Tenderness sweeps over his face. He looks at me as though memorizing every line (and believe me, there are plenty) and every contour. Tears well in my eyes. Before I can avert my gaze, his expression changes and I know he saw the tears. "Bye, Greg." My heart feels like it's being ripped from my chest as I walk the twenty yards to my doorstep.

I feel his eyes on me and, mustering as much determination as I can, I squeeze my hands into fists. Like a well-trained soldier, I force my attention forward. Everything in me screams to turn around and run back to him. But I stand firm.

I can't be a pastor's wife. The price is just too high.

"Claire, why didn't you call us? We would have come and picked you up." Darcy's voice scolds me over the phone.

I've been trying to be really nice to Darcy lately. During her last ultrasound, her doctor said she's a few weeks further along than they originally thought. Which is not fair. I always knew about two weeks after I was pregnant. Good for beginning prenatal care, but gee whiz, it makes the wait that much longer. This new date means Darcy was three full months pregnant at Christmastime when she found out. Which means she's eight months along, raging with end-of-pregnancy hormones, exhausted from lack of sleep, and prone to unexplained and unprovoked tears. Which is why I have been trying to be nicer than usual. "To tell you the truth, Darce, I just called the first person who came to mind."

Oh, shoot. There's zero chance she'll let that pass without comment.

"See? You still love Greg."

Do I know Darcy or what? I hate being right all the time. "What's love got to do with it?"

Hesitation gives silence a chance. I smirk.

"Are you joking?"

"A little bit." But I'm serious, too. "Love isn't the issue with Greg and me. It's about where we want to be ten or twenty years from now. And our visions of tomorrow don't match."

"A wife should adapt to her husband."

Excuse me while I barf.

"Precisely why I will not be walking down the aisle with Greg."

"Oh, Claire, honestly. Sometimes you're so stubborn."

Okay, enough of this. "Yes, well. I mainly called to let you know about my car situation. You'll have to bring the kids home after church tomorrow."

"Want me to come get you for service? Rick is covering for Sam at the hospital, so he can't go."

It's on the tip of my tongue to say yes, then I remember Greg said they'd be announcing his departure tomorrow. If I know Pastor Devine, he's going to make a big deal out of the whole thing. I would spend the entire service in tears.

"I think I'll pass. I'm not feeling real great."

"Claire," she says softly. "You've missed several services in the past few weeks. Are you all right spiritually?"

"What?" Irritation builds in me. "Yes, I'm fine. There's just been a ton of stuff going on. You know that."

"Yeah." It doesn't take a mind reader to figure out that she's not exactly convinced. I just can't face Greg. But there's no way I can tell Darcy.

"Hey, look. Since Rick's working, come in with the kids and I'll fix us a great Sunday dinner, okay?"

"I thought you weren't feeling great."

"Don't bite the hand that feeds you, Darcy." Okay, starting to lose cool. Must end conversation before gasket-blowing commences. "Do you want to stay or not?"

"You know I'd love to."

So we leave it at that.

The next day Ari shows up driving her dad's Benz while Darcy drives her SUV. I stand at the door so that not one of my children can get past me without a hug. After all, I haven't seen them since Friday.

"Does your dad know you're driving his car?" I ask after I turn Ari loose.

"We dropped him at the hospital this morning."

"Why did you do that?"

The boys give their obligatory hugs and run off to do their own things.

Darcy holds out a set of keys. "Rick and I agree you need a car worse than I do right now. I hate to even get out of bed." She struggles to sit. "I know Ari isn't supposed to be driving, but Rick thought under the circumstances it would be okay."

I give a "that's fine" nod, and Ari grins with victory. But no time to deal with Missy Smug-girl. "I can't drive your SUV." I can't believe she'd even loan it to me.

Shoving herself back so that the recliner footrest flies out, she stretches and grunts. "Don't be silly. I can barely even fit under the wheel anymore. Rick's been after me to stop driving until after the baby's born anyway."

I stop just short of an insistent "What part of *no* don't you get?" But the practical me realizes this is the ideal solution until I figure out what's wrong with my van.

I nod, and from the delicate lift of Darcy's brow I can tell she expected more fight from me. A smile stretches her lips. "Oh, good. I didn't feel like arguing." The smile turns into a yawn. Her eyes close. "Do you need help with dinner?" she asks sleepily.

I can't resist a little laugh. The mother-to-be is already asleep, she just doesn't know it yet. "Lay there and rest," I say. "I'll call you when it's time to eat."

"Mmm . . . 'kay."

In a moment I can only attribute to gratefulness over Darcy's loaning me the SUV, I slip her shoes from her swollen feet and set them next to the recliner. Then I snatch a light afghan from the couch and spread it over her. Being right under the air-conditioner vent, I assume she'll cool off pretty quickly.

"That was really nice, Mom."

I turn in surprise to find Ari at the bottom of the steps.

"Well, Darcy's really nice, too." I smile at my girl. "Come to the kitchen with me while I finish dinner."

To my surprise and delight, she does so without so much as a rolling of the eyes, unless she does it behind my back— which is possible. "So," I ask, pulling out the ingredients for a salad. "Did you have a good weekend?"

She gives a little shrug and to my utter shock heads to the cabinet and pulls out the large white ceramic bowl I always use for salad. "I went out with Paddy last night."

"You two back together?"

"I guess." She takes a knife and the cutting board and sits at the table. I'm wondering if we're in a real-life version of *Invasion of the Body Snatchers*, because this is *not* the daughter I left at Rick and Darcy's house on Friday.

"Are you happy to be back with him?"

She grins slowly. "Yeah."

Small talk takes over the conversation for the next few minutes until we finish making the salad. I stand and turn toward the oven. I figure the lasagna (homemade, not Stouffer's) is just about ready.

"Hey, Mom?"

Trying to concentrate on not burning off my fingerprints, I give her a distracted "Huh?"

I kick the oven door closed and feel panic rising as the heat begins to seep through the pot holders.

"Can I go with Paddy and his parents to Mexico?"

Good thing I am so close to the rack. I drop the lasagna onto the counter. "You want to go to Mexico?"

Ari's hopeful expression clouds over. "They're going with a

couple of other pastors' families. They're going to be building a church from the ground up."

My skeptical nature rises, along with the disappointment of knowing her true motives for being so nice to me. Darn it. Oh well, it's not like I've actually lost anything. And I got a salad made.

"If your dad pays for it, I don't have any objections to you going with them. It's in July, right?"

Her face brightens about six shades. How can I be so happy for her after she blatantly set me up with her goodness to me? When she grabs me in a fierce hug, I know why.

And who knows? Maybe the trip will do her some good.

This week Emma and I are focusing on my feelings of inadequacy as a parent. Fifteen minutes into the hour-long conversation and I'm still talking about Ari.

"I just don't know how to be close to her," I'm complaining. "I look at Linda and Trish and they adore each other and sometimes I'm so jealous."

"Why's that?"

"You mean, why am I jealous?"

"Yes."

"Linda has a way of taking bad situations and turning them into learning experiences that Trish actually responds to."

For instance, the whole pizza situation. Trish has been good as gold ever since that night. Linda didn't even have to ground her. Ari was livid with Rick and me about the fact that Trish was only reprimanded. I tell this to Emma.

"Can you understand why she might be upset when her punishment is so severe and her friend's is so light for the same offense?"

I hesitate, because I do see why Ari would be upset. But the girl has done some crazy things. Sneaking out. Changing boyfriends like you'd change socks. I'm worried about her.

Not the best thing to tell Emma.

"I think Ari senses you don't respect her or trust her to make the right decisions. So she automatically chooses the things she knows you wouldn't want her to do."

"What do you suggest?"

She pauses a second. Then: "You might sit her down and tell her you're ungrounding her because you believe you can trust her not to behave so irresponsibly in the future."

As we hang up, a battle is raging inside of me. A war I have a feeling Ari is going to win.

When a person's phone rings at three in the morning, it can mean any number of things—rarely good. So, when mine rings, yanking my subconscious from a warm, comforting, passionate Greg-dream, I'm sorely tempted to ignore said ring. Especially when caller ID won't reveal the caller.

I really want to bury my head under my pillow and sink back into Greg's arms. But then I wonder: Do hospitals show up on caller ID? What if Mom has had a stroke? The thought sends me popping up like a jack-in-the-box. I make a dash for the cordless before the hospital gives up.

"Hello?"

"Mom?" A young girl's voice greets me from the other end. Definitely not a hospital. I breathe a sigh of relief, knowing my own little girl is safely tucked away in her own bed, just down the hall from me, sound asleep.

"I'm sorry," I say, in my most sympathetic and motherly (because, doesn't it take a village?) voice. "I think you have the wrong number, hon."

"It's me, Mom." I hear tears in this child's voice. And something familiar in the way she sniffles.

Ari?

I never knew it was possible for fear to grip every muscle and tendon of your body in one split second. But that's what it does as my mind wraps around the fact that while I've been blissfully dreaming of being in Greg's arms, my daughter has not been in her bed where I thought she was.

"Where are you?"

A sob bursts from her and she begins to babble, slurring her words and I have not a clue what she's trying to convey, other than the fact that she's apparently hammered and in some sort of trouble.

"Ari! Ari, stop crying and talk to me."

She's so hysterical, she's making me hysterical, and that's not going to do either of us any good.

"Ms. Everett?"

A male voice. Also familiar.

"Who is this? If you've hurt my daughter, I'll . . ."

"It's me, Ms. Everett. Patrick Devine."

"Paddy? What the heck is going on? Why is my daughter calling me crying in the middle of the night instead of sleeping like I thought she was?" *And what do you have to do with it, bucko?* But inwardly, I'm relieved to hear she is with Paddy. It doesn't mean I'm not going to kill them both, but at least I know she's safe. "Never mind. Just put her back on the phone."

"Uh, I can't."

"What do you mean you can't? You'd better do as I say right now."

He clears his throat. Never a good sign. My lungs begin to burn and I realize I've been holding my breath. Air leaves my throat with a cool *whoosh*. "Spit it out, Patrick. What's going on? And don't lie to me. I can smell a lie a mile off."

"Ari was at a party."

"What? You encouraged my daughter to sneak out of the house and took her to a party?" I'm burning up now. No, I've passed burning. I'm flat-out burned up. Last year he talked his way out of being caught red-handed kissing another girl, but he's not going to be able to talk his way out of this one.

"No, ma'am. I didn't take her to a party. She called me from the party. She was—uh—dumped by some college guy. And if I ever get my hands on him . . ."

"Okay, spare me the macho garbage. There is no way my daughter would go off to a party on her own with someone I don't know."

My mind skitters back to the incident at the pizza place with the college guy. Apparently I don't know my daughter as well as I thought I did. What is it with her and older men?

"All right. Let's start over." I take a deep breath. "Where is my daughter?"

"In my car. I'm driving her home as we speak."

I imagine Ari passed out in the backseat of this teenage kid's sports car.

"All right. Why did she call you instead of me?"

"Fear?"

"Fear? Of me?"

I get a "think about it" silence. I guess I do tend to overreact. Or more precisely, act outside of the norm. I'm not crazy about Patrick driving and talking on the phone at the same time. But I can't bear the thought of losing this connection to Ari until I can actually see for myself that she's all right. "How close are you to getting here?"

"Pulling into the parking lot right now."

I glance out the window and, sure enough, the Mustang is pulling into one of the few empty spaces. With all my motherly indignation, relief, anger, and overwhelming joy to see my daughter home safely, I fling open the door. In my SpongeBob SquarePants pajamas and an oversized T-shirt, I run barefoot from my door to Patrick's car.

My view of Ari is pretty close to the one I had envisioned, only she's in the front seat, and not the back.

"Thanks for bringing her home, Paddy."

He nods and motions me aside. With the kind of tenderness normally reserved for men ten years his senior, he leans in, unhooks my daughter's seat belt, and gently lifts her from the car. I lead the way inside.

"Lay her on the couch and then come into the kitchen and tell me everything you know."

Trembling, I fill the teakettle and set it on a burner. Then I roam the cabinets for anything herbal and non-caffeinated, grab a chamomile teabag, and sit at the table waiting for the kettle to whistle.

Patrick steps partway into the kitchen and leans against the wall. The kid's face is white as a sheet and I start to see this whole thing through his eyes. Ari uses him when she's alone and blows him off whenever she gets a better offer. My Ari? At this moment, I don't like my daughter very much.

"Tell me what happened."

With a swipe of thick dark hair, he takes a seat in the chair I kick out across from me.

"Don't leave anything out," I warn. "I'll eventually get it all out of her anyway."

He nods miserably. "She called me because . . ."

I hold up my hand. "Wait. Back up the story and tell me how she got to a college-boy party in the first place."

"She met this guy at the apartment pool. He thought she was in college, too, so he invited her to go."

"Oh, gee, I wonder who could have possibly led him to believe she was a coed."

His lip twitches a little and I know the poor kid got the joke. I feel a little guilty for rubbing salt into the wound. "Sorry, Paddy. Go on."

"That's about it, I guess."

"Do I even want to know how she got to the party? And please, don't say Trish was there, too."

"No." He glances around the parking lot and that's when I notice Darcy's SUV is missing! I gasp. Oh, she is in so much trouble.

"The party didn't even get started until around ten. So it wasn't in full swing until midnight. She waited until she knew you were settled in for the night and snuck out."

That explains that. I was down for the count long before midnight. I groan. "With Darcy's SUV. Please tell me she didn't wreck it?"

"No. At least she knew better than to drink and drive." He gives me a look of compassion.

I am amazed at how clueless I am. I've always prided myself on my savvy sense of reality. The way I hardly ever take anything at face value, but rather fall back on cynicism and sarcasm as my way of getting to the truth of any issue. Keeping it real, rather than allowing anyone to pull the wool over my eyes. Only guess what? This kid—my sixteen-year-old daughter—has me totally blinded. I've been one of *those* moms. The kind who insists that all the other kids are bad, but my kid would never ever drink or have sex.

My heart jumps into my throat and forms a boulder-sized

lump. "So, this college jerk plied her with alcohol and then what?"

His jaw twitches and anger flashes in his baby blues. "He took her upstairs . . ."

Oh, Lord.

"Apparently, that's where the real party was. He tried to get her to do cocaine."

Oh, thank God. Wait. What? "Cocaine?"

"Yeah. Thankfully, she had enough presence of mind to tell him where to get off. Then she called me from her cell. And I made her call you to prepare you for her condition."

I am so filled with love and gratitude for this kid. I reach across the table and pat his hand. "Thank you for being there for her."

He nods. "I'll be over tomorrow to see her."

Something in the way he says it sends a shot of sadness through me. "Had all you can take, huh?"

His shoulders lift and lower. "Yeah." When his gaze reaches mine, I detect a glimmer of moisture.

Ari, open your eyes, you foolish girl!

And just like that, she appears, clutching her stomach, her eyes wide with horror as she breezes past us into the half bath right off the kitchen. Patrick and I sit in silence as my daughter hurls in the next room. I hear her moan, and I know she's dropped to the floor, exhausted and miserable.

And I take that as my cue. I shove up from my chair and give Patrick a "better get going" half smile. He nods.

"Can you see yourself out, Paddy? I need to go take care of my daughter."

He stands, casts a lingering, heartbreakingly sad glance toward the bathroom and retreats to the living room. As I kneel beside my reeking daughter, I hear the front door close softly.

I know there is no point in kicking Ari while she's down. There will be plenty of time for her to regret her abominably poor judgment. Like when she wakes up tomorrow. When Patrick comes over and ends things with her once and for all, which I fully believe he will do, when she's not going to Mexico because, even if Patrick weren't about to dump her for good, there's zero chance I'd let her go now.

I find it hard to drum up much sympathy for her as I help her back to the couch, run a fluffy washcloth under cool water, and lay it folded across her forehead. Her chest rises and falls steadily within a couple of minutes.

I sit there and watch her sleep. I am filled with anger, outrage, hurt. How could she do this? To herself? To Patrick? To me?

Two hours later, I'm sitting at my kitchen table. Knowing there's no way I'm going to be able to sleep, I exchange the chamomile tea for a freshly brewed cup of full-strength caffeinated Cain's coffee and am soon mulling over all the things that have happened since that stupid tornado a mere four weeks ago.

I thought I was doing the right thing by bringing my kids back to me, even if we had to live in a crummy townhouse for a few weeks. Now I'm not so sure. Or at the very least I should have found someplace not inundated with college guys.

Oh, Claire, how stupid can you be? I slap my palm to my forehead. How could I not have known that a complex full of college-age guys would be too much temptation for my kid to handle?

It's five-thirty in the morning but I couldn't get back to sleep now even if I could pick up where my Greg dream was interrupted. I grab my coffee mug and lift out all the napkins I used to sketch my new story at Ellie's Barbecue. As I transcribe my barely readable notes, yesterday's experiences come to mind. Penny in the laundry room, the van breaking down, Brandi, Greg . . .

Hmm. Greg's offer to have me stay at his place until my house is fixed . . .

By the time I am seriously considering the offer, the clock reads almost seven. Greg's an early bird, so I grab the phone and punch in his number.

Two days later, most of the neighborhood turns out to lend a hand moving Greg's stuff into storage and mine into Greg's house. Even Van shows up during breaks. (And is it my imagination or is he taking quite a few breaks more than necessary? Glad I'm not paying by the hour.) He seems content to ignore the looks he's getting from Greg.

I can't help but be a little bewildered at these two guys. They're both acting pretty macho—like I'm the little lady and they're about to fight a duel over who wins my hand. I'd be flattered if I weren't so depressed over the whole breakup with Greg.

By noon, everyone is starving, so Darcy, whom I refuse to allow to lift a finger to help with the move, shows up driving Rick's Mercedes. She's picked up a full meal for us, complete with barbecued ribs, fried chicken, potato salad, baked beans. You name it, it's here. We end up having an impromptu block party—half Greg's going away, half my welcome back.

John Wells corners me just as I bite into juicy, spicy, tangy barbecue.

"Pork is going to be the downfall of America," he says.

I wipe away a smeary face full of sauce and smirk. "No doubt a conspiracy created by foreign enemies bent on our destruction."

"I would not doubt it one bit." He gives me a wink. "So, you've taken up residence on our quiet street once more."

He's fishing for something, but for the life of me I haven't a clue what it is.

"Yes, I have. It's nice to be home." Literally. Living in Greg's house is going to take me back to childhood.

"I take it you and Mr. Lewis are finally engaged to be married then?"

"Not that it's any of your business, Mr. Wells, but no, we aren't. He's moving away for a year or so and I need a place to live where I won't constantly worry about my kids. Does that satisfy your curiosity?"

"Quite. And how about your van? I notice it has been absent."

Taking a bite, I chew and talk, I admit, mostly to bug John. "Had to put it in the shop. They called today and the motor is shot."

"Unfortunate."

He has no idea. Rick is encouraging me to buy a used one. He even has a friend with a three-year-old Dodge Caravan for sale for fifteen thousand. Blue Book confirms that's a great deal. But I just don't know if I can even swing that much. And with my pay schedule, setting up accounts that have to be paid on a monthly basis is scary.

But I know John didn't come in here to talk about my van. "What's up, John?"

"I wanted to take a minute to chat about your son. I've already decided that he will have the part of Peter Pan."

"You have!" Finally, something going right for a member of my family. "Thanks, John. He's going to be thrilled."

"Yes, well. Callbacks aren't over yet, so keep it under wraps until we announce it officially."

"Oh, sure. No problem."

"Now, on to the issue we discussed previously."

"What issue?"

"That of you allowing me to tutor Shawn."

"John Wells, you're a bulldog disguised as a handsome older man."

His smile shows his beautifully white teeth. I swear John's had tons of dental work done. There's just no other explanation. He leans in a little, allowing me a whiff of musky cologne. "So you admit to thinking of me as handsome?"

I give him a tap on the shoulder. "Handsome *older* gentleman, John."

"You break my heart, Ms. Everett."

"I'm sure you'll recover." I give him a dry grin and he laughs outright.

"I'm sure you're right. But back to the subject of your talented son."

"John, I've already told you. I can't just hand him over for you to brainwash with all those anti-God, liberal, immoral ideals you hold."

"First of all, I am not anti-God. To be against God, one must first believe He exists. And I simply do not."

"I stand corrected."

"Liberal. Immoral." An exaggerated sigh escapes. "I'm afraid you're right about those."

"You're impossible, John Wells." So why do I like him so much? Not in an I-want-to-date-a-man-old-enough-to-be-my-dad kind of way, but more in an I-wish-dad-were-still-around kind of way. "Impossible and forbidden to brainwash my kid."

"What can I say to assure you I will in no way try to brainwash the boy?"

"Oh, I don't know, how about, 'I believe in God, His Son,

Jesus, and the Holy Spirit, and I promise to never ever be immoral or liberal again'?"

I give him a whopper of a wise-guy grin.

His eyes flash with a seriousness I've rarely seen, and his expression drops.

"John? Is everything all right?"

He expels a long slow breath and lowers himself to the only kitchen chair vacant of moving boxes. "What you say makes a lot of sense. I wish I could believe."

Heat spreads over me and I lean close, my heart filled with so much emotion. "John, believing is easy. Much easier than trying to explain God's amazing world any other way than the hand of someone bigger than you."

"Do you really think so, Ms. Everett?"

"I truly do."

"Then I promise to try."

"Try?" There is no try. In the words of the one and only great Jedi master, Yoda, "Do or do not. There is no try." But I'm almost positive that's not something I should say while trying to convince an atheist to believe in God. Besides, he's sort of looking up at me and there's this grin . . .

I suck half the oxygen from the room and my jaw drops. "John Wells, you big rotten heathen. Were you acting just then?"

A chuckle leaves his throat in a most mocking way. "And that, my dear, is why you need this liberal, immoral atheist training your son who longs to be an actor."

Disappointment yawns inside of me like a gaping wound. I should have known it couldn't be that easy. What am I, stupid?

John stands and presses a kiss to my forehead. He winks and heads toward the kitchen door.

His affection for me is clear, and I know, despite the teasing, it's not in a patronizing sort of way. His affection for Shawn is evident as well.

Lord? What's the answer here?

I think about Little League and music lessons. I know more about John Wells than I ever knew about those coaches and instructors. Could it be that God dropped John in our laps so that Shawn could have a future as an actor and John could hear the Gospel from people who care about him?

With that thought to spur me on, I sprint across the kitchen. "Hey, John, wait up."

I find him halfway through the living room and headed to the door. He stops and waits for me to join him.

"Okay, listen," I say. "Here's the deal."

"The deal?" He lifts an eyebrow a la Sean Connery. I make a mental note to tell Linda. "I'm offering free coaching for your son. And you want to strike a bargain?"

"Crazy as it sounds. Yeah."

His mustache twitches, and his eyes squint with amusement. "All right, I'm listening. What are your terms?"

"I want Shawn to do chores for you to pay for the lessons."

He scowls. "I will not allow it."

"He has to learn that things aren't going to be handed to him on a silver platter just because he's talented. Think about the spoiled, indulgent actors out there. Especially the young ones. Is that what you want for Shawn?"

"All right. Yes. That is a very good argument. I will consider it."

"No, you have to agree."

His eyes scan my face and I guess he sees that this is nonnegotiable, because he nods. "You drive a hard bargain, Ms.

Everett. But I agree. And as a matter of fact, I have a project I'm working on and I could use the boy's help."

"Good."

He holds out his hand. "Are we agreed then?"

"Not yet."

"Do go on."

"There are ground rules. You can't ever try to sway him to liberal, immoral, or atheistic beliefs. I know we were joking around earlier, but I am dead serious. If he comes home even one time and says something that makes me uncomfortable and I trace it back to you, that will be the end of it."

"You have my most solemn word that I will not squash his most holy faith. Time and disappointment will do that without my help."

"I disagree. I believe God will give my son a very bright future." I smile and take his arm. "After all, He gave us you, didn't He?"

"You think your God brought me here just to give your boy lessons?"

"Partly."

He gives a mocking tsk, tsk, tsk. "You think more highly of yourself than you ought."

"Quoting Scripture, John? Interesting."

"Just because I don't believe the Bible to be true doesn't mean I don't find it an entertaining read. Especially the Song of Solomon." He gives me a suggestive lifting of his dirty-old-man brow.

I shove away from him. "You're impossible."

"And you, my dear lady, are silly if you think there are cosmic forces working to bring you into my life so that I can coach your boy."

"One of these days, John," I say with bold assurance, "you're going to come to me and admit it."

For some reason, I can't quite bring myself to tell him I met Brandi. I have a feeling it's not an easy subject. So, I renew my efforts to pray for them both. And if God wants to use me to bring these two together, I'm willing.

The lawn has emptied out, everything is moved in, and only Greg and Darcy remain of the helpers. Even though I told him it wasn't necessary, he's upstairs putting beds together. See? The man is way too good for me.

Darcy looks like she's about to fall over. She's trying to help me put dishes away. But one look down at her swollen feet and I grab the plate from her hand and push her by the shoulders into the living room. "You're outta here, sister."

"Claire, I want to help."

"Darcy, honey, you've been on your feet all day. You're exhausted. That baby will be here soon, and you need to save your strength for labor and delivery."

Tears well up in her eyes. Sheesh. I hurt her feelings even when I'm trying to be nice. I really should just stop talking altogether.

"I'm sorry, Darce. I'm not trying to be mean. I just don't want you to hurt yourself or the little one."

She gives a vehement shake of her head. "You didn't hurt my feelings."

"Okay. You're just emotional. I get it." I smile into her round little water-filled face. "Go home and get off your feet, honey. You'll be a new woman in the morning."

Fresh tears flow down her cheeks and she grabs onto me, slamming me into the baby as she gives me a fierce hug. "This is the first time you've ever used a term of endearment with me, Claire. Like maybe you might actually love me a little bit."

Oh, for the love of . . .

Lord? Is this my punishment for unconfessed sins?

"Okay, Darcy. All right. Take it easy." I pull out of her embrace and snatch a Kleenex from an opened box labeled "living room." "Here. Take this."

She dabs at her nose and eyes, never taking her gaze off me. Clearly she is waiting for me to confirm or deny her assumption.

"You know I love you."

Her eyes grow big. Enormous. I'm glad she's not still holding my plate, because I swear she'd drop it.

Come on. I haven't been so awful that a little "I love you" sends her over some kind of emotional edge.

"Oh, Claire. I'm so glad. I just kept praying and praying. And God answered my prayer tonight." She hugs me again while I speechlessly allow the embrace. I'm too stunned to do anything else.

She loosens her death grip and grabs her purse from the key table by the door. "I'll be over tomorrow if Rick can do without the car."

I switch on the porch light as she steps outside. "Stay in bed, Darcy. I can get the rest put away myself. Your ankles look like softballs. I want you to take care of yourself." Her face crumples and I don't dare use any terms of affection. "Really. Go home and rest up. We want a healthy little Darcy Jr., don't we?"

She nods and her expression brightens. I stand at the door and wait as she pulls away. I breathe a sigh of relief and turn. I stop short at the sight of Greg standing in a white T-shirt and denim shorts. He is way too good-looking to be a pastor.

Good-looking in a normal, rugged sort of way. Not all spruced up and trying to look good for TV. Greg just is. Understated. I adore that about him. If things were different right now, I'd be in his arms.

"That Darcy loves you a lot, doesn't she?" he asks with a tender smile.

"Darcy is a nutcase." I shake my head and close the door.

"So anyone who loves you must be nuts?" I've annoyed him with my less-than-gracious response to his observation.

"Not everyone," I say cheekily. "Just her. My ex-husband's wife? You don't think her devotion to me is a little off the wall?"

He shrugs and takes two steps to intercept me. "Maybe people just can't help themselves."

"You mean I'm irresistible?" I'm flirting. And it's not fair to either of us, but it's so easy and natural to fall into with him.

I think he might take me in his arms, but he doesn't. He just reaches forward and tucks my hair behind my ear. "You're letting it grow."

A shrug lifts my shoulders. "Not really. Just no time to get it cut. Too preoccupied with everything."

He nods. We're never at a loss for words with each other, but this silence is a little awkward. Finally, he speaks. "It never occurred to me, you know?" He's looking past me to the bare wall.

"What? You should have hung a picture there?" Oh, why do I have to resort to lame jokes all the time?

"That you wouldn't want to marry me if I were in full-time ministry."

"It's not you, Greg." I let off a sigh and drop onto the couch. Greg sits next to me.

He takes my hands. "Help me to understand. Please. I know

this isn't because you don't want to serve God. Your faith is as strong as anyone's."

"I wouldn't be a good minister's wife. Trust me."

"I just want you to be you. Stand beside me."

"And share you with five hundred people?"

He gives a boyish grin. "I'm hoping for more like a thousand-member church eventually."

"I have no doubt you'll achieve that goal."

"But it has to be without you, huh?"

Has he missed the last two weeks where we've been broken up?

I nod.

He expels a frustrated breath.

Almost afraid of the answer, I ask, "Do you want us to move?"

Giving my hands a squeeze, he releases me. "Of course not."

"Hang on. Let me get my checkbook," I say, needing to remove myself from this situation that's about to make me cry. "We never really settled on a rent, but I figure eight hundred dollars a month is a good number for a place like this. You know you'd get three times that much in the city."

He pulls me back. "I told you no rent. The house is paid for. I'm debt-free. I don't need or want your money. You and the kids are doing me a favor by living here."

"You know it's only for a few months until my house is done. Then the house will be empty until you get out of school."

"I know. But having someone living here, even for a few months, makes me feel better."

"All right, Greg." I know he's only doing this for me. And I feel bad for taking shameless advantage of the situation but I justify myself with two thoughts: One, I grew up in this house, so somehow I feel like I've retained some ownership rights. Two, I need my children to be away from the terrible influences lurking about that college-kid-infested apartment complex.

And speaking of the kids, all four of mine and Greg's Sadie are now barreling down the stairs like a herd of elephants. "We're hungry," Tommy announces.

"There's tons of leftover barbecue," I say. "Darcy brought enough to feed an army."

A collective groan emerges. "If I see another barbecued rib I'll barf," Ari whines, and the others follow her example with "yeahs" and "me too's."

Greg stands up and stuffs his hands in his front pockets. "How about I take you all out for pizza as my way of saying good-bye?"

"Yeah!" The crowd rallies.

"Uh, not a good idea," I say to Greg with my eyes big like I'm telling him to read my mind so I don't have to spell out the reason in front of the K-I-D-S.

Grinning, he ignores my not-so-subtle hint. "So, what do you say? Barney's sound all right?"

Ari's face brightens. "Yeah. Let's go to Barney's."

College hangout and my daughter all wide-eyed and hopeful. "Not a chance," I break in, amid images of frat boys and pizza and pitchers of beer at these tables. The image morphs into drunk, leering frat boys, with my daughter loving every second of the attention. I shudder. "How about Pizza Hut?"

Greg shrugs. "Sounds good to me."

I bend to grab my shoes from the floor in front of the couch, and when I straighten up, I catch a knowing grin on Ari's face and Greg smiles back.

Reality hammers home. "You set me up! Talk about your classic bait and switch."

The kids, including Sadie, break into laughter. Greg glances at me, as though afraid I might be angry. My heart turns over in my chest. I give his arm a light punch.

"Conspiring against me, huh?"

He looks deep into my eyes and I want to melt into his arms and promise him I'll be here for him when he's finished with Bible college.

"Come on, Mom," Tommy says, in the surprise twist of the night. "Give the guy a break. It's his last night here."

Unable to look away, I give a simple nod. "Okay. We can go."

There is no more opportunity for closeness or serious talks. Or good-bye kisses. And as I lie in my bed that night, I can't stop thinking about him. The way it felt all family-togetherish tonight at Pizza Hut. The way his fingers brushed mine as we both reached for the Parmesan cheese at the same time, the way his lips tilted at the corners and lines crinkled at the sides of his eyes every time he smiled. The way his gaze lingered on me when he dropped us off. His eyes said so much.

At four in the morning, I'm still fighting memories and trying to put him out of my mind. One problem: his cologne lingers everywhere. Finally in sleep-deprived desperation, I make a decision: tomorrow I'm moving one more time—from the master bedroom to Ari's room. The girl is going to be ecstatic at the promotion. And maybe I'll be able to get some sleep.

14

I get a call from Rick the next morning. "I think it's finally time," he says. My stomach drops.

"Darcy's in labor?"

"Of course not. She's got two more weeks. You know first babies are usually late."

Yeah, so are second, third, and fourth babies if I'm any example. "Time for what, then?"

"Remember how we said part of Ari's punishment for sneaking out and going to Barney's that night would be that she has to volunteer at the crisis pregnancy center?"

"Yes. Only you switched places with another doctor and stopped doing it." Ari was just thrilled to dodge that bullet.

"I know, but we've hired another ob-gyn so my schedule is slowing down some and I'm starting back at the clinic today. I think it's time to get her thinking about someone besides herself. Can I pick her up?"

I agree and hang up the phone. Ari and I have had the "Do you know what might have happened?" discussion since Patrick brought her home from the party. A rather lengthy one, as a matter of fact. She just doesn't seem to get it at all. Which frustrates me to no end. Why don't teenagers have any sense? Well, Paddy does. Revised question: Why can't all teenagers be as levelheaded as Paddy? Oh well. Might as well ask: Why aren't there any blue horses? Absent of common sense, hopefully seeing what can happen to girls who don't use good judgment will jar Ari out of her rebellion.

I pad down the hall to her room—the master bedroom. "Ari," I call, opening the door. "Get up. Dad's coming to get you in an hour."

"*Mmm.*" She turns over and covers her head with her comforter.

"No time for snooze this morning."

"Go away, Mother. It's not Friday. I don't go to Dad's today."

Go away? Yeah, that's not going to fly. I tell her so by yanking her comforter from the bed, leaving a ball of one-hundred-ten-pound girl in the middle of the full-sized canopy bed.

"Ma!" she moans. I sense the agony of defeat in her sleepy voice.

"The two of you are starting your volunteer work down at the crisis pregnancy center today. You have ten minutes to be up or I'm bringing a glass of water to dump on your cute little head."

She sits up and gives me a glare. "Don't you think I've been punished enough?"

I cock my head to the side and stare right back at her. "Well, let me think about that." I open my eyes wide and press my finger to the side of my mouth. "No, not really."

"I lost Paddy. I lost my license. I'm grounded all summer from going anywhere with friends. How much more punishment do I deserve?"

Good Lord. If John Wells saw Ari in action, he might reconsider coaching Shawn and turn his attention to her.

I don't even answer what I assume to be a rhetorical question anyway. "Get up and get dressed. I'll go fix you some breakfast."

"I don't want any."

"Well, I'll fix you something anyway and if you don't want it, don't eat it."

"I won't," she calls after me.

"Don't then."

I'm deep into the fourth chapter of my "Brandi" story when I realize something. This is the first book I've written without a contract since I started selling them without full chapters. I always vowed never to do it again. But I've somehow fallen in love with this story. It's so simple: a young woman who runs a restaurant and the kooky characters she encounters as she learns to love her ailing estranged father again. They're all each other has.

In the past twenty thousand words I've laughed, I've cried, and I've come to a decision. I will not write another book that doesn't touch a place deep in my heart.

I don't know what Stu's going to say about it, but I don't care. If he drops me and I have to start all over again, that's what I'm going to do.

I'm waiting to hear about the romance proposal. If it sells, I'll write it. After all, sending out a proposal and having it accepted is still a God thing. I just believe that He's in control.

By noon, I'm still pounding away on the keys when the door knocks open and I catch a glimpse of Ari just before she stomps up the steps.

"Claire?" Rick's voice calls from the living room. "You in here?"

I get up from my desk in my dad's old office and walk in there. "What happened?"

"I made her play nurse while I gave exams all day."

"She didn't see anything, did she?"

"Of course not. I kept her on the other side of the sheet. But she's still mad."

Traumatized is probably more like it.

I partly question the wisdom of this (and I'm not entirely sure it's legal) and partly I applaud his genius, because after three hours of watching little pink toes braced in stirrups, she's going to know what happens in the doctor's office to girls who get pregnant.

"I'm taking her back on Thursday."

"How many more times do you think are necessary?"

"I think all summer should do it."

"*All?*"

He shrugs. "What else does she have to do? She's grounded from everything."

He has a point there.

"All right."

His eyebrows go up. "No arguments?"

"Not for now. You love her too much to let anything happen to her." I give him a pointed look. "If it seems it's too much for her, I want you to let her off the hook."

"I understand. Anyway, I'm going to switch her to a different job. I just wanted to give her a strong dose of reality."

"I'm glad." I smile at him. It occurs to me that a year ago this conversation would never have been possible.

"Where are the boys?" Rick asks. "I want to say hi before I head to work."

"Tommy's at The Board working on his 'moves.'" I grin.

He grins back. "He's pretty good."

"Really good. The next Tony Hawk."

"What about Shawn? Is he around?"

I shake my head. "He's at the theater. Rehearsals started for *Peter Pan*." I still haven't broken the news to Rick yet that

Shawn's going with Everett as a stage name. My son hasn't really given an explanation as to why he's doing this, but I figure it's because I write under Everett. It's a crazy connection kind of thing, I imagine.

"Jakey's playing Nintendo?"

I chuckle. "No. He's in the tree house with Sadie."

"Sadie?" He frowns. "I thought you and Greg broke up."

"We did. As a matter of fact, he's on his way to Tulsa." I glance at my watch. He's probably just now arriving, most likely.

"Then why are you living in his house and keeping his daughter?"

My defenses are rising. What's it to Rick where I live or who comes to play with my kids? "I had to get Ari out of those apartments and Greg wanted someone in the house so it doesn't sit here empty."

"Ari could have come and lived with me." He's sulking. He does occasionally when we discuss the fact that I took the kids back a mere two weeks after I dropped them at his house. At first he took it as my lack of faith in his ability to take care of them, to nurture them properly. I had to enlist Darcy's help to make him see the whole thing for what it was: the kids and I need to be together. He's the one who left and they don't see him as the main parent. He's the part-time guy. They didn't want me to be the part-time gal. Simply put: they need us both, but they need my presence more.

"It was better this way." I'm not getting into this argument with him. "Do you want me to call Jake in so you can see him?"

"No. I'll go out there." He heads toward the kitchen where

the back door is located. Then he turns. "Darcy told me what you said."

Alarm jolts through me, because I say a lot of things. And more often than not it gets me into trouble. "She did?"

His expression softens. "Hearing you tell her you love her meant more than anything good that's happened to her in a long time."

I want to ask him if she's got a few screws loose, but I refrain from resorting to sarcasm since he's being so serious and appreciative.

"She's been praying hard that tensions would loosen between us before the baby is born. She just doesn't want the kids to have to play referee between us."

I don't bother to answer because, quite frankly, I don't know what to say. He seems to get it, because he gives me a nod and walks away.

Darcy. Now there's someone who would make a good pastor's wife. Why can't I be more like her?

Okay, I know I'm going crazy. One thing is for sure. Emma gives bad advice, evidenced by my loosening the reins of Ari's grounding. I already cancelled the rest of my sessions with the so-called life coach, and she grudgingly refunded half of my money.

But talking out my feelings did seem to help. My mind flitters back to the notice on the bulletin board in the laundry room. It was free. All I have to do is agree to be a test subject. I fish through a stack of papers on my counter. Yes, I, too, have a paper pile. Those flyers and coupons and old notes from teachers—papers I can't bear to throw out because they might some day come in handy. I finally pull out the elusive flyer from the bottom of the pile.

I glance at the clock. Do I really have time to get a private session in? Ari is upstairs sulking, Tommy is gone again, Shawn is having his private lesson with John, and Helen has invited Jake to come to her house and spend the day with Sadie.

Flyer in hand, I pace the kitchen floor for a few minutes trying to decide if I really want to go there again. I'm fully aware that my window of opportunity for today is slipping by.

Finally I just do it. I dial the number. After six rings I'm just about to hang up when I hear a breathless, "Hello?"

"Ina?"

"Who?"

Heat moves over my face. "I'm sorry. I must have the wrong number."

"Wait! Did you say Ina?"

"Um . . . yeah."

"Okay, hang on. Ina's here. Ina!" she yells.

I hear a muffled voice respond, "I'll be there in a second."

"Ma'am? She'll be here in a second. I'm sorry if I seemed rude."

"Not at all." Just clueless.

"Okay, here she is."

"Hello?"

"Yes?" I say. I swear the voice . . .

"This is Ina. What can I do for you?"

"Actually. Do you know you sound exactly like the other girl?" If there were money exchanging hands, I'd be tempted to think someone was yanking me around.

She hesitates. "We're twins. Identical twins. Twin sisters, actually. People get us mixed up on the phone all the time."

"And in person, too, I bet."

"What do you mean by that?" She sounds defensive.

"Just that you're look-alikes, right? Wouldn't people mistake you for each other until they get to know you?"

She gives an airy little laugh. "Yeah. You're right. What have you been doing, following me—er—us around?"

Methinks perhaps I'm not connecting with this life coach. Or maybe the problem is that this life coach isn't connecting with much herself. Like reality, for instance.

"Um, listen, Ina. I think maybe I did get a wrong number after all."

"Wait. No. Don't go. I'm a little scattered today, that's all. I really need a subject for my thesis. I can help you. I promise I can. And we can even do it all over the phone. So no need to leave your home unless you want to."

She seems so desperate, my heart goes out to her. "Okay, where do we start?"

"Oh, thank you." I hear her draw on a cigarette and blow out the smoke. "Tell me about yourself, first of all."

"All right, but no names."

"Anonymity will work fine for my thesis. But I'll need to fax you a consent form and will need a real signature when we're finished in order for me to use the information we come up with. Will you agree to that?"

"I can't have my name published." I roll my eyes at that, considering my occupation.

"That's fine. I only need to use it on the consent form."

Without divulging my name, I spend the next hour sharing the details of my life with this young woman. She asks me to make a list of all the things I am satisfied with and the things I'm not satisfied with. And because we're working toward her thesis, we'll speak twice a week. We'll try to make the satisfied list longer and the other list shorter as we progress.

Despite the disconcerting beginning to my conversation with Ina, I hang up feeling strangely hopeful. Maybe Ina is a better fit and talking things out with an impartial third party will help me to put things into perspective.

I don't know why, but somehow I expected to hear from Greg from time to time. I miss him. Badly. When two weeks pass with no direct word from him, I realize he's moved on. With that thought in mind, I finally accept Van's invitation to take me to dinner, even though Emma—the so-called life coach—had encouraged this.

"Anyplace but Red Lobster," I say when he asks where I'd like to go. I may never be able to eat there again after the heartbreak of my last date with Greg.

Van picks me up wearing a pink Polo shirt and a pair of Hollister jeans exactly like a pair I bought for Tommy a couple of weeks ago. I'm thinking Van might be a little younger at heart than I am. Or younger in style, at least.

I'm intrigued when he takes me to the Golf-a-Rama. Not exactly the kind of place a mid-thirties woman expects to be taken on a first date.

"I feel a little guilty coming here without the kids," I say.

Pretty boy smiles. "We'll bring them next time."

I defy any girl to try to convince me her heart rate doesn't double at the sight of his brilliant smile. I say that to rid myself of the guilt. If I had to choose between Van and Greg (sans pastoral ambitions), I would choose Greg in a split second. But I don't have that option and Van's the one who asked me out. Do I have to remain dateless forever?

I smile up at him; if I had inherited the family dimples like Charley, they'd be winking right now. "Taking a little bit for granted, aren't you?" I am fully aware that I'm shamelessly flirting with this guy.

Like a pro, he flirts back. And for the record, it's all too obvious he has a lot more experience with this than I do, even if I am several years older.

"Am I?" He takes my hand and our fingers intertwine.

"Well, you promised me dinner. Not putt-putt golf."

"Say no more, beautiful lady. Your dinner awaits you."

He takes me to the taco stand. "Oh, Romeo, Romeo, you shouldn't have gone to so much trouble, Romeo."

"Hey, you're worth it." He grins and squeezes my hand as we approach the counter.

Van and I eat nachos, play golf, ride go-carts, and I feel like I've regressed ten years. Don't get me wrong. I had a good time. But . . . maybe it's because Van is only twenty-nine—almost a decade my junior—that I can't seem to muster any real interest beyond the cuteness and good nature.

We get back to my house (Greg's, actually, which makes this whole thing even more awkward). I know Van's counting on a good-night kiss. I'm pulled with indecision as he opens the door on his five-year-old Camry. I even let him hold my hand on the way to the door.

"I had a great time, Claire," he says in that husky, I'm-getting-a-good-night-kiss tone of voice. He stops at the door and leans his shoulder casually against the doorframe. Guys like this know what they want, and they're used to getting it. So I have to be careful. Put it out there on the table that I'm not going to make out with him on my ex-boyfriend's front porch.

He tugs on my hand to pull me closer.

Oh, gee, he's making his move. "Hey, look, Van."

"Yeah?" he asks, distracted. His gaze smolders, and he zeros in on my mouth.

My stomach flips, and I'm almost sure it's not the nachos. Oh, boy. Give me strength.

"I'm not going to kiss you," I say when my mouth is mere inches from his.

He pulls back, his brows yanked up like they're connected to a string. "How come? Didn't you have a good time?"

I cast him a tolerant smile. "You know I did. I had a great time."

"Worried about the onions in the tacos?"

"What? Oh, my breath." Well, there is that. But curiously, I hadn't even thought of it.

"I have spray," he says with a boyish grin.

"Thanks, but it's not necessary."

"No kiss? For real? Not even a tiny one?"

"I'm afraid not. I like you. Really. But . . ."

"Oh, no." He gives me a mock jaw drop. "You're brushing me off, aren't you?"

"I'm sorry. But I don't see this going anywhere." I laugh at his fake heart failure as he clamps his hand to his chest. "I know you're not used to rejection from women."

"At least not until they realize what am immature jerk I am. Never after just one date. And I always at least get kissed." He leans in. "Was it the putt-putt golf that gave it away?"

"Maybe a little."

"I can be more grown up. How about I take you to the opera next time?"

I shake my head. "Good night, Van. I really did have a good time. Thanks."

This time he leans in and does kiss me . . . on the cheek.

I watch him walk down the steps, and I can't help but wonder if there will ever come a day when I can date again. Because if I can let go of a guy like that, then Greg truly has ruined me for anyone else.

15

List of things I'm satisfied with and not satisfied with. Okay, I'll start with my satisfied list.

WHAT I'M SATISFIED WITH

I stare at those words, racking my brain, trying to come up with something. Anything rather than pathetically conclude that at over three-and-a-half decades of life, I haven't found the state of contentment the apostle Paul wrote about in the epistles. Finally, I write:

1. Jesus

Okay, Jesus definitely satisfies me.
Smile.
Frown.
Hmmm. If Jesus is more than enough, then why do I want more?

Oh, man. Am I going to have to scratch Jesus off my list? What's wrong with me? I cringe as I make a mark through the Name above every name. I feel like I've just committed a sin.

But this is about honesty. How can I expect Ina to help me get to the bottom of why every area of my life seems to be filled with discontent if I am not honest about the basic things? I guess I have to face the truth about my own spiritual condition. Bottom line: Jesus *should* be more than enough for me. But He's not.

Fifteen minutes later, I come to the conclusion that I've pretty much exhausted my "satisfied with" list. And there's still a big fat blank space staring at me.

THINGS ABOUT MY LIFE I AM NOT SATISFIED WITH
1. Relationship with God (apparently)
2. Ari's destructive behavior
3. Direction my career is taking
4. I have no home of my own
5. My van is in the shop

I'm going to stop there. There are many more things I could write down. Like my extra ten pounds, Darcy's assumption that I'm part of her family with Rick, Greg's absence from my life.

Okay, on second thought, Greg's going on the list.

6. My inability to hang on to a man.

Having finished the list, I set it aside and grab my laptop.

Since it's Saturday, the kids are with Rick and Darcy. So I've decided to go work where I can watch my "inspiration" in action.

I pull into the parking lot of Ellie's Barbecue just before eleven. Only one other car is visible. I hop out and grab my laptop, but the door to the restaurant is locked when I try to go inside. Brandi is preparing for the day—filling salt and pepper shakers, etc. She glances up and her face lights with a smile.

"Hey there," she says a minute later when she opens the door for me. "Nice new ride." Her eyes scale past me to Darcy's SUV.

"Oh, I wish. It's borrowed."

"Must have some good friends."

"Believe me, you don't want me to go into it. And even more so, I don't want to."

She gives a little laugh as I step inside and head for the same booth I occupied last time.

"I'm ordering lunch. Can I stay and work?"

"Of course."

So I do. Brandi's smile is unstoppable. For three hours customers come in and out. One leaves, another arrives. Brandi's pleasant demeanor never fails. I wonder if she ever just wants to toss a plate of food on someone or tell them to get their own drink. As a former server myself, let me just say that I was not as patient as Brandi. While she's cleaning up the dining room after the rush is over, I ask her just that.

A smile steals over her lips as she grabs a salt shaker from the table next to mine. I watch as the snowy white grains pour from a large container into the smaller. "I like to make people happy. When someone comes in and they're obviously angry or sad or hurting, I consider it a mission to bring out a smile."

"Do you ever fail?"

Her own smile widens, bringing her dimples to the surface. "Not very often."

"I guess it must run in your family."

She gives a soft laugh and glances at her grandmother.

"Grandma is the only one I can't make smile on a regular basis."

The old lady leans closer as though she's really going to be able to hear us all the way across the room. She frowns like she knows we're discussing her. I give her little wave. Then turn my focus back to Brandi.

"I was talking about your dad."

The light in her eyes dims. "What about him?"

"I'm sure he feels the same way about acting that you do about serving people. You both want to make your audience smile."

Her lip curls in the same bitterness I saw the last time I spoke of John to her. "My father lives to please only one person: John Wells."

In part, I want to respect her unspoken desire to drop this subject that obviously brings her so much pain. But I feel that tug to draw it out. "He's giving my son acting lessons for free."

Her eyebrows go up. "Well, that's the first unselfish thing I've ever heard of him doing. Don't get your hopes up. In a year you'll probably get a big fat bill in the mail."

I can't help but laugh. "I doubt it. But if I do, I'll tell him to lump it."

Making people smile must be an inherent goal of writers, too, because I watch closely and when I see her mouth curve upward, my spirit soars.

Brandi looks across to her grandma, who is cleaning up in the kitchen and keeps peeping out from the order-up window. "I'm going to take a break, Grams."

"Do you want something to eat?" the old woman calls, much to my surprise. I figured she'd complain about how lazy young people are these days. That's what I get for judging a book by its cover. Smile.

"No, thank you, Grams." Brandi's gaze shifts back to me. "More coffee?"

I glance at my empty cup. "No, you take your break."

"It's okay. I'm going to get myself some." She grabs the pot and comes back to my table. "Want some company, or you getting back to work?"

"I'd love to stop and take a break."

"Good." Brandi slides into the seat across from mine. She sips her coffee then stares a little past me. I get the urge to turn around and see what she's looking at, but something in me recognizes a pensive moment.

Silence yawns between us, and it's starting to get pretty uncomfortable when she finally says, "I know he came back to make amends. I just don't know how to forgive him for what he did to my mother."

"Cheated?"

She shook her head. "There was no need to cheat. He never committed to her. My mom went to New York in rebellion against my grandparents. Imagine a girl from this area thirty years ago."

I get the mental image.

"Anyway, just when she was on the brink of starvation, she landed a walk-on role in one of my dad's stage productions."

"Broadway?"

Amusement lights her brown eyes. "So far off Broadway it might as well have been Connecticut. Anyway. John got *discovered* and left the theater. Left Mom two months' pregnant. When she finally found him again, I was two months old."

I see raw pain, bitterness, anger—all those things in her eyes. "I'm sorry, Brandi."

"You know what I'm most sorry about?"

I shake my head.

"I'm sorry that my mother got mixed up with a man who swore to love her forever. A man who got her pregnant and then became too full of his successful new life to share that life with the woman who adored him."

"What happened?" I ask quietly.

Brandi sips her coffee, swallows as she sets her cup back on the scarred wood tabletop. "He gave her money, sent her back here to her parents, and sent money every month the whole time I was growing up."

"And your mother is . . . ?"

A short laugh bursts from her throat. "Mom married Jerry Ray Boggs when I was ten years old." She clutches her coffee cup between both hands until her knuckles grow white. "Jerry Ray liked me a little too much, if you know what I mean. So, Mama left me to live with my grandparents and off she went with Jerry. She ODed on heroin five years later."

"Oh, Brandi." Oh, man. God, give me words. I feel so inadequate to hear this.

Caught up in her memories, Brandi goes on as though I've never even spoken. "Of course, John never knew any of this, so he just kept sending money here." She gives me a little grin. "I remember the first letter we got from him after Mama moved off, Grandma took it, unopened, and marched it right back down to the post office. Wrote 'Return to sender' on the envelope along with a short note—all on the outside of the envelope, mind you—that conveyed the message we didn't need any of his dirty money and he could just go to the devil."

Well, he's taking her advice. I hate it. I hate that John was a jerk. I hate that Brandi has to live with the heartbreak of those choices. I am most impressed at what a wonderful human being she's turned out to be. I reach across the table and pat her hand. "You are an amazing woman to have survived such a life and still have any sense of goodness and compassion in you."

Her eyes fill with tears. "Thank you, Claire. It's funny. I know my dad has come back to love me and to build a relationship with me, but somehow I just can't play Daddy's little girl with him."

"Maybe you don't need to do that. Maybe for both of your sakes, you could just start with getting to know one another."

A barely discernible nod inclines her head. "We'll see." She frowns and leans forward. "You and he aren't . . . ?"

It takes me a second to get where she's going. My eyes go big. "Good grief. No way."

Relief washes over her and I realize that Brandi cares a lot more about what goes on in her dad's life than she wants to admit—even to herself. "Sorry," she mutters. "It's really none of my business."

"Trust me. John's a good neighbor, and besides being an atheist, is becoming a good friend. But there's nothing even remotely romantic going on between us."

She tips her head to the side and purses her lips as though coming to a conclusion. "I see . . . you're the daughter he never had."

Pain lurks just around the edges of that comment and I see how deeply she wants to love her father—to be able to put her heart out there and be assured he won't trample it.

"You could say that I'm a very poor substitute for the daughter he actually does have." I glance at my watch and close my laptop. "Time to go."

I stand and give her a look. "Listen, Brandi. I don't know

what's right for you. My heart is telling me you should call John and set up a meeting. But regardless of what you choose, the unforgiveness will eat you alive."

She stands. "Tell me about it. I can't even date because of him."

"You're a Christian, aren't you?" She reads my books, so I assume . . .

"I guess," she says with a shrug. "I went to Sunday school some as a child. I still pray every night at bedtime."

I jot my phone number on a napkin and hand it to her. "Anytime you want to talk, day or night, give me a call."

Her dimples wink as she smiles and tucks the number into her apron pocket. "Thanks, Claire."

I drop the cash to pay my check, along with a nice tip, onto the table and head to Darcy's SUV. I can't help but think about Penny, the Laundromat girl, and John, my atheistic friend. Now Brandi. It's like the song says: people need the Lord. I've stayed tucked away in my little corner of the world, writing my little books, avoiding close relationships so that I don't have to leave my comfort zone. No wonder I didn't really know just how much need there was until this relocation forced me to open my eyes.

Sunday-morning service is depressingly empty without Greg's subtle presence. Over the past few months, Sunday morning service has been my favorite because once I talked him into attending the later service so I could sleep in, I have relished the warm smile as he greeted me. That shoulder pressed against mine during the whole service (since he only led worship on Wednesdays), sharing a Bible.

I miss him so much.

Blinking back hot tears of self-pity, I glance across the

church and locate Helen in her regular spot. Surprise shifts through me when my gaze locks onto Sadie's. I frown, only because I'm wondering why she isn't in kids' church with the rest of the six-year-olds.

Apparently the little girl mistakes my frown as a challenge because in a flash, her pink tongue shoots from her mouth and right in my direction. Then she does it again. And again.

Heat moves across my face and I fight an inner war. I want to reciprocate. Really bad. I'd like to say that my spiritual strength took over, Joyce Meyer's teaching about rising above offense, but that's just not the case. I'm about to totally give in to my flesh and stick out my own tongue when Helen catches Sadie in the act. Greg's mom glances at me with horrified apology. I nod and give the best (and I know a little guilty) smile I can muster.

After service, she beelines for me, dragging Sadie behind her. I know I'm about to get an apology. I paste a look of utter innocence on my face because although I know I was about to do the same thing, for once I didn't get caught doing the wrong thing. I will savor this moment and happily let a six-year-old take the fall.

"Claire, I'm so sorry about Sadie's actions." Helen pulls Sadie forward. "Apologize to Claire."

The little raven-haired beauty clamps her lips together and shakes her head. Defiance shoots from every line of her face, but her eyes are filled with unshed tears.

"Helen, it's okay."

"No it isn't." She focuses her stern gaze on her granddaughter. "Immediately, or no TV for a week."

Sadie's lips are still clamped together so tightly they're white. She shakes her head wildly. Tears spill over. Even I can tell there is more than anger involved here. More than stubbornness.

"Helen. Let's drop it. Okay?"

Helen sits and pulls Sadie forward. "Why are you being so stubborn? You're usually such a good girl."

Everything in me wants to snort. Yeah, right. But a modicum of self-control takes over and I remain silent.

Sadie relaxes her lips and glares up at me with such venom, I think I might need an antidote. She points a little finger at me. "She made Daddy cry."

I feel the blood drain from my face.

"Sadie, that is between your father and Claire. Do you think he'd want you to be mean to her?"

Sadie stomps so hard, I'm afraid she might have fractured her foot. At any rate, I can tell it was painful because a grimace covers her face. But she seems to shake it off in light of her principled stand. "I'm not saying sorry. She made Daddy cry, and that's why he left me."

I really want to crumple into dust. I know one thing, I'm not waiting around for the kid to apologize. "Excuse me, please."

Helen places her hand on my arm. "Claire, she doesn't understand."

"I know. It's all right. Really, I have to go."

"I do understand."

I hear Sadie sob behind me. "I want my daddy!"

Pain squeezes my heart as I hurry out of the church.

In the parking lot I hear a voice calling me. "Hey! Hey, Claire!"

I stop because a rusty little VW Bug is heading toward me. The kind before they got the new bodies and became "Beetles." The sun is glaring off the windshield, so I can't make out the face, but I do see a dark arm poking out of the window and a hand waving frantically. A head sticks out just before the VW screeches to a halt.

"Penny?"

Her grin is so wide, it envelops me with its infectious properties and I smile despite the heartbreaking scene I've just left. "I'm so happy to see you!"

"Same here. I just had to check out the best church in town."

"Was I right or was I right?"

"Well, I haven't checked out all the others, but this beats any I've gone to since Mama's church back home."

The girl's obviously brainwashed because childhood loyalty notwithstanding, there's no way she's ever been to a church as great as this one. "Got plans for lunch?"

"Not really," she says.

"Want to join me? I thought about going to Ellie's Barbecue out by Bennett Springs."

"Mmm. Sounds good."

"Great, follow me to my house and we'll leave your car there. You can ride with me."

She agrees and I walk to my borrowed SUV. Alone. The kids are staying two weeks with their dad per Darcy's request. She says she's nesting and needs someone to take care of with Rick working so many hours and her getting uncomfortably close to her due date. I didn't see them in church, so I figure they went to the first service.

Kids are so unpredictable. I almost expected an outcry at the suggestion they spend two weeks with Rick and Darcy, especially after the way they reacted about staying there before. I suppose they see this differently, though. Because there was no fussing about it.

In a few minutes I'm pulling into my driveway. Penny parks alongside the curb.

"This is your house, huh?" she says as she gets in.

"Not exactly," I say as I pull back out. "The owner left town and needed someone to keep an eye on the place."

"Lucky you. Sure beats the apartments."

"You got that right, girlfriend." Darn it! There it comes again. The lingo. I roll my eyes. "Sorry."

Laughter bursts from her throat. "You don't need to be sorry. I'm used to it."

Now my face burns. As much as I don't want to see differences, I do. Not in a class or caste system. More a cultural thing. I guess it's sort of like how my brother, Charley, has a thick Texas drawl even though he grew up in Missouri and has only lived in the Lone Star state for the past five years.

Then again, I guess only a weak mind is so easily influenced. I've always known Charley was weak, but what does that say about me?

Oh, well.

By now we're passing my house and Penny gives a low whistle as she looks it over. The broken part of the roof has been removed and the boards are in a pile at the side of the house.

I stop the SUV in the middle of the road. "That's my house."

"I didn't picture it being this bad."

"I used to have a massive oak tree next to the house."

"How long before you get to move back in?"

"Two or three months, I guess. One of the rooms has more damage than the rest."

"Who's the old man?"

"Huh?" I think maybe Penny might be hallucinating just a bit.

"In that yard."

I tear my eyes from my dilapidated house to see John Wells waving.

I take my foot off the brake and pull the SUV to a stop next to John's curb. I wave him over as an idea hits me. An idea that is quite possibly not that great of an idea, but nonetheless, when I get something into my head it's hard not to follow through. He walks to my window.

"You look very nice, Ms. Everett." His lips twitch.

"Thanks. Church."

"Has your soul been sufficiently lifted?"

"It has. You ought to try it sometime." I look at Penny, whose bemused look reveals that she doesn't get the joke. And, of course, there's no reason she should. "John's the neighborhood's token atheist."

She snorts.

"If you're going to discuss me as though I'm not here, please introduce me to this young lady."

"John Wells, meet Penny. We met while I was living at the apartments."

"My pleasure."

"Thanks," Penny says with her wide smile. "My pleasure, too."

And now for my bright idea. "Hey, John, we're going out for lunch. Want to tag along?"

"Inviting me on a date? I'm honored, Ms. Everett."

"Okay. You can delude yourself into thinking this is a date. But remember, it's not really."

He chuckles and looks past me to Penny. "Ms. Everett is our token heartbreaker. There's one on every block."

We wait for John to wash his hands and lock his door.

"Thanks for inviting me," Penny says suddenly. "It's been a tough week. I feel better already. Just going to church and being invited to lunch."

"I'm glad for the company. The kids are gone for a couple of weeks. I always eat too much when I'm alone."

"I hear you."

I can't help but roll my eyes. She has the perfect body, and I have a feeling she knows it.

She unhooks her seat belt when John emerges from his house. "Guess I'll let the old guy sit up front."

I grin. John would hate being called the "old guy," but come on. He is.

He slips into his seat and looks at me expectantly. I look right back at him, because, frankly, I'm not that great a driver. I drive too fast and sometimes birds distract me. "Are we having a picnic in the vehicle?" he asks, and I hear Penny snort from the back.

"Seat belt, Sir John Wells."

"Never wear them."

Okay, one thing I have discovered about John is that he loves women. I know it won't take much to get my way.

"Please? I would feel awful if we crash and you get hurt."

He raises an eyebrow and I see acquiescence on his lined, Sean Conneryish handsome face.

"For you, Ms. Everett." And just like that he clicks his seat belt into place.

I reward him with a broad smile. "Thanks."

As I pull away from the curb, my stomach starts to churn. I'm not sure this is such a good idea, after all.

"So, tell me about yourself, John," Penny says.

Oh, good. His favorite subject. That ought to distract him for the time being.

And for the next ten minutes he regales us with a tale about the time President Reagan came to see him while he was performing on Broadway. His voice gets thoughtful as he recites from memory a note the late great president sent backstage. It was simple: "You made me forget you were acting. Good job. Ronnie."

"Wow, that's amazing." Penny says, although I know darned well Miss Barely Twentysomething couldn't possibly remember a president before Clinton. "My folks voted for Carter and Mondale." Okay, maybe she paid attention in history classes.

"Ah, were your parents from Minnesota?" John grins.

Penny's laugh echoes throughout the SUV. "California. I think they were the only people in the state who voted on the Democratic ticket that election."

John looks over his shoulder and sends her a wink. (What is it about old guys and winking, anyway?) "I didn't vote either time, but I had great respect for Reagan. It was a sad, sad day when he passed on."

"At least he's in heaven," I can't resist saying. I'd rather talk religion than politics anyway. I know where I stand on Christianity. I'm a little wishy-washy when it comes to politics. And we'll just leave it at that.

John seems to have my number. He laughs out loud. "Heaven? The fairy-tale kingdom where all good people and good dogs go when they die."

"Now, John. You've read the Bible, you say. You should know that no one is good. No not one."

"Touché. So why try?"

"I'm so glad you asked." I grin and turn my gaze to him.

While he's a captive audience, I think the time might finally have arrived to share the gospel. "Listen, John . . ."

"Ms. Everett. While it is true I don't believe in an afterlife, I'm not quite ready to test my theory. Will you please turn your attention back to the winding road?"

"Yeah, I'm still debating whether my salvation is holding up considering the past few years of my life," Penny chimes in from the back. "I'm not ready to test my fear of hell."

"All right, fine." I focus, and just in time, because I'm about to miss the parking lot. I set the whole heaven versus fairy-tale land debate on the back burner for now because, judging from the whiteness of John's face, I think I might have to do CPR.

"John, you okay?"

"Why did you bring me here?"

"Don't you like barbecue?" Penny saves me a reply by asking.

"I do not."

"Well, that's okay." I wave off his frustrated response—totally playing the innocent. "They have seafood, too. And fried chicken."

"That is not the point." He glares at me, and I realize once again what a terrible, awful actress I am. "When did you discover that my daughter and her grandmother run this place?"

Penny holds up her hand. "Look, I can tell this is a private conversation, so how about I go in and use the bathroom and when I come out, you'll either be in a booth waiting for me, or in the car waiting for me so we can leave."

She doesn't bother to wait for an answer, but opens the door and heads inside.

"Ms. Everett, I'm not pleased with your duplicity."

He's lucky I'm a wordsmith or I wouldn't even know what

he meant. But I get it. He's basically calling me a liar. A deceiver.

"Hey, John. I just wanted barbecue and invited you along."

"Revelation twenty-one, verse eight," he says with Stu-like smugness. "Read it."

"How about telling me what it says?"

"In essence, it tells where liars go."

I'm getting a little ticked off at this God-mocker's Scripture referencing. "Oh, yeah? Where does it say atheists go?"

His mustache gives that telltale twitch. "At least I admit what I am. That's much more than I can say for you. I can read your face. You brought me here to try to play some sort of peacemaker between us."

Caught with my hand in the proverbial cookie jar, I shrug. "Well, 'Blessed are the peacemakers, for they shall be called the sons of God.' "

His lip turns down and I see the first real scowl I've ever seen on John's face. "You're beginning to annoy me."

"What? It's okay to quote it as long as you don't believe it?"

"How about we drop this and go inside before Penny thinks we're leaving?"

"Really?" Okay, I thought we were gearing up for a knock-down-drag-out fight and an immediate trip back to town.

"I'm not a fool, my dear. I've been invited to dinner by two beautiful women. How can I pass up the opportunity?"

John is smooth. Very smooth.

Only when Brandi sees us, she glares at John and smiles at me. To my surprise, she meets us at the door with menus. "Follow me."

She seats us in my favorite booth. "I'll be back with some water."

"Thanks. We have another person with us."

"That'll be me." Penny smiles broadly and plants herself next to me, forcing me to scoot in. I prefer to have a seat to myself, or at the very least have the outside. But I swallow hard and decide to try to contain my claustrophobia for the next thirty minutes to an hour.

Brandi returns, unaware that her father hasn't taken his eyes off of her since we stepped inside. Brandi leans on one hip. "So, how'd you get him to come out here?"

I grin. "Seat belt, locked door, and seventy miles per hour. He didn't have a chance."

"Indeed?"

"He's afraid of where atheists go," I whisper, trying to get a rise out of him.

"I can tell him where to go," Brandi says, her expression turning hard as stone.

John, ever the gentleman, clears his throat and looks at the menu. "I believe I will have the grilled trout with steamed zucchini and a house salad. Oil and vinegar dressing."

"Fine." Brandi finishes taking his order, then turns to Penny and me. "Ladies?"

I'm miserable. Truly. Why can't I just mind my own business?

The next forty-six minutes pass in a blur. The studied indifference of Brandi and John feeds Penny's unabashed interest as she keeps glancing from them to me with a definite smirk. Brandi's usual grin is nowhere in sight as she makes a minimal effort to keep us supplied with food and drink.

Sigh. There's nothing to do but tough it out and acknowledge my attempt at reconciliation is a complete failure.

I do notice, however, that when we get up to leave John drops three crisp one-hundred-dollar bills on the table.

"Nice tip, John," Penny says and winks. "If you ever come into Shoney's, be sure and ask for me. I work there Thursday, Friday, and Saturday nights."

"I'll remember that," John says, giving her a tolerant smile. We are out at the SUV and about to pull away when Brandi bursts through the door. "Hey! Wait!"

John heaves a sigh and rolls down his window.

"I don't want your money, John Wells."

"I want you to have it. You're my daughter."

Anger burns in her eyes. "Listen. I didn't need your money growing up. And I don't need your money now." She flings the bills at him.

Very calmly, John folds the money and reaches out before she can stop him. He tucks the money into her apron pocket. "It's a tip for exceptional service." Without another word he rolls up the window and sits straight as an arrow, his gaze directly ahead.

Brandi stands motionless, her face reflecting indecision and pain. I help her make her decision to keep the cash that's probably more than she makes in a week in tips. Sending her a little wave, I shift into reverse and back away.

Once we get on the road, the silence is palpable. Finally, I can stand it no longer. "Now who's the liar, John?"

My words, out of nowhere, jolt him from his thoughts. "I beg your pardon?"

"Exceptional service, my eye. We got everything *except* service from your daughter."

John Wells sits for a second in stunned silence. Then he laughs aloud. Penny joins him and, relieved, so do I.

"Sorry for the bushwhack, John," I say when I pull up alongside the curb in front of his house.

He takes my hand and presses a kiss to my fingers. "Your heart was in the right place. It's been a long time since someone cared about me, Ms. Everett. I can't help but be touched by your generosity."

Sudden tears well up in my eyes, blinding me. I blink them back. "Don't give up. She'll come around eventually."

He gives me a sad little smile and there's that wink again. "From your mouth to God's ears."

16

That night I pull on my pj's at eight o'clock and slip *The Wizard of* Oz into the DVD player. I crawl into bed. Lonely. The phone rings just as Dorothy steps from black and white into the Technicolor land of Oz.

"Hi, Mom."

"How did you . . . oh, caller ID."

Not much slips by Mom. She's finally getting it.

"So, what's up?" I ask, hitting the pause button on the movie.

"I couldn't stop thinking about you," she says. "I can tell something is wrong. Want to tell me what it is?"

"Oh, nothing." I know she won't buy it. And she knows I know it. Why do we go through the trouble of this little routine? Will I ever just come right out and admit my life stinks? For some reason I'm compelled to follow through with the comfortable ritual whereby Mom asks, I deny, she fishes, I give in, she gives bad advice, I get ticked, we hang up. Then act like nothing happened. No big deal.

Let the games begin . . .

"Something is wrong," Mom fishes.

Here's where I give in, knowing I shouldn't, but needing the unconditional love that only a mom can give. "Greg left for Oklahoma a few days ago." Tears burn my eyes. "I just really miss him."

"Have you had a change of heart about marrying him?" She has that hopeful tone that makes me feel even worse.

"Not really." I reiterate my position because it seems as though she needs a refresher. "Not pastor's-wife material, remember?"

"That's just ridiculous." Okay, it's a little sooner than usual, but Mom has just kicked into bad-advice mode. "You give yourself far too little credit. Besides, I think you've misunderstood the role of a minister's wife. Not all wives are involved in the day-to-day ministry of the pastor. Some stay home and take care of kids."

"I know," I say a little testily, because quite frankly, I'm tired of discussing it. Why am I the only person who realizes what a horrible pastor's wife I would make? And "stay home and take care of the kids"? What does she think I've been doing for the past sixteen years?

"Well, if you're going to be cranky, I'll get to the point."

Please do, I think, but would never have the guts to say out loud. Besides, I thought the point was that she couldn't stop thinking about me and my inner pain. I guess I don't have the guts to go with that one, either.

"I've decided to move back home."

I'm in the middle of an inhale when she says this, and for the life of me, I can't seem to blow out the breath. It just stays in my lungs until I feel like my entire core is on fire.

"Claire, are you still there?"

The breath leaves me in a puff. "Can you say that again, Mom?"

"I said I'm moving back."

I kick my legs over and over under the sheets, squeeze my eyes shut, try *hard* not to scream.

Mom's not buying it, though. "Good grief, Claire. What's all that noise?"

Immediately, my tantrum ceases. "What do you mean?"

"Don't you want me to move back?" Her tone moves me to guilt.

"I just never thought you would. You love being with Charley and Marie and the kids. And, Mom, what about the new twins? Can you really leave those babies?"

My mind is racing. I mean, I hated that she moved last fall. Hated it with a passion. I needed her help with the kids while I was recovering from carpal tunnel surgery. Turns out, I got along okay and learned to stand on my own. Does that mean this news of her return also foretells my regression into the same needy soul I was before?

"I love those babies, that's true. But I'm just too old to keep up with them. Marie's going to have to find a different babysitter or stay home with the kids."

"But where are you going to live, Mom? You sold your house, remember?"

"Until I find a place, I'll naturally have to live with you."

Oh, dear Lord. Say it isn't so.

Don't get me wrong. I love my mother. She's very cool. Well, cool might be a stretch. When I was thirteen years old, my friend Kimberly Jones loaned me a Petra record. (Remember records? My kids call them "really big CDs.") Mom took a listen and banned the Christian rockers with a vehemence I'd seen only once before in my short life—the time Charley begged to be allowed to watch *The Return of the Jedi.*

Mother's refusal on that was a result of our church's wishy-washy stand on the movie. Dark side/light side. All very confusing. Church opinion was split down the middle and Mom's close-knit clique was on the "*Star Wars* is of the devil" side, so Charley got the short end of the stick.

The little wimp cried about it for two days because all of his little grammar-school friends were going to see it. Finally I got so sick of his whining, I snuck him out of the house one night and walked him down to the movie theater, paid for tickets, sprang for popcorn out of my hard-earned babysitting money, and told him I'd beat the heck out of him if he ever told on us.

Sensitive boy that he was, he had guilt nightmares for a week until he finally tiptoed into my parents' room at midnight one night and confessed (fully aware that Mom and the angels would protect him from my wrath).

Charley's repentance absolved him of his sin, and that night he slept like a baby, while I lay in bed imagining scenarios whereby my little brother might go missing and never be seen again. The next morning I was sentenced to two weeks' grounding from watching *Hart to Hart*.

I've never gone out on a limb for Charley since. And I didn't get to beat the heck out of him either, because Mom, foreseeing the possibility, warned me off under threat of missing not only two episodes but the entire season of the TV show. After weighing the joy of pummeling my brother against the torture of months and months without Stephanie Powers and Robert Wagner, I had to go with what would make me the happiest. It was a close call, but I chose the millionaire amateur sleuths over the instant and short-lived gratification of inflicting pain where it was deserved.

Anyway, back to the paradox that is my mother. Christian rock was a definite no-no in our house, while twice a week she scrubbed the kitchen floor in time to Barbara Mandrell's "You

Can Eat Crackers in My Bed Anytime." Needless to say, I have consistency issues that plague me to this day.

"So—uh, when are you coming, Mom?"

"Well, I won't if you don't want me to." Oh, groan. Manipulation that leads to guilt and the inevitable apology—mine, of course.

I cover the receiver with my hand and heave a great big sigh. Take my hand off the receiver. "You know I want you to." Forgive me, Lord. "You'd have to share the master bedroom with Ari, though."

I pause. Smile. That'll keep my kid from sneaking out at night. Mom's got better radar than Big Brother. I'm warming up to the idea when she deflates my balloon. "Don't be silly. We'll put a bed in the basement and I will sleep down there. I refuse to uproot those children again."

Uproot? Is she referring to the massive oak tree that uprooted and slammed into my house? My defenses are rising and I want to ask her if she is blaming me for a tornado, but I think sometimes it's better to let things go. So that's what I do, because she'll just backtrack, do the don't-go-twisting-my-words routine—and quite frankly, I don't think it will do any good anyway. So, like I said, I let it go and point the conversation toward her imminent homecoming—and my imminent return to my childhood.

"When's it going to be, Mom? I'll need to get the basement ready."

"Next Friday. My plane lands at 3:30 in the morning."

"Mom! In the morning?"

"It was the cheapest flight I could get."

"You know I would have made up the difference if I'd known about it ahead of time." Good grief. Like I don't lose enough sleep these days. Between missing Greg and watching

Ari like a hawk, I haven't slept more than four hours a night in ages.

"You have to save your money now that you're homeless and that dirty rotten scoundrel stole your money."

I have tried to explain more than once to my mother that the insurance check has already cleared. I'm just waiting for Van's bill and it's all taken care of. But for some reason, she keeps thinking the thirty grand it's going to cost to fix my house is coming out of my pocket. I've exhausted myself trying to convince her. "Fine, Mom. Three-thirty it is."

"Thank you, hon. Now, have you heard from Greg?"

Oh, ow. Twist the knife, Mom. Why don't you just drive it in deep and give it a good swift crank?

"No, I haven't. But I saw his mother and Sadie at church today."

"Oh, that's nice. Did Helen mention whether or not she's heard from him?"

Should I tell her what happened?

Sure, why not.

"She didn't really have a chance. Sadie stuck out her tongue at me and accused me of making her daddy cry and then leave her." The images replay in my head and I'm living it again.

"The poor little girl. I did question the wisdom of his leaving her."

The other line beeps. I'm saved! "Hey, Mom, I need to let you go. I have another call."

"Oh, I hate that call waiting. They never should have invented it."

"I know, Mom. It's rude. I'll talk to you tomorrow."

"Fine. Good-bye, then."

I click the other line and say hello.

"Hi, Claire. It's me."

My heart nearly stops and then soars at the sound of Greg's voice.

"Hi. How's Tulsa?"

"Lonely."

Well, what'd ya expect, bud? Okay, that's what I want to say. But why kick a man when he's already down, you know? "I'm sorry. Maybe it'll get easier."

"I hope so. I pray so. Classes are good."

"I'm glad." Oh, man. John's right. I am a liar. I wanted classes to be bad. Horrible. Filled with heresy and half-truths. I hoped the instructors would be crosses between Jim Jones and Reverend Moon. I wanted the bathrooms to all be caked with filth. I wanted traffic to annoy him and the Oklahoma wind to sweep down the plains to frustrate him. In short, I wanted him to realize that God couldn't possibly be the One who sent him away, because . . . it's not what I want. I want him to forget the whole idea of being a pastor and just come back to me so things can get back to normal.

"Listen, Claire. The main reason I called is to apologize for Sadie."

Something inside of me just dies when he says that. Couldn't it have been because he misses me? Or perhaps because he sees my face everywhere he goes? I have this really bad feeling Greg's already moving on. I want to throw the phone against the wall and watch it and Greg shatter. Instead I paste a smile on my face. And yes, I know he can't see me; it's to psych myself up.

"No need to apologize. Maybe she'll feel better if she knows I was this close to sticking my tongue back out at her. But your mom looked up at just the right time."

He laughs. The rich, comforting sound sweeps over me like a warm summer rain. I lean back against my pillows and close my eyes. I'm savoring the sound of his voice, and relishing the fact that I can still make him laugh. "What can I say? I'm pretty much still a six-year-old at heart."

"I didn't even know she stuck out her tongue."

"Oh. Guess I just told on us both, then."

He chuckles. "Actually, Mom told me what she said about you being the reason I left."

"Don't worry about it, Greg." I'm so gracious, I scare myself. "I understand kids. I have four of them."

"I remember. I was hoping to be their stepdad."

Oh, be still my beating heart. Need I remind him that he was the one who changed direction midstream?

The laughter dies out and silence yawns between us. I think he's trying to find a way to gracefully say good-bye now that he's done what he called to do. And I'm just about to let him off the hook by making up some lame excuse to go, when I hear the intake of breath that signals he's about to speak.

"Mom is moving here with Sadie until I graduate."

Okay, talk about being blindsided. I so didn't see that coming. And with the information that his mother is moving, I feel my last emotional link to Greg slipping away.

Two weeks later, my life has suddenly gone from peaceful to crazy.

Mom is back in all her glory. So far things aren't too bad, although I occasionally have to bite my tongue over a stray comment or two. She's taken over the downstairs and seems fairly happy there.

Darcy calls me eight times a day to ask my opinion as to whether or not she will ever go into labor or will this baby just stay inside of her until she explodes?

Eight times a day I assure her the baby will, in fact, make his or her appearance in due time. And no, I don't see a tummy explosion in her future.

Ari is still stomping in and out of the house on Tuesday and Thursday mornings as she goes to and from the Hope House.

I take those times to call Ina, my life coach. And this is what I've learned: according to Ina, life shouldn't be filled with stress and anger. I have deep, deep resentment against my mother. Apparently, I mask this resentment in comedy and sarcasm. Not exactly rocket science. I'd already figured all that out from being an avid fan of Dr. Phil.

One thing the good TV doctor and I never got around to working on, though, is something Ina has put her crazy, neurotic finger on: I'm so afraid my daughter will feel the same way about me as I do about my mother that I've closed myself off to complete vulnerability with her.

I didn't know that, but I do see it. And I think I might have put my finger on why Ari is sneaking out, too.

She wants my attention.

This is where my life coach and I have come to after today's telephone session. I'm grateful for the breakthrough and decide to return the favor. I'm worried about Ina. I heard her light up at least ten times during the hour-and-a-half session. She's jittery, and quite frankly, I think she's on the edge. Physician, heal thyself.

"Hey, Ina. If you ever want to talk, I'm here for you, too."

She hesitates and puffs smoke. "I'm not sure that'd be very professional. Know what I mean?"

"In a normal situation, I'd agree, but remember I'm your project. It's not like I'm paying for your help. Come on. Talk to me."

Silence looms.

"Okay, it's all right. But can you at least talk over what's bothering you with your twin sister?"

"Who?"

"Your sister? The twin that sounds just like you? I talked to her the first day we met."

"Oh." She drops into silence once more and I'm about to just let her go until I hear sniffles from her end.

"Ina? Are you okay? Did something happen to your sister?"

"I don't have one."

"Okay. So you lied. What was that for?"

"I'm so sorry. I was just having a really bad day when you first called and I sounded so desperate and crazy over the phone, I was afraid you wouldn't want me to coach you. I've only gotten one other call and it was a pervert who wanted phone sex."

"Ew."

"Tell me about it."

"You know, Ina, sometimes it helps just talking out a problem."

"It's just that I don't have any family around here. They're all in California. My boyfriend broke up with me a few weeks ago and I see him everywhere with his new boyfriend."

"Boyfriend?"

She heaves a sigh and I hear a fresh sob rush to her throat. "Yeah. He dated me all through our undergrad work and through the first year of grad school. One night we're talking about how great it will be to finish our master's degrees and get on with our careers and I say, 'And we can start planning that wedding.' And he just looks at me like this is something we haven't been discussing for the past five years, and says, 'I'm in love with Brian.' Brian! Can you believe it?"

Okay, I don't even know who Brian is. And good grief, her boyfriend was gay? How could she not know after five years?

She answers both questions as though I've spoken out loud.

"Brian is a guy who works at my hair salon. It was just so obvious he was gay. But how could I have not known that Joe was into that lifestyle, too? What's wrong with me that I didn't see the signs?"

"Listen, Ina. It's like any relationship. When one person cheats, we always blame ourselves. What did I do? How could I not have seen? The truth is cheaters are masters of deception, so unless they're incredibly stupid or just want to get caught, it's unlikely they will be."

"Sounds like you're speaking from experience."

"I am. Only my husband wasn't gay, and we had four kids together, so when he left me, he also walked out on a family."

"I guess it could have been worse," she says glumly. "At least he didn't marry me and sleep around on me with guys."

"Definitely could have been worse."

"My mind tells me I'm better off without him. That I never really even knew him in the first place. But my heart just drops every time I see him with someone else."

"I understand."

"You know what's even worse?"

"What?"

"Are you a Christian?"

How can she have been coaching me through several sessions and not know this?

"Yes, I'm a Christian. Why do you ask?"

"Because I've been going to church again, and I've been thinking about things I've just let slide lately. My convictions had become muddy and I didn't even have a straight theology like I did when I was growing up. But I know his lifestyle is wrong. I just . . . I'm afraid for him. Eternally, know what I mean?"

"I'm sorry, Ina. I do know what you mean."

"So it's just everything. Life is hectic. I go to school full time and teacher assist for two freshman psychology classes— which means I do all the work while the professor just does the actual lecturing. He even asked me to get his coffee the other day. I was like, 'Honey, if you want coffee, you can get it yourself. I'm not a maid.'"

"You go, girl." Yowser. I never realized until this minute that Ina must be African American. I pictured a Swedish or German girl. I mean . . . Ina.

"Hey, you remind me of someone."

"I do?"

"Claire? Is that you?"

I draw a sharp breath. I haven't shared my name with Ina. And hadn't planned to until the end of the project, just in case she happens to read my books. I just thought it might be less awkward to wait. "My name is Claire, yes. Do . . . do I know you?"

"Oh, man. Claire, I'm really sorry. I just didn't put two and two together until just this second."

"Okay, the suspense is killing me. How do we know each other?"

Hesitation on the other line is making me nervous. My mind plays a slide show of everyone I know who is in grad school. Only one person comes to mind . . .

"It's me. Penny."

"Penny?"

Funny crazy Penny?

Okay, somehow it all fits together. But that doesn't make me feel any better knowing I've been spilling my guts to a twenty-four-year-old. "How come you said your name was Ina?"

"Same reason you didn't want your name published. Anonymity."

"Oh, my goodness." The whole situation strikes me as funny, and I start to laugh. And laugh. I should have known it was Penny. Now that I see it all in hindsight, I honestly don't know how I missed it. I guess I was just so absorbed in my own troubles that I didn't really think about "Ina" as a person but more of a faceless "safe place." Now my safe place is on the other end of the line chain-smoking Marlboro Lights, stressing over school, and heartbroken over an ended relationship.

Penny and Ina are one and the same. How weird is that?

We have a good laugh about it and resolve to continue our

talks, only as friends. Penny has enough issues in her life and is definitely not qualified to coach me.

In the meantime, the door slams, the advent of Ari's return from her quality time with Dad.

"I have to go, Penny. I'll call you Thursday."

After I hang up with Penny, I start thinking about Ari. Despite the fact that we had some breakthroughs during the winter, I feel like we've regressed lately. I've been so preoccupied with getting our living situation ironed out that I've pretty much let motherhood go. Slipped back into some old ways. But all isn't lost. Tommy really is doing well with his sponsor. He will be competing at a local competition for the chance to go regional. If that happens, well . . . I'm not sure what happens if that happens, but according to Tommy it's pretty exciting. And, unless I miss my guess, it will be time-consuming.

Shawn is thriving under John's tutelage and so far I've noticed nary a sign of atheistic tendencies, so John must be keeping his word.

My Jakey is having a hard time with Sadie's absence. They're so cute sending daily e-mails to each other. Words are misspelled and there's barely any punctuation or capital letters, but Jake seems to understand exactly what Sadie is saying. He's in a period where I've limited the Nintendo again. I'm going to have to get better about limits there. I start with good intentions, but always end up letting him spend too much time, then I have to pull him off altogether in order to break the addiction. After three such cycles in less than a year, I'm thinking it might possibly be time for another plan. What that plan will be remains to be seen.

Anyway, there are some kinks to work out, just like in any

family, but for the most part, I think the boys are doing all right.

But Ari . . .

Now that I see she needs me, I wonder, what can I do to let down some of my own walls? Put myself out there and risk her rejection?

I leave my office and go upstairs. I give her door a tap, then enter.

"I really wish you'd stop barging in my room." She's lying on her bed reading a magazine.

"Well, I won't. So, can we lose the attitude?"

She rolls her eyes.

Inwardly I cringe. This is not going the way I pictured it.

"Want to come with me to pick up the boys?"

What is it about teenagers and their eyes? She gives me this you've-got-to-be-kidding look. Just right there, plain as day. But she says, "No, thanks. I want to read."

"Are you sure? I thought we'd go out for barbecue at Ellie's for lunch and then maybe spend the afternoon swimming at Bennett Springs."

"What's Ellie's?"

"A little barbecue spot I found awhile back. The owner's granddaughter is John Wells's daughter."

Her eyes go big. "Wow. I didn't know he even had a daughter."

I guess the kids don't pick up on as much gossip as I thought they did.

"Yeah. Her grandmother raised her. But he retired from the stage and moved here to mend the relationship."

Ari swings her legs around and sits up. Apparently smelling a drama, she grins. "What do they have besides barbecue?"

I quickly put on makeup and call down the basement steps, "Mom, we're going to get the boys. Do you want to come with us?"

She shows up at the bottom of the steps. "You couldn't walk down the steps and speak to me in a civilized tone?"

"Sorry."

Mom hates yelling. I'm a yeller, I can't help it.

"I'm taking the kids to eat lunch and then swimming. Do you want to come along?"

"No. It's too hot. I'll have supper ready when you get home."

"There's no need for you to go to the trouble, Mom. I'll pick up McDonald's or something."

She scowls, as I knew she would. "These children eat way too much junk food, if you ask me." Which I didn't.

Nevertheless, she heaves a sigh. "But I suppose it's my own fault for failing in my own mothering. I should have made you help me in the kitchen more."

How does she do that? Blame me by blaming herself?

"All right, then. I won't stop at McDonald's."

On the way to the theater to pick up Shawn, Ari and I talk small talk for a few minutes, then I cut to the chase. "How's it going over at the crisis pregnancy center?"

"It's all right. The hardest part is trying not to show my contempt for all those idiots who didn't use birth control. I mean, what's the point of sex ed if they're just going to have sex without protection?"

I don't reply right off the bat because I'm not sure how much of what she's saying is actually her own feelings, and how much is to get a rise out of me.

"And don't worry, Mother. I'm not having sex."

Oh, thank you, Lord.

"But if I did, I'd be smart enough to buy condoms."

My face heats up. In my day, we didn't talk openly about sex and condoms and stuff like that. I didn't know what gay was until I was thirteen years old and my friend Gina gave me the 411. I still didn't believe it until I was a little older. So to hear my daughter speak so openly and without the slightest embarrassment or reservation is a little disconcerting. I suppose a faction of our society would applaud her attitude and ability to open up, but not me.

"I'm glad to hear you're abstaining, Ari. But . . ." Oh, man, I don't want to lecture. I really don't. Penny/Ina was right. I'm terrified she's not going to like me.

"But what, Mother?" Her tone is guarded, like she knows I'm about to lecture and she's getting out the mental cotton balls to jam in her ears.

I brace myself and forge ahead. "But don't you think those girls heard all of the same safe-sex talks you've heard?"

"Duh. That's the point. What about 'condoms' didn't they understand?"

"Okay, first, don't say 'duh' to me again."

"Sorry," she mutters.

"Second, don't say 'condoms,' either."

"You want me to say . . ."

"No! Don't say either and just let me talk."

"Fine."

Why does every conversation with her have to end in an argument where I am the inevitable loser? Even when I pull rank and win through sheer force of will, she wins because I can't stand to have her mad at me. And boy, can this kid hold a grudge.

"My point is, most of those girls probably would feel the same way you do if they were in your shoes. Have you gotten close enough to them to befriend them? Ask their stories? The fact is, maybe they don't deserve your disdain. Birth control, even 'condoms' aren't fail-safe. Believe me, I know."

"Oh, gross, Mom."

"Well, you brought it up." Sort of. "So, answer me. Have you bothered to try to get to know even one of them? It might do them a world of good to have someone to talk to."

"No. I'm not a counselor."

"No one said you have to be. How about being a friend?"

She gives me a twist of a smile. "You want me to hang out with pregnant teens? Aren't you worried I might catch something?"

Yeah, maybe some sense! But I refrain from vocalizing my smart-alecky reply.

"Besides, all I'm allowed to do is clean toilets and sort through the baby clothes. People give a lot of junky clothes to the place just because the girls who go there can't afford to buy baby things."

"Sounds like that might be an issue with you."

"It is. I mean, don't get me wrong. I still think those girls are stupid, but the babies shouldn't have to wear clothes with barf stains just because their moms are poor."

"I agree."

Causes. The first sign a person is truly learning to think about someone or something other than themselves. It's a step in the right direction.

"Are you thinking of doing anything about it?"

"Me?" She gives a short laugh. "What can I do? Take my college money and spend it all on baby clothes?"

Not while there's breath in my body. I look askance at her

and smile. "I'm sure you'll figure it out. Or do nothing. It's really up to you."

She's reflective as we pull alongside the theater and I think I might actually have gotten through to her for a change.

Watching traffic go by always calms me for some reason. The whoosh, the flash of color. I don't know. Who can really understand the intricacies of the mind? Ari and I are sitting here, Ari reflecting—not telling what she's thinking—me watching cars, when suddenly there goes a truck I recognize all too well. A 1980-something Chevy with the broken words MIL 'S C NTRA TING on it. I catch a flash of red as he passes. I'd know that red cap anywhere.

I give a sudden gasp and Ari sits up straight, her defenses on high alert. "What's wrong?"

"I just saw Milt's truck."

"Milt who?"

"The contractor who swindled us out of ten grand." Keeping my eye on the black smoke coming from the exhaust pipe of that truck, I nod.

"The dead guy?"

"He's not dead, Ari. I saw his cap. It's too much to be coincidence. This guy is obviously better than anyone could have imagined. Good enough to fake his own death."

"Call the police, Mom!"

"Ari, get out and wait for Shawn. I'm going after him."

"I'm coming, too."

"No. I don't want to take any chances you might get hurt."

She obeys instantly because she and I both know how I drive when I'm anxious or in a hurry.

"Be careful." She slams the door and I peel out. Horns honk

all along the street as my tires squeal. I weave and bob in and out of traffic. "Drat you, Milt. I'm catching up with you."

Just when I think I'm going to lose him, I hear the delicious roar of a train. I can make out the cab of his truck two vehicles behind the front car and at least six in front of me. I slam the SUV into park (we're stopped anyway—it's not like I'm blocking traffic). I fling open my door and run past two minivans, one Dodge, one Ford, a Camry, a PT Cruiser with a wood-grain strip down the side. I'm getting closer, hoping the train is good and long. I pass a little convertible, and finally a Taurus.

I am reaching for the handle before I even get to the truck. In a flash I swing the door open. "All right, Milt. Where's my money, you jerk?"

"What the—?"

My eyes widen and my jaw drops. This enormous fellow isn't Milt. Not even close. "Lady, what do you think you're doing?"

"I . . . I thought, well, this is Milt's truck."

"Milt was my dad."

"You mean he really is dead?"

He nods as sadness creeps into his eyes. "He died of a heart attack a few weeks ago."

Mortified, I step back. "I'm so sorry."

"You say he owed you?"

"He, uh—was supposed to fix my roof."

The train is still chugging by, but I can see the end in sight. "I better get back to my car. The train's about over."

The man strokes his sandy-colored beard. "Meet me at Kentucky Fried Chicken. I'm getting take-out for my crew's lunch. We'll settle this."

I nod and slink back to Darcy's SUV just as the train clears the track and the crossing gate lifts.

At KFC, Milt's son is getting out of his dilapidated truck by the time I pull into a parking space. I can barely look him in the eye. This man looks a lot like Tim Allen in *The Santa Clause*, during the period where he was gaining weight, but his hair wasn't white yet.

I hold out my hand. He takes it grudgingly. "Mr. Travis, I am very sorry for the misunderstanding."

"How about just telling me your name and we'll get this straightened out."

I spend a few minutes explaining about the tornado, the estimate (minus the desperate need for me to avert my gaze every time his dad bent over), the deposit. Phone calls. Going to the police. All of it.

"I didn't call you back, but we did send a check back to you with a letter of explanation and apology that we couldn't do your roof. At the time we didn't have the manpower."

"I never received the check."

He nods. "It was returned to us. We stopped payment."

"Sorry. The apartment I moved into had trouble getting my mail to me."

Sweat is beginning to bead across his forehead and he seems to be a little breathless.

"I'd better let you go. Can I give you my address so you can send me the check?"

He shakes his head.

"No? What do you mean, no?" I'm bristling and just about to tell him off again when he reaches back into his truck and grabs a business checkbook. "I can write you one right now."

I suck in a breath of humid eighty-six-degree June air. "Oh."

"I need to see your identification first."

I go to my SUV, grab my purse, and pull out my wallet. I leave my driver's license in the wallet, but hold it out.

With a nod, he hands me the check. I tuck it in my wallet. "Thank you. And please accept my condolences on your father's passing."

Mr. Travis is sweating profusely now and seems to be breathing a little too heavily. His face has gone white and I'm not sure he's all that focused.

"Are you okay?"

Suddenly, he clutches his chest and hits the ground.

From the corner of my eye I see someone running toward us. "Call 9-1-1," I command.

I drop to my knees beside him. He's not breathing!

CPR, I know. You can't be married to a doctor for eleven years without learning basic life-saving techniques. I begin compressions and mouth-to-mouth. Frantically, over and over.

"Jesus, please touch Mr. Travis! Don't let him die in the parking lot of Kentucky Fried Chicken." I don't know why I said it. It just seemed so unfair for a fat man to die that way. Like it was just inviting uncouth, so-called comedians to make light of a man's death just because of the irony.

I breathe a sigh of relief as finally, after what seems like hours, his chest begins to rise and fall. I sit back, holding his hand. Exhausted from my efforts. I hear applause and look up. That's when I notice that a crowd has formed around us. Poor Mr. Travis.

The paramedics arrive—sirens and lights—and give me an "Atta girl," before telling me to get out of the way. I do so. I stand, and hang back, but I don't want to let him go. I'm wondering, does Mr. Travis know Jesus? How is it possible that a man almost died right in front of me and the last Christian he would have seen was someone who yelled at him over money his dead father owed her?

I step forward as they load him in and the door is closed. "What hospital are you taking him to?"

"St. John's." The paramedic is a young woman who can't be bigger than five foot two and looks about the size of a ten-year-old boy. She gives me a gentle smile and pats me as she walks by to climb into the passenger side. "Ma'am, this man would be dead if you hadn't known to do CPR. You saved his life. You did good. Don't look so sad."

I'm that easy to read?

I need to call his family. Is his mother still alive? How would she hold up, this woman who lost her husband only a few weeks earlier? Without even feeling guilty, I look around his pickup. The only thing I see is a cell phone. I wonder . . .

I snatch it up and open the contacts list. I see "Mom" and I see "Tom." Otherwise, everyone has first and last name, and I figure those aren't people who are particularly close to Mr. Travis. I press the button for "Mom." After six rings, there's still no answer.

Next I try Tom. On the fifth ring, he picks up. "Hello?"

"Uh, hello. Are you a friend of Mr. Travis?"

"I'm his brother. What's going on?"

"He collapsed at KFC. They've taken him to St. John's hospital here in town."

"What? Who did you say this is?"

"Claire Everett. I was with him in the parking lot when he collapsed. I found his cell phone in the seat of his truck. I didn't mean to snoop, but I wanted to let his family know as soon as possible." So he doesn't die before the hospital gets around to notifying anyone that he's been brought in.

"Thank you, Claire. I appreciate it." He pauses. "It's going to be three hours before I can get back to town."

"Is there another family member I can call?"

"Mom never hears her phone."

"I tried to call her first."

"Claire, I hate to impose. But can you please go by my mother's house and tell her about my brother? I'll be there as fast as I can make it."

"I'd be happy to." I walk to Darcy's SUV as he gives me directions to his mother's house.

My own cell phone is ringing when I get back inside the SUV.

"Mom?" Ari's angry tone responds to my greeting. "Were you planning to leave us sitting outside the theater all day?"

"Listen, Ari. There's been an emergency. Ask John to take you home or call Darcy. I'll explain later."

"There's no way Dad will let Darcy drive now that she's past her due date."

"Ask John then," I snap.

"Are you okay? What's the emergency?" The worry in her voice warms me and quite frankly gives me hope that all is not lost in our relationship.

I relent and give her a quick rundown.

"Wow, Mom. You're a hero."

"Let's not get carried away."

"Seriously. They should write about you in the hometown-hero section of the newspaper."

"Okay, thanks for the vote of confidence. So, you'll get a ride for you and Shawny?"

"Yeah, I'll get Tinker Bell—I mean Peter Pan—home safely."

I hear the grin in her voice. The brat. She and Tommy have

been calling Shawn "Tinker Bell" since he went to the first audition.

"Be nice." We say good-bye and hang up as I turn off the main street into a residential area.

The streets are becoming unfamiliar as I enter an older section of town. Not torn up. Just old. Like a good wine. The houses are well taken care of, but were obviously built years ago. Most are redbrick and two-story. Nice lawns stretch yard to yard and I even see a few garden spots. Sprinklers chigger away here and there. I have to smile. Don't they know it's politically incorrect to water your lawn when it's so hot? Some people think we're in for a water shortage.

Finally I come to the right address and pull into the drive. A row of shrubs fences in the yard and a ceramic rabbit sits just off the driveway. When I ring the bell, a yippy dog starts barking its head off.

"Cricket! Stop that. Stop that right now!" I hear, just before the door opens a crack.

"We don't buy anything from door-to-door salesmen."

"No, ma'am. I'm not here to sell you anything."

"Well, I have a church already."

This is a relief. Maybe her son is a Christian after all.

"Your son Tom asked me to come over."

The door flies open and she unlocks the screen. "What happened? Is my Tommy okay?"

"Yes. It's your other son."

"Timmy? What's happened?"

"Well, he collapsed in the parking lot at Kentucky Fried Chicken. They've taken him to St. John's."

"Oh. Oh my goodness. I have to get there."

"I'll take you."

She gives me a wary look and I don't blame her. How many

news reports focus on the victimization of the elderly? I show her Timmy's cell phone. "This is Timmy's. Do you want to call Tom and confirm?"

She takes it and does just that. When she's done, she nods at me. "Please wait here while I go get my purse and change out of my slippers."

I get her to the hospital fifteen minutes later. And within ten more we're speaking to a cardiologist. "We've stabilized him, and we're waiting for some test results. My guess is that we're looking at bypass surgery."

"Oh, my poor boy. I just can't bear it. First Milt and now our son." Tears form in the faded gray eyes. I slip my arm around her.

"Are you a family member?" the doctor asks.

"No. I was just there when he collapsed. I notified the family."

"You're the one who gave him CPR?"

I nod, keeping my focus on Mrs. Travis, whom I'm afraid might pass out.

"Mrs. Travis," the doctor says, "if it weren't for this woman, your son wouldn't have made it to the hospital. Someone was looking out for him that she was there at the right time."

"Doctor," I say, fully aware that Mrs. Travis doesn't need to feel beholden to me. She has enough to think about. "Why did you want to know if I was a family member?"

"Tim stopped breathing long enough that we're not sure if there's any brain damage."

"Oh, dear." Mrs. Travis places her hand to her throat.

"Let's not borrow trouble, Mrs. Travis," I say. I look at the doctor. "What should the family expect for the next few hours?"

"We're waiting for test results and will probably operate tonight."

"Can I see him?" Mrs. Travis asks in a shaky voice.

"For a minute." The doctor's smile is kind.

I step back to let Mrs. Travis have her privacy, but she looks up at me like a lost lamb. "Will you come with me? I'm just not feeling very strong."

I stay with Mrs. Travis for two and a half hours until her other son arrives.

They thank me, take my number, and I leave the hospital, feeling like the hand of destiny has been guiding me. I don't believe in coincidence in most cases. I believe my steps are ordered by God. And God knew Tim Travis was going to need help in the parking lot of a greasy chicken place.

Wow.

18

The noise in The Board is crazy, with mind-numbing Christian rock music and two hundred people squeezed inside of the building for the competition, all trying to talk loud enough to be heard. I fully expect to have another crippling panic attack. True, I haven't had one in a few weeks, but we're closed in, the place is noisy, and my son is going to be doing things on a skateboard that make me want to grab his hand and run home with him.

We're sitting in the bleachers—Tommy's fans: Rick and Darcy (who should be home in bed), Shawn, Jake, Ari, and me. And surprise . . . Mom.

First prize is a thousand-dollar savings bond and a trip to the regionals. Second prize is a five-hundred-dollar savings bond and a trip to the regionals. Third prize is a hundred-dollar savings bond and a trip to the regionals. Tommy could care less about the savings bonds; he's just hoping to get into the top three and make it to the next round.

My stomach is a ball of nerves. The first two boarders wipe out three times. I think there's definitely something wrong with my joy over two young teenagers who fall. The third boy gives a performance that—for all I know—is perfect. His score reflects it. Next up is Tommy.

Mom closes her eyes and hollers, "Dadgum, I can't watch. Tell me when it's over." There's a lot of noise in the place, but her voice must have carried because someone taps her from behind.

"My grandson was the first one up. I know just how you feel." Mother turns, and so do I, to find an older gentleman smiling warmly, his eyes just about the gentlest I've ever seen.

"I'm Eli," he says, and it's pretty obvious he's interested. My mother blushes as she accepts his proffered hand. "Edith."

Oh, the blush deepens when he covers her hand with his other one. And I wish I had a camera because I know darned well she's never going to admit to it.

Darcy nudges me and we snicker together. Mom glares and yanks her hand away and jerks around, once more sitting straight as a board. She closes her eyes. "I'm not watching."

Undaunted, Eli leans forward. "You have to watch, Edith. What if your grandson does something truly exceptional? Do you want to miss it?"

Mom doesn't answer, but her eyes pop open.

"Okay, he's up," I say, forgetting all about the geriatric flirtation going on right under my nose.

Tommy takes my breath away. And not just because of the danger of the sport. He flies through the air. Poetry in motion. Like a work of art. His moves are flawless as far as my un-trained eye can tell and from the crowd's reaction, I think my assessment must be correct.

His score is the highest of the four who have competed so far. He looks into the crowd as he walks to his seat. When our eyes connect, he beams with pride. I give him the victory sign, and he smiles even broader.

We sit impatiently through six more competitors. When all is said and done, Tommy gets third place. He's ecstatic. Personally, I think he was robbed.

I'm a little let down that Tommy doesn't want to celebrate

with us because Shane, the youth pastor/sponsor, has planned a party for all the kids who participated in tonight's competition.

We walk into the night air. I can smell the scent of rain. I love summer rains. I look forward to sitting on the covered porch and watching as it comes down around me.

I'm about to kiss Tommy good-bye and take my other kids home to watch a movie when Darcy taps me on the shoulder. "Claire, I think I'm in labor."

Alarm shoots through me like lightning up a flag pole. "Are you sure?"

"Not positive," says the new mom-to-be (imminently, it appears), "but I think so."

"How long have you been having pains?"

"A couple of hours."

"Darce! Why didn't you say something?"

"I wanted to see Tommy skate. Besides, I'm almost two weeks past due as it is, what's a few more hours?"

"What does Rick say?"

"I haven't told him yet. I wanted to ask you if you think I'm really in labor. It hurts like monthly cramps and tightens my stomach."

Okay, she's married to an ob-gyn and she's asking *my* opinion? What's wrong with this picture?

"Rick!" I call. "Stop horsing around with the boys and get over here."

He jogs over and grins at Darcy. "You going to let her talk to me like that? Tell her you're my boss now."

A giggle leaves her and then a grimace slides across her face.

"She thinks she's in labor," I say. "Take care of her."

Darcy grabs my arm. "Wait. Aren't you coming with us?" Panic shoots from her eyes.

"I need to get the kids home, Darce. Rick will call me when you're close to delivering, and I'll come to the hospital then, okay? Isn't that right, Rick?"

"Huh? Oh, sure. First babies take forever." Clueless as ever, Rick starts with the doctor routine. "What are your symptoms?"

Darcy tenses immediately, and I don't think it's a contraction. "Cramps and stomach tightening," she grouses.

Still not taking a hint, Rick continues his routine. "How long have you been having contractions and how far apart?"

"Just shut up, Rick!" she explodes. "Stop asking questions. You're not even my doctor. Just be my husband!"

Rick looks so taken aback I almost feel sorry for him. He slips an arm around her. "All right, sweetheart. Let's get you to the hospital. I'll call your doctor on the way."

"Claire . . ." Darcy's eyes plead.

I give Rick a talk-to-her look.

He tries. "Let's get you all settled into a room and get your labor going good and then we'll call Claire. Okay? You don't want her to sit around for hours and hours do you?"

Tears well up. "I need my best friend to be with me."

Oh, for the love of pete. "All right, Darce. Let me get the kids and Mom home. I'll be thirty minutes behind you at the most."

The next morning, a tired and dejected Darcy waddles, still pregnant, into her enormous pillared home and, according to Rick, cries herself to sleep.

False labor.

I fall into bed at eight in the morning, silently cursing Rick, who should have known the contractions were Braxton Hicks in the first place. What kind of obstetrician is he, anyway? I'm just dozing off when the phone rings.

Curses!

My caller ID identifies Stu.

"Hi, Stu."

"Good morning."

"What's up?"

"I have some not-so-great news."

He's got my full attention now. "That's about all you deliver lately."

"Sorry to be the bearer of more. The publisher decided not to buy the romance proposal."

I'm stunned, really. Even though I wasn't crazy about the idea, I figured it was easy money. Money in the bank. Money I am going to need within a couple of months when my savings runs out. Especially since I'm having to use this ten-thousand-dollar check Tom Travis gave me, plus another five thousand from savings, to buy the new/used van.

"Did they say why?"

"It's a pretty overdone plot. You knew that when you started. I can't believe you even tried it."

"Hey, I risked my life to get a research book for that story. And besides, you're the one who said that's what they wanted."

"The time period. Not the same-ol', same-ol'. But that's not all."

Great. What's he going to tell me now, they've finally figured out I'm nothing more than a hack author and have no business being a writer?

Stu forges ahead, oblivious to my inner self-deprecation.

"The numbers for *Esmeralda's Heart* haven't been as great as we'd hoped for."

"What about the other publishers you sent it to?"

"They've all rejected. I didn't want to say anything because of the tornado and house situation."

Nice of him to wait until I have to buy a new van and I've been awake all night to spring the news.

"All right. What do you want me to do?"

As soon as I voice the words I know he's the wrong person to ask, so I cut him off before he can start the lecture. "Hey, Stu. Mind if I call you in a couple of days? I was up all night with a friend who thought she was in labor, and I'm just about to hit the sack."

"That's fine. Let's think about some career planning to get you over this hump. And we'll talk in a couple of days." He says it like it's his idea. Stu's arrogance bugs me. He's always been a little full of himself, but when the publishers were clamoring for me, and he knew I could get any agent I wanted, for the most part, he was all for reining in the bossiness. Now he'll be unbearable.

I fall asleep to the mental images of me telling Stu off with poetic turns of phrases and a smile.

I wake up at five in the evening to yummy smells coming from Mom's kitchen. This was her kitchen for many years, after all. Despite my annoyance and the fact that we hardly agree on anything, I love my mother, and quite honestly, I'm happy to have her home.

I push back the covers and pad down the hall. Make a stop at the bathroom then follow my nose to the kitchen. "Mmm. Smells great, Mom."

She beams under the praise. "Thank you. Tex-Mex chili and cornbread."

"Yum." I grab a cup from the cabinet and pour my "morning" coffee. "We'll turn up the air conditioner and pretend it's winter."

Mom gives a chuckle. She finishes mixing the cornbread and pours it into a sizzling pan. "Have a cup of coffee with me, Mom?"

She casts a glance at her watch. "Maybe half a cup. I have to shower and get ready."

I frown and rack my brain trying to remember what Mom has planned for tonight.

"I'm playing canasta with Eli and a couple he knows."

Mom has a date? How depressing is that?

"Who the heck is Eli?"

"You remember. The man at the skateboard thing last night."

"Mom! You can't go out alone with a man you don't know. This is the twenty-first century. Dating isn't the same as it was when you were a young thing."

Did I really just say "young thing"?

"Don't worry, I checked him out with Tommy before I agreed to go."

"Oh, well, that's good—take the word of a fourteen-year-old boy."

"My decision. I'm going."

"Fine. But at least take your cell phone, and don't forget to turn it on."

"Yes, Mother." She grins and so do I.

"Speaking of Tommy, where is he? And the rest of the kids."

"Shawn is at his lesson with that vile man down the block."

"John's a great guy, Mom. Too bad he's not a Christian, you could—"

"Oh, no. He's not my type."

My mom has a type? That's just wrong. Wrong like *Dr. Quinn, Medicine Woman* being cancelled. Wrong like Cheryl Ladd doing menopause commercials. Wrong like New Coke. Some things just shouldn't be. And my mind just won't wrap around the thought of my mother dating.

And kissing. Ew! Go away, thought. Bad, bad mental image.

"Okay, forget John. I guess Ari the Grounded is in her room?"

"Nope. She's still at that Hope House."

I bristle. Just when I think Ari is coming around, she pulls a stunt like this? Takes advantage of her Granny while I'm asleep. "Mother, Ari should have been home by noon. Rick finished at eleven thirty."

"I know. I'm not completely ignorant." She scowls at me. "Rick called and said he was giving her permission to stay and work on a project there."

And just like that anger floats away on a cloud of curiosity. "What kind of project?"

She shrugs. "Some kind of fund-raising something or other. I'm sure she'll be hitting us both up for money soon enough."

"Not that she's likely to be getting any out of me." I sip my coffee and set the cup back on the table. "Stu called this morning. My latest proposal was soundly rejected by all."

"They're idiots. Every last one of them."

I appreciate the support. Really I do. But right now stating the obvious isn't helping me.

"I'm thinking of parting company with Stu."

"Good! I never liked him anyway."

"Really?"

"Really. He's just a little too big for his britches, if you ask me."

I laugh at that. I know what she means. But Stu is about five foot five and probably weighs a hundred and twenty pounds soaking wet.

"I'm not positive. But I need to find an agent who is on my side and is willing to help me. Stu was so great in the beginning. He went to bat for me. Seemed to really be on board with where I wanted my career to go, but he doesn't want to pitch anything but romance."

"Are you working on other things?"

I nod. "I have two different ideas. One a fun, comedy type. The other is about a girl who owns a restaurant and her relationships with the customers and family. They're both great ideas that I really believe in."

"Have you asked Stu about pitching them?"

I give a glum nod. "I sent him the proposal for the first one."

"The comedy?"

"Yeah. He says no one wants that stuff from me. They want romance."

"Honey, the Bible says there are seasons in our lives. Seasons that God creates for us. Maybe the season for you and Stu to work together is over."

"Maybe."

Mom stands, pushing back her chair. She walks around, kisses me on the head, and pats me on the shoulder. "You'll figure it out. I have to go get ready for my date."

I can't help but grin. She says "date" almost like she's trying the word on for size. Like when a kid gets his first job and keeps saying, "I have to go to work." Or new writers who say "my editor" or "my agent." It's fun.

Just as she's about to disappear through the doorway, I remember something. "Hey, you never told me where Jakey is." He'd better not be playing Nintendo.

"Oh." Mom peeps back around the corner. "Helen and Sadie came by and asked if he could go over and play at their house. I know I should have asked, but you were asleep and I didn't want to wake you. I just didn't have the heart to say no."

My heart jumps into my throat. "It was just Helen and Sadie?"

Mom's eyes twinkle. "Yes. But I understand they all three came in for the fourth. Apparently Greg has a few days off to celebrate. And they wanted to come home to do it. Now don't forget about the cornbread and stir the chili again in a few minutes." And with those instructions, Mom dashes off to get ready for her date. While I settle in for an evening in front of the television with a bowl of comforting chili.

Ari's so excited when she comes home that I think I'm going to have to peel her off the wall. "Mom!" she calls as she slams through the door.

I jump up from the table and rush into the living room, my heart in my throat as I picture her with broken bones or blood pouring out of some wound. Instead she's waving a newspaper around. "I'm published," she says as soon as she sees me.

Excitement rushes through me. "You are? Let me see. What is it?"

"A letter to the editor about those stained baby clothes at Hope House."

"You wrote a letter to the editor?" I'm so impressed and proud. "And he printed it?"

"He sure did. In last night's paper. Only he made it into an article instead of the letter to the editor page. When Dad and

I got to Hope House today, there were tons of donations. Nice things, Mom. Some people just went out and bought new stuff."

"Oh, my goodness. Give it here and let me read it."

My name is Arianna Everett Frank, and I am sixteen years old. I volunteer at Hope House—our local home for pregnant teens. I hated it at first. I thought I was too good to work at a place like that. But I got into some trouble, and my parents thought volunteering at a home like that would open my eyes.

And guess what? They were right. No, I didn't learn that I should abstain from sex. My Christian beliefs already taught me that. No, I didn't learn that pregnancy is difficult. My stepmom is going through that right now and believe me, I'm in no hurry.

I smile at this. What a great kid.

What I have learned is this: The world is divided into two kinds of people. Those who have and those who don't. The Haves never worry where their next meal will come from or how to buy clothes for their new babies, while the Have Nots must often depend upon the Haves for their next meal or clothes for their babies.

My job at the Hope House is sorting the donations. Anger is a mild word for what I feel day after day as I sort through stained and ripped clothes. Clothes I wouldn't put on a dog, let alone a sweet, beautiful baby.

Why do people think that just because someone is poor that she'll take anything?

My dad is an obstetrician, and he volunteers twice a week so these girls can have good prenatal care. My mom is an author, and she donates her books for the girls to read while they're waiting for their babies to be born. But just because the girls don't have the money to pay doesn't mean my dad only gives them half the care he would provide for someone with insurance. My mom doesn't give ripped up or discarded books just because there's no royalty in it for her. Beyond that, my mother saved a man's life last week. He had a heart attack right out in the open. She gave him CPR and kept him alive until the paramedics arrived. What if she had stopped to think about his breath? Or didn't push hard enough on his chest because she just had her nails done?

Come on, people. Don't send us clothes you wouldn't wear. If they're ripped or stained, we're throwing them in the garbage anyway. So why bother?

Volunteering at Hope House has changed me. Every baby should have an equal chance starting out. Life is hard enough as we grow. Let's give the babies clean clothes and soft blankets. You can make a difference.

Thank you,
Arianna Everett Frank

Tears well up as I hand it back to her. "This is fantastic."

"Thank you." She folds up the newspaper and sets it on the coffee table. "The best part is that donations started coming today. That's why I stayed late. It was incredible."

She hugs me fiercely. "Now I know how you feel when you get a letter from a reader who says your books have touched her life. I love making a difference."

"Don't forget to watch that cornbread, Claire!" Mom's voice carries down the stairs.

"I'm watching it." I shoot Ari a grin. "Congratulations. Do you want to come into the kitchen with me?"

"I can't. I want to go call Paddy and tell him."

"Paddy? Are you two . . ."

Ari shakes her head; her eyes reflect such sadness after being so filled with joy a second ago that I wish I hadn't asked. "He says we can only be friends. I don't blame him. His friendship is better than nothing. So, I'll take it."

I watch my daughter walk toward the steps and I realize that her dad was actually right about making her volunteer. Come to think of it, he's the one who gave Tommy permission to be sponsored, too. And look how that's turning out.

I mull this new twist around in my mind. As much as I hate to give him credit in the kid department, I have to say, God must have given him some wisdom.

I'm just finished taking the cornbread out of the oven when I hear the front door open. "Mom!" Jake calls out.

"Shh, Jakey," I hear Greg say in low tones. "Your mom might be sleeping still."

"No I'm not," I say, as I enter the living room.

My heart does a loop-de-loop at the sight of him. And as I stare into his eyes, I'm speechless. Love bursts through every valve of my heart, and I want to tell him so. I step forward, but he turns and reaches for the door at the same time. I know it's not intentional, that he didn't know I was moving toward him. But it's enough to bring me to my senses. Stopping dead in my tracks, I push aside these thoughts of romance.

"So, how long are you here for?"

"We're going back on Sunday after church."

"Okay, then I guess I'll see you in church."

He nods. "Hey, I read Ari's article."

My chest swells with motherly pride. "Isn't it great?"

"You're pretty great, too. A real hero." A smile tips his lips and for a second, he looks like the old Greg.

"I was just in the right place at the right time."

"Sounds like God to me."

"Yes. Definitely."

He gives me a lingering look, and I know he wants to talk. I hold my breath.

The click-clack of Mother's black one-inch-heel pumps signals her descent on the stairs.

"Mom's got a date," I whisper to Greg.

He smiles just as she enters. "Greg! Nice to see you."

"Thank you. It's nice to see you, as well."

"Staying for supper?"

"No. Mom's cooking lasagna."

One thing I get to take away from my relationship with Greg: I learned how to make lasagna because I knew he loved it so much.

Silence becomes awkward in this moment when I want to beg him to stay—but won't—Mom wants to put in her two cents' worth—but doesn't—and Greg just wants to escape.

Which is what he does.

19

Two evenings later, the house is in an uproar because of Shawn's nerves. Tonight is the opening for *Peter Pan*. He's exercising his voice in all manner of funky-sounding exercises. "Hee hee hee hee, hoo hoo hoo hoo, ha ha ha ha."

Which has the expected effect on his siblings. The house is filled with echoing choruses of "Hee hee hee, hoo hoo hoo, ha ha ha ha."

On one hand, who can blame the other kids for cracking up? On the other hand, Shawn has to do what he has to do so that he can be heard across the auditorium without harming his vocal cords.

"Can the mockery, you guys."

"Just exercising my voice so I can project when I cheer on my brother," Tommy says. He grins that heart-melting, no-way-I-can-resist grin.

I smile. "Nice try."

"Mom! Mom!" Shawn takes a break from all the *hee, hoo-hoo*'s and sounds nearly panicked as he glances at the clock. "I have to go right now. I'm going to be late. Mr. Wells doesn't permit tardiness."

Good grief, the kid's a basket case.

"Calm down. Everyone out to the van."

Yesterday I cashed the check Tom Travis gave me, pulled the rest out of the bank, and bought the three-year-old Dodge

Caravan. It's nice to have my own wheels again. The way I drive, I was petrified I'd wreck Darcy's SUV. Now the fifty-thousand-dollar truck-slash-minivan is safely tucked in the Frank garage next to Rick's Mercedes.

I drop Shawn at the stage-door entrance and find parking two full blocks away from the entrance. When you live in a small Missouri town, anything new like a children's theater is going to draw a crowd. Only who knew they'd all get here an hour before curtain?

Thankfully, the performers were allowed to reserve seats for family and friends. The number of seats directly correlate with the actor or actress's importance in the show. Shawn, being the title character, has the entire third row roped off. I frown a little because even with Rick, Darcy, Mom, my kids, and me, there are a few more empty seats reserved. I just don't want to be accused of hogging.

The dilemma is solved as the curtain goes up. Helen, Sadie, and Greg slide into the row and take the last three seats. Greg sits next to me. "Shawn invited me. Do you mind?"

Is he kidding? My heart is lodged firmly in my throat. I smile. I can't stop staring into his eyes. He looks different somehow. At peace. I hate to admit it, but Bible school possibly might be a good thing for him.

He seems as mesmerized as I do. His hand slides over mine. I automatically turn my palm to his and our fingers clasp.

I gather the first full breath since our breakup and settle in to enjoy my son's debut.

And enjoy I do. He's brilliant, flawless. There is no doubt that he is Peter Pan. Jenny Devine snagged the role of Wendy and plays the part to perfection alongside my boy. During the thimble scene where Wendy wants a kiss, I glance back at Pastor and Tina Devine. Tina catches my gaze and grins.

For some reason, I start to think about her role in the church. She sings, takes care of some behind-the-scenes stuff, but I've never once seen her lead a Bible study. I've never known her to organize a bake sale. Polite, yes. Godly, definitely. Committed to the ministry and doing her part, but not so overrun with responsibility that she isn't enjoying every second of her children's lives.

I take a second to look at Greg. He looks back and squeezes my hand. I don't know. *Could* I be a pastor's wife?

During intermission, I make a little stop at the ladies' room. Tina Devine had the same idea. We both wash our hands at the same time using antiseptic-smelling soap. We smile at each other's reflection in the wall-length mirror above the sinks. "Jenny's knocking them dead," I say.

Her eyes brighten. "So is Shawn."

"She wasn't too disappointed about not getting to be the next Sandy Duncan?"

Laughter bubbles from Tina's lips. "Not too bad. She told me later that as soon as she saw Shawn's audition she knew he was going to get that role. She was afraid she wouldn't get to be in the play at all since she hadn't tried out for Wendy."

"John has a sharp eye. He picked the perfect lead actors."

"I agree," she says, punching the button to start the air dryer. "I notice Greg's sitting with you. You guys back together?"

Heat crawls across my face. I shake my head. "Shawn invited him."

She hesitates. I can tell she'd like to help but doesn't want to pry.

I open it up by stating the obvious. "Greg's going to be a pastor."

"I know. I think that's awesome."

You just can't help but warm up to a woman like this who says "awesome." Only, I don't know what to say. Because I don't happen to think this situation *is* awesome. She picks up on my negative vibe.

"You're against it, I take it?"

My shoulders lift in a shrug. "It's really not my place to be for it or against it. That's Greg's decision."

"But you don't like the idea?"

"Not so much."

"Mind if I ask why?"

"I'm too cranky to be a pastor's wife. I couldn't be nice to someone who wasn't being nice to my husband."

She laughs again. "You just have to let *him* deal with those people."

"Really?"

"Greg has the temperament for it. He's got a lot of experience dealing with critical people. He's a schoolteacher, after all."

She's got a point there.

"Look." Her bony hip is leaned against the counter and she's facing me. "You and Greg love each other. Your ministries complement each other—"

This is where I stop her.

"I don't have a church ministry. And," I confess, "I don't even like doing nursery."

"You don't have to. I don't."

Well, that's true.

"Being the wife of a pastor is like being anyone else's wife. If he's a good man, he puts you before his church responsibilities. And you don't demand his attention when you know he's needed at the church. Otherwise you end up competing. And that's not good."

"But what about me? What about the things I want to do? I have a career. I answer to a lot of people. I have book tours and conferences to attend. I miss church sometimes when I'm on a rigid deadline. How can I be what he needs me to be?"

"You support each other. And you let God deal with the details. I have a ministry inside the church and dreams outside the church. My husband supports both. And so will Greg."

I guess I know that.

My stomach is in knots as I walk back to the auditorium. Greg stands to let me through and I'm so close to him I can feel his breath on my face. I can't help but picture us the way we used to be. As I sit, he takes my hand again. Just before the curtain rises for the second half of the play he leans close and whispers against my ear. "We're talking later. This separation is crazy."

Welcome back, Alpha Greg.

My son receives a standing ovation when he walks onto the stage at the end of the show. He stands there in green tights and a Robin Hood hat (and I know he's going to catch a lot of flack from Tommy about that later on). After he sweeps off the hat and takes a gracious bow he, very gentlemanlike, extends his arm toward backstage and Jenny Devine glides toward him. They join hands and bow together. I glance back at Tina again and we share a laugh. So maybe Ari blew it with Paddy, but there's always Shawn and Jenny.

All family and friends of the actors are invited to an after-party in the enormous foyer of the theater building.

I'm shocked to see Brandi grabbing a glass of punch.

"This is a huge surprise." Never thought I'd see the day. At least not so soon. Maybe God is in the process of working a miracle for these two after all. I have a feeling John's atheistic days are going to be coming to an end soon.

"Hey," she says. "Go figure, huh?"

"I'm so happy you came. I bet it means a lot to your dad."

"Oh, well. It would have meant a lot if he'd showed up at one of my school plays, too." She gives a shrug and I can tell she's trying to rein in her emotions. "But I guess two wrongs don't make a right. Right?"

I smile. "Right."

"Besides, it's not like I had to pay to get in. He sent us tickets."

"Your grandmother came?"

"Fat chance."

Now that *would* have been a miracle.

"Well, you showed up. And that's what matters most."

She gives a nod and looks at me with what I can only describe as reflective admiration. "Thanks for caring about John. I know he thinks of you as a daughter. I don't know, seeing the two of you together that day at the restaurant made me see him as more than just a jerk who ran out on my mother. I'm not ready to be a daughter to him. But at least there's a place to start."

I give her hand a squeeze. "I'm so happy for you. Your dad's basically a good man. I think he's sorry for abandoning you. He could have chosen anywhere in the world to settle down after retirement. But look where he came."

I happen to glance past her and I see Greg staring at me across the room. She turns and follows my gaze. "Oh, the hero who came to your rescue the day your van broke down."

"Yeah." I can't help the stupid grin spreading across my face.

"Go to him."

"Thanks. I'll see you later."

We walk toward each other like two lovers running along a shoreline, arms outstretched, waiting for that embrace. Only, newsflash, Rick steps between us.

Doggone it. What does he want?

I force myself to focus on his stark-white face as Greg joins us.

"Darcy's in labor."

Why does Darcy go into labor every time one of my kids has an event?

"Think it's for real this time?" I ask, not facetiously.

He nods. "Her water broke."

For an OB, Rick's not being very calm. I swear he's about to lose it. "Want me to drive you?"

Predictably, he scowls. "I think I can manage. But you know Darcy doesn't think she can have this baby if you're not there."

Somehow, although I know he's glad we get along these days, I think Rick has to be a little bugged at how much his wife loves me. And I know it bugs him that I act superior. But my own issues notwithstanding, Darcy has grown on me— like a lone freckle on your arm. A comfortable familiar freckle that you wouldn't know your arm without.

I blow out a frustrated sigh that my plans for a long talk followed by a few minutes of making out with Greg have just been thwarted for the night. "What about the kids?"

"She wants them, too. Says they have to see their new baby brother or sister before non-family members."

"All right. Get her to the hospital. I'll go rally the troops."

In typical new-dad-to-be fashion, Rick dashes off to boil water or something while I turn to the current man in my life.

With a long, regretful look, I let Greg know I'd rather be with him. "They're making me do this against my will, you know."

Leaning forward, he presses a warm kiss to my cheek. I want to lean into him and get lost in the strength of his arms. But that option is not on the table just yet.

"I'm sorry, Greg."

"It's okay." He's such a great guy. "You go do what you need to do. We'll talk tomorrow."

So, after dropping Mom at home, the kids and I change into comfortable clothes and head for the hospital.

We are allowed to go into her room as soon as we get there.

Rick practically yanks me in. "Thank God you're here. She's threatening to leave me."

"What?"

"She says I knew she'd be in all this pain and didn't stop her from getting pregnant."

"Oh, for crying out loud, Rick. Go get something to drink. I'll talk to her. And make sure you don't get anything caffeinated."

Darcy bursts into tears the second she sees me. "Claire, what should I do? It hurts so much."

"Well, what did you expect, Darce? You've watched every delivery show on Discovery Health and Lifetime TV at least ten times."

"I know. But I think mine hurts worse than theirs."

Oh, good grief. "Look, there's no shame in having an epidural. And trust me, you won't regret it."

"Really?"

"Really. And after you get it, make sure you tell Rick you still love him and don't think he's a monster."

So we call the nurse, who calls the doctor, who calls the anesthesiologist. Rick is so grateful that I've convinced little Miss Pollyanna-turned-Godzilla to have the epidural that I have to back up and frown really hard to keep him from kissing me. I do, however, allow a very quick side hug.

I leave them to their making up and head for the cafeteria. My cell phone rings. Stu. I still haven't made a decision yet concerning him. I mean, I know what I want to do, but just don't know if I can really do that to him.

"Hi, Stu."

Turns out I don't have to make the decision. Stu dumps me right then and there. We have an amicable parting whereby we wish each other well. I'm okay. On the way to the cafeteria, I happen to spot Mrs. Travis at the first-floor nurse's station.

Her face brightens as soon as she sees me. She takes my hand and turns to the three nurses behind the counter. "This is the woman who saved my Timmy's life."

The women smile politely. Somehow, to these nurses who save lives every day, I'm not quite the hero everyone else is making me out to be.

Mrs. Travis tugs on my hand. "Please come and speak with my son. I know he wants to thank you personally."

"There's no need for that." Oh, boy. This is worse than having a fan crying because I sign a book.

"Please. He has wished so many times this week that you'd show up. And here you are."

I don't have the heart to tell her I didn't come to check on him. I knew he was doing fine because I called the hospital a couple of times during the past week to check on his progress.

"All right," I finally relent.

We walk slowly, keeping Mrs. Travis's pace until she turns into a semiprivate room. Tim Travis is sitting up in bed, looking at least twenty pounds lighter than he did the last time I saw him.

"Look who I found in the hallway, Tim."

He frowns a second, and I feel a little embarrassed. The guy doesn't even recognize me?

"It's the woman who gave you mouth-to-mouth."

Oh, sheesh, now I'm totally blushing.

A smile spreads across his big, good-ol'-boy face. "Oh, yeah. Sure, I remember now." He holds out his hand and I step forward. I expect a little shake. Instead he pulls me into a big embrace. I clear my throat and avert my gaze when he turns me loose. "Sorry I didn't recognize you right off. I have a little short-term memory loss from the lack of oxygen to my brain."

"I understand."

He frowns. "Who are you?"

I'm about to tell him when he grins. "Just kidding."

I join his laughter as his mother huffs. "Your condition is nothing to joke about, son."

He looks at me. "Who is this woman?"

I snort. Mrs. Travis scowls and gives a dismissal wave. "You're hopeless."

His eyes twinkle pleasantly as our laughter dies and I take in the sight of all the tubes sticking out of his body. "How are you feeling, Mr. Travis?"

"Please call me Tim. You make me feel old."

I scrutinize him. If I had to guess I'd say he's around forty, maybe forty-five. Definitely too young to be having a heart attack. I bet KFC is going to be a place to avoid at all costs from now on.

"Then how are you feeling, Tim?"

"Weak. But alive."

"I'm glad."

"I heard you praying."

Words escape me, so I just nod, which is just as well because Tim's not done.

"I've never been into religion, but as soon as I heard you tell God I couldn't die without knowing Him, I knew it was true. I asked Him to just give me more time."

My heart catches in my throat as the sweet presence of the Lord fills the room. I step forward and take Tim's hand. "Would you like me to introduce you to Him?"

Tears shimmer in his eyes and he nods. Mrs. Travis joins us and takes my other hand. "Me too."

Shock zips through me. How does a person get to be this old and not know about God? I think about the parable of the vineyard workers. All started at different times of the day and yet each received the same wage when the work was over. That's how it is with God. You can grow up knowing Him, like Darcy's baby will, or you can come to God at middle age, like Tim. Or you can wait until you've reached your twilight years, like Mrs. Travis. Regardless, your place in heaven is just as secure as the next person's.

I relate this story to my new friends. I share my Jesus with them, and as I head toward the door a few minutes later, it is with the heady knowledge that God has just performed the greatest heart surgery. He's removed stony hearts, and has given two new people hearts of flesh.

Mrs. Travis walks me to the door. "You know, my Tim is single."

"Geez, Ma!"

"Well, you are!"

Impulsively, I reach out and give her a quick hug. "I'm flattered, ma'am. But I'm off the market."

"You're not wearing a ring."

I give her a tentative smile. "Not yet."

At twenty minutes to midnight on July seventh, a full two weeks overdue, a baby girl entered the world and greeted her parents, Rick and Darcy Frank. Two hours later, she greeted her very sleepy brothers and sister. And a very relieved Aunt (good grief) Claire.

"So, what's her name?" Ari asks, as she sits in the courtesy rocker and stares down at her wrinkly new baby sister.

Darcy looks on with maternal adoration. "I was thinking Claire."

I gasp, and Rick and I both say "No!" at the same time.

Darcy gives us a twinkly-eyed grin. "Gotcha."

"You little trickster," Rick says, and tweaks her nose like she's a little girl. Gross.

"So, really, what's her name?" I ask.

"I was thinking Lydia. I've always loved that name."

I reach for Lydia and take her from my protesting daughter. She's an angel. And I adore her already. "Come to Auntie Claire," I coo, fully aware that I am now in too deep. Darcy has worn me down with her love for me. She's become a true friend. Some folks might think this baby has joined our two families together, but that's not entirely true. Darcy has.

I place Lydia into her mother's waiting arms, and bending over, I press a kiss to the baby's temporarily cone-shaped head. Then I maneuver around the infant to give Darcy a hug. "You did great, Darce."

She beams. "Yeah."

"I had a little something to do with it, too," Rick says. Then he blushes, so I spare him the sarcastic retort that's on the tip of my tongue. "You did good, too, slugger." I slide a glance to Darcy. "I'll say one thing for him. At least he makes pretty babies."

"You got that right," she returns, without skipping a beat.

"Oh, gross, you guys," Ari groans. "Can we just go home? Jake's falling asleep in the chair."

None of us rises before ten the next morning. That's the great thing about summer and Saturdays. No one is in any big hurry to get up and get cracking. I slowly wake up to the sound of the doorbell.

Swinging my legs around, I make my way downstairs. A delivery guy stands there with a box of flowers. He looks me over and I can only imagine the view he's getting. "Late sleeper?"

"Late night." Smart aleck. I'm tempted not to tip him, but the thought of who those flowers are from perks me up and I grab a five out of the emergency bowl on the table next to the door.

He gives me an obnoxious wink. "Enjoy the flowers."

"Jerk," I mutter, as I close the door and head into the kitchen. Mom's in there.

"Why didn't you get the door?"

"I was reading my Bible. Besides, I figured it was time you got up." She looks at the box. "From Greg?"

"I'd imagine." I slide off the ribbon. I've never gotten a dozen long-stemmed roses. And they are exquisite. Tenderly I remove one and bring it to my nose. I close my eyes and inhale the heady scent.

I pull out the card and take it and my roses to my office where I can read it alone.

Wear a dress and be ready at seven tonight.

I pick up the phone and dial his number. His voice is low and husky as he says, "Hello."

"I just got a gorgeous box of roses. Know who they might be from?"

"Who is this?" But I can hear laughter in his voice.

"They're beautiful."

"And so are you." I feel a little guilty that I set him up for that, especially since my hair is sticking up and I don't have one speck of makeup on my face. I'm so not beautiful.

"Did you read the card?"

"Yes, and you know I hate dresses."

"Wear one anyway."

"What if I don't have one to wear?"

"How about that little black number you wore for Linda and Mark's second wedding?"

I forgot about that. "All right. I can do that. Where are we going?"

"You'll find out. Just wear the dress, and let me take care of the rest."

I float through the day, preparing for my date with Greg. Somehow, he's figured out that I'm ready to be his wife, come hell or high water. Or in this case: whether he's a pastor or not.

The dress is a little snug, darn it. Not so tight it's cutting off the blood circulation, but definitely a wake-up call. I pull on the three-inch strappy sandals Linda forced me to buy. Then, because there are still thirty minutes until Greg picks me up, I call her. I haven't spent that much time with my friend this summer. She's been busy decorating her new house, and I've been busy trying to get mine fixed. But I know I must speak with my best friend and analyze what will happen on the date.

"I'm so happy!" she exults, when I tell her about the flowers and the date. "I've been praying for this."

"I'm wearing the dress we got for your wedding."

A throaty laugh escapes her. "I knew that dress would come in handy again. Don't forget to wear the heels."

"Got them."

"Claire, I know you're going to be exactly the wife Greg needs. So stop worrying!"

"If only I could." I'm still not one hundred percent convinced, but I figure if this is something he's got to do, then I'm going to do it, too. After all, like Tina said (and she's been a pastor's wife for twenty years, so she should know), I don't have to do anything I'm not called to do. Just love and support my husband.

The bell rings at exactly seven o'clock. I open the door for Greg. Decked out in a new black suit, banded collared shirt underneath. No tie. He looks incredible. I'd like to tell him so, but the kids are milling around the living room so there's no chance for a private word. Plus, it's a little hard to think about romance when Tommy is crunching Doritos and laughing at *The Three Stooges* marathon playing on the Superstation. Catchy game music is playing from Jakey's handheld Game Boy, and Shawn is practicing lines. Auditions for *Oklahoma!* begin in a month. Ari is leaning against the entryway between the kitchen and living room, arms folded loosely across her chest. She watches me with a quirky grin and I know she's as hopeful about this evening as I am.

In the midst of my chaos, Greg's gaze pulls me away as it sweeps over my dress. Tenderness and admiration shine from his eyes as they lock onto mine.

"Humph!" Tenderness and admiration, however, are the last things shining from Sadie's eyes. The little girl is sending unsubtle death rays from beneath her bristly dark lashes. I toss Ari a "you sure you can handle her?" raised-brow look. My daughter grins. Oh yeah. She can manage the little monster.

"Come on, Sadie. We're making cookies and watching a movie." Good. Take command. Don't ask her, tell her what you're doing. Brave move. I watch with paused breath to see if Sadie will be stubborn or give in.

Sadie eyes her. "What kind of cookies?"

"You'll just have to come to the kitchen and find out."

With a long-suffering eye roll, Sadie deposits her little pink plastic purse onto the coffee table and heads toward the kitchen.

"Kiss me good-bye, honey," Greg says.

Sadie huffs and whips around. She gives him a grudging peck on the cheek, shoots me a glare, and follows Ari into the kitchen.

I can't help but be a bit dubious about the night. But Greg doesn't seem concerned.

I grab my purse from the end table next to Jakey's chair. He never even looks up. I kiss his head, then turn back to Greg. "You sure Sadie's going to be all right here with my kids?"

"Sure she will. Once she starts mixing up cookie dough, she'll forget all about being left out of our date."

"Not to be nosy or anything, but did your mom have plans tonight that kept her from keeping Sadie?"

"You could say that. No more questions." He bends and presses a kiss to my lips.

"All right, all right," Tommy pipes up. "You guys take it outside. I'm eating here."

"Sorry, man." Greg chuckles, then turns his attention back to me. "Ready to go?"

Is he kidding? I tell the boys good-bye and precede him as he opens the door and steps aside like the gentleman he is.

"Where are we going?" I ask, after we settle into his Avalanche and he starts the motor.

"I thought I said no questions."

"I know, but can't you give me a teeny-tiny hint?"

"Nope. I want you to be surprised."

Ten minutes later he has no idea how surprised I am as we pull up in front of his mother's house. Disappointment sweeps over me. "You made me wear a dress for dinner at your mom's?"

I cringe at my pouty tone. Good grief. I'm worse than Sadie.

"I'll make it worth your while. Just wait."

He opens the truck door for me. My heels click-clack up the brick walk to the porch. My legs are wobbly, and I'm about to lose my battle with the three-inch heels because the warmth from Greg's palm seeping through the back of my dress is making me weak-kneed as he guides me up the steps. Thankfully, he drops his hand and unlocks the door, which is the only reason, I'm sure, that I don't land on my face.

He sweeps me through the house and straight to the dining room. The beautiful cherry-wood dining-room table glimmers in the candlelight. I catch my breath. Two plates covered by sterling silver domes are in place, along with a pitcher of tea. Greg doesn't drink wine, which would have been a lot more romantic than tea. But I can't help but be glad he chose the tea rather than going with a wine substitute just to be romantic. Sparkling cider in wine-shaped bottles always feels a little junior high to me.

I hear a door close somewhere in the house and I jerk around.

"Get that worried look off your face. That was just my mom leaving."

"She didn't have to do that!"

He pulls me close. "Yes, she did."

Without a word, I surrender to his embrace. I wrap my arms around his neck as his mouth covers mine and I absolutely melt into his kiss. I could stay here forever, I really could. I love this man so much. How could I have ever listened to Emma Carrington? The wacko, yoga-doing, higher power (but not necessarily God)–believing life coach. What was I thinking? What would she know about God ordering a person's life? About God equipping a woman to stand beside her husband in the ministry and support him? Why did I waste so much time listening to a lie?

Way too soon Greg pulls away and seats me in a cushiony dining-room chair. Which is just as well, because after that kiss, my legs are about to give out on me.

Instead of sitting in his own chair, he drops to one knee in front of me.

My heart pounds so loud in my ears that I'm afraid I might not get to hear the actual proposal that only a moron wouldn't be able to figure out is coming.

"I know you still haven't figured out where your career is going," he begins. "I know you're not in your house yet, and I know you're not altogether crazy about the idea that I'm going to be a pastor. But I think when you find the kind of love and companionship that we have, you have to stop trying to wait for everything to be just right and step out in faith."

He takes the velvet box from his pocket. "You're the only woman for me, Claire. Now and for the rest of my life. I love you too much to let you go. Maybe it's selfish of me to even ask this knowing your reservations, but will you marry me?"

Well, what's a girl to say when she's looking at a princess-cut rock being offered by the man she loves? "Yes." And there it is. Short, sweet, to the point. And it takes an incredible weight off my heart to finally say it.

His jaw drops a little, and a smile splits his handsome face. "Are you sure?"

I nod and, I must admit, my eyes are watery with unshed tears. I cup his cheek and look deeply into his eyes. "I'm still carrying some emotional baggage from Rick's unfaithfulness. It might take awhile before I completely trust you. And I can't promise I won't say something stupid and single-handedly bring down your ministry. Or if I don't bring it down completely, I'm for sure going to embarrass you at some point."

He laughs. "I know you, Claire. I know you have insecurities because of the past. I want to be the man to prove that not only *can* a man be faithful, but that you are more than enough for me. I could never want anyone else."

There is no denying the sincerity of his words. "I believe you mean that, Greg." And I do. At this moment anyway. Even as relief crosses his face, I feel I have to press. "But what about the rest of what I said?"

"Oh, honey. Don't worry so much. You say the right thing a lot more often than you say the wrong thing."

Oh, if only that were true. "What about that time when I laughed so hard at poor Mr. Cain's incontinence?"

Greg's lips twist, and I can tell he's trying to keep back a grin. I slug him in the arm. "See? That's the kind of stuff I do."

"First of all, you didn't laugh at Eddie's incontinence, only the way he told about it. And believe me, you weren't the only one fighting to keep a straight face that day."

That's little consolation since, if memory serves, I'm the only one who actually gave in to the moment of weakness.

"So you're not perfect." He takes my hand once more. "But you're perfect for me."

He keeps his dark gaze on me while he slips the cool ring on my finger and wraps his hand around mine. Rising on his knees, he meets me at eye level and I meet him in the middle. His lips cover mine and I can feel the tension in the muscles of his neck as my arms wrap around his neck. It's a kiss of commitment, confirmation, definitely passion. I understand when he breaks our embrace a moment later.

"Are you wondering why I brought you here to ask you to marry me?"

"A little."

"This is only if you agree . . . but Mom has decided to buy a condo in Twin Oak Hills. She wants to give us this house as a wedding present."

"The *Father of the Bride* house?" I am awestruck. My insides are jumpy, shaky, quaky. If I could harness all this energy and bottle it into a fitness supplement, no one would ever have another lethargic workout.

Greg gives me a questioning smile. "I don't get it."

"My all-time favorite house is the one in the movie *Father of the Bride*. This one looks just like it, almost."

A smile lifts the edges of his lips. "Just like it, almost?"

"Close enough."

"So, I assume you're happy with the gift?"

"Are you kidding me? Only, can we really take such an elaborate gift? Shouldn't your mom sell it to buy the condo?"

"Trust me, she can afford it."

Joy shoots through me. My dream man, my dream home.

Three months ago, I had my future mapped out. My career, my perfect yuppie marriage to Greg. Then a tornado hit, and suddenly I realized I had no idea how to salvage my splintered life. But God knew He had a plan that didn't include the things I thought were important.

In hindsight, I guess I was pretty clueless to try to figure it out with anyone else's help but God's. Emma was a disaster and gave the kind of advice one might expect from someone who doesn't know God. But it definitely wasn't the right advice for me. And Penny, well, her heart was in the right place, but she had her own issues. The one thing I can say that I did take away from that experience is a good friend.

I glance across the table at my future husband/pastor. And I think, *Man, how'd I get so lucky?* But I realize I couldn't have gotten to this place on my own.

Greg looks up from his meal and smiles at me.

And all I can think is, *Thank you, God, for not giving me what I thought I wanted, because what you had planned is infinitely better.*

READING GROUP GUIDE

1. Claire has worked hard to forgive her ex-husband for his adultery. But clearly she still struggles. Do you have an issue in your life for which you feel you must continually repent? By faith, can you trust that God is delivering you from this, even though your feelings don't always back it up?

2. Claire struggles with the various input on how she should punish Ari, which has disastrous consequences. Has there ever been a time when you've taken someone else's advice against what you knew in your heart to be true?

3. Claire battles insecurity. Do you? How do you push through those times and forge ahead to do what you feel like God has told you to do, regardless of your feelings or your fear?

4. At first, Claire has misgivings about Shawn being coached by an atheist. Why do you think she changes her mind? If you have children, do you feel it's your job as a parent to guard your child from someone who might influence them in a negative way? How did Claire balance the need to protect Shawn with the knowledge that his faith would grow by being challenged?

5. Claire has decided that it may be time for her to end her relationship with her agent. Her mom talks to her about "seasons." Have you ever had a season that you knew was over, yet you clung to it, refusing to move forward? Is there a way to prepare yourself to face change?

6. Claire breaks it off with Greg because she "knows" she can't be a pastor's wife. Is there something that's holding you back from living your dream? Some failing or inadequacy you see in yourself? Do you truly believe God covers our inadequacies with His grace?

ABOUT THE AUTHOR

Tracey Bateman published her first novel in 2000 and has been busy ever since. Tracey attended Southwest Missouri State University, where she majored in English. She began developing her writing career after her fourth child was born. She became a member of American Christian Romance Writers in the early months of its inception. Currently she serves as the president of American Christian Fiction Writers board. She lives with her husband and four children in Lebanon, Missouri.